W

MW01128203

NOVELS

A Daughter of the Snows (1902)
The Cruise of the *Dazzler* (1902)
The Kempton-Wace Letters (with Anna
   Strunsky; 1903)
The Call of the Wild (1903)
The Sea-Wolf (1904)
The Game (1905)
White Fang (1906)
Before Adam (1907)
The Iron Heel (1908)
Martin Eden (1909)
Burning Daylight (1910)
Adventure (1911)
The Abysmal Brute (1911)
The Scarlet Plague (1912)
The Valley of the Moon (1913)
Mutiny of the Elsinore (1914)
The Star Rover (1915)
The Little Lady of the Big House (1916)
Jerry of the Islands (1917)
Michael, Brother of Jerry (1917)
Hearts of Three (1918)
The Assassination Bureau, Ltd (completed by
   Robert L. Fish, 1963)

NON-FICTION

The People of the Abyss (1903)
War of the Classes (1905)
The Road (1907)
Revolution (1910)
The Cruise of the *Snark* (1911)
John Barleycorn (1913)
The Human Drift (1917)

SHORT STORY COLLECTIONS

The Son of the Wolf (1900)
The God of his Fathers (1901)
Children of the Frost (1902)
The Faith of Men (1904)
Tales of the Fish Patrol (1905)
Moon-Face (1906)
Love of Life (1907)
Lost Face (1910)
When God Laughs (1911)
South Sea Tales (1911)
The House of Pride (1912)
A Son of the Sun (1912)
Smoke Bellew (1912)
The Night Born (1913)
The Strength of the Strong (1914)
The Turtles of Tasman (1916)
The Red One (1918)
On the Makaloa Mat (1919)
Dutch Courage (1922)

PLAYS

Scorn of Women (1906)
Theft (1910)
The Acorn Planter (1916)
Gold (completed by Herbert Heron, 1972)

SELECTED COLLECTIONS

Letters from Jack London (1965)
Jack London Reports (1970)
No Mentor But Myself (1979)
Jack London on the Road: The Tramp Diary and
   other Hobo Writings (1979)
The Library of America editions (2 vols, 1982)
Letters of Jack London (3 vols, 1988)
The Unpublished and Uncollected Articles and
   Essays (2007)

The day Jack and Charmian London sailed from the foot of Broadway, Oakland, for their South Pacific adventure aboard the *Snark* in 1907.

(Joseph R. Knowland collection at the Oakland History Room, Oakland Public Library. Public domain.)

JACK LONDON
San Francisco Stories

Edited and with an introduction by
MATTHEW ASPREY

Preface by RODGER JACOBS

SYDNEY
SAMIZDAT
PRESS

SYDNEY SAMIZDAT PRESS
SYDNEY, AUSTRALIA

Originally published October 2010
2nd CreateSpace edition July 2011
Revised edition June 2014
Set in 9 point Palatino

For reprint rights, contact:
twelvemilereef@yahoo.com

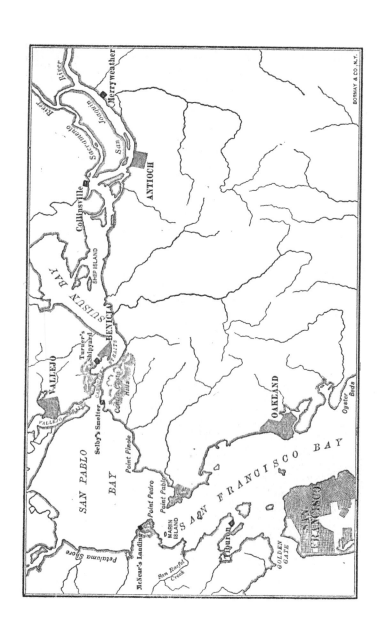

Contents

III. THE BAY AREA

IV. SAN FRANCISCO PAST AND FUTURE

EPILOGUE: 18 April 1906

Acknowledgments

The editor wishes to dedicate this volume to past and present denizens of the Green Tortoise Hostel in North Beach, San Francisco.

Additional thanks to Rodger Jacobs, Peter Doyle, and Clare Anderson for their encouragement.

Dale L. Walker's mammoth 20-part story-by-story commentary on *The Complete Stories of Jack London* (three volumes, edited by Earle Labor, Robert C. Leitz III, and I. Milo Shepard; Stanford University Press, 1993) was an invaluable guide to the assembly of this material. It can be found at www.jacklondons.net.

of damage from the 1906 San Francisco earthquake when the pilings beneath the bar settled in the mud and could never be shored up.

Jack London loved to drink at Johnny Heinold's Saloon and now, I thought to myself as I walked through the door one cool summer day many years past, I am going to sit down and get drunk at the exact same bar where one of my idols traded wild tales with his boisterous drinking companions.

The bar is dimly lit with gas lights. A brownish oily creosote is seeping out of the aged wood and the smoke from the wood-burning stoves and cigarettes has stained the walls.

I sidled up to the bar with its original but worn through brass rail and ordered the first of an unending series of bourbon and waters. The bartender tried to impose the tourist spiel on me but I dismissed his rehearsed lecture with a wave of my hand.

"I probably know more about this place than you do," I said. I simply wanted to be left alone to soak up the booze and the history.

Once I assured the bartender that I was not going to be climbing behind the wheel of a car, not me, he began pouring the liquor with a free hand. It seemed that I was imbibing from a bottomless glass.

Golden time arrived quickly; that's the moment when the drinker abruptly finds his boat cast on the other side of the shore. Lucidity is gone. Senses are dulled to the point of numbness. The stability of the ground beneath your feet is no longer a certainty (Well, it never is in Oakland). And the brain returns forgotten memories and offers up tantalizing hallucinations and fantasies as the optical gaze turns inward.

Through the filter of my mind's eye there marched an endless procession of spooks and ghouls that were oozing out of the stagnant air of Heinold's Saloon like the creosote from the wood.

There were hundreds of nameless and faceless ghosts, aimlessly shuffling around the room, wishing and hoping that they could locate the other pieces of their disintegrated souls so that they can be whole again. There were longshoremen and sailors and sea captains from all corners of the globe. There were soldiers who shipped off to war from the Port of Oakland, enjoying their last drink at Heinold's before rushing to greet their grim fate on some foreign battlefield.

Not all of the ghosts were anonymous. Some of them were men of great repute, anxiously taking advantage of my blinding inebriation to reveal themselves.

Robert Louis Stevenson, who passed time at Heinold's before embarking on his final cruise to Samoa, brushed past my shoulder in the form of a cool breeze. Pieces of Robert Service's soul lingered in the air, cursing his lack of physical properties because there is so much poetry to be composed about life on the other side.

The disembodied spirit of Ambrose Bierce, the ultimate cynic, treads the boards at Heinold's Saloon. In *The Devil's Dictionary*, Bierce defines a ghost as "the outward and visible sign of an inner fear."

And in time I could almost discern the apparitional form of Jack London, his stocky frame poured into a bar stool. He is like vapor, bathed in a glowing yellow light, wearing a bulky waist-length rain slicker. His hair is tousled, as it is in most photographs of him, and his sunken eyes are haunting beyond words.

Jack doesn't utter a word. He flashes that wry grin of his, cocks his head slightly to the left, and fixes his spectral gaze on my face, occasionally glancing with envy at the strong bourbon concoction in my hand. I find myself, in this moment of communion with the

In 1893 London signed on to the schooner *Sophie Sutherland* and voyaged across the Pacific. The next year he was on the road as a hobo with Kelly's Army. It was only in 1895 that he was able to attend Oakland High School. After graduation and a brief stint at the University of California in nearby Berkeley, London sailed north to the Yukon for the Klondike Gold Rush. His experiences in the Northlands would lead to the creation of such classic works as *The Call of the Wild* (1903), *White Fang* (1906), and 'To Build A Fire' (1908). London would soon become one of the world's most popular writers.

Never losing his love of travel and adventure, Jack London always returned to California. He eventually bought a ranch north of San Pablo Bay in Sonoma County. He died there at the age of forty on November 22, 1916. He had published over forty volumes—novels, short stories, non-fiction, and essays.

II

THE IDEA FOR THIS collection can be traced to the autumn of 2009. In San Francisco for a spell, I took Don Herron's enthusiastic, super-generous, long-running Dashiell Hammett Tour. I hired a Chevrolet Camaro and hit the road south to Monterey, but Steinbeck's Cannery Row had become a yuppified street of tourist hotels. I drove down Highway 1 to the Henry Miller Library in Big Sur. Then I returned to San Francisco to look for Jack London.

After reading Rodger Jacobs' 2003 essay 'Ghost Land', I caught a BART train to Oakland. From the 12th Street station I walked to Jack London Square. This modern waterfront was centred around a block-long Barnes & Noble bookstore, now closed. In this very contemporary setting it was jarring to see Jack London's Klondike cabin, reconstructed from the original logs. Well, half the logs; the others were used to build an identical cabin in Dawson City, Yukon. It was even more surprising to come upon Heinold's First and Last Chance Saloon, which is still in business. Due to damage from the Great Earthquake the floor slopes and the clock is stuck forever at quake hour. The bar still uses gaslights. The roof is creosote-blackened and papered with innumerable business cards from another age. You can ask the barman for a glass of white rum and drink at the actual tables where London studied as a boy and later worked on *The Call of the Wild* and *The Sea-Wolf*. They have a photo to prove it.

I drank the glass of rum and thought of Jack London's enduring fame as the tale-teller of the Klondike and the Pacific. But what had London written about his home town, the Bay Area of more than a century ago? In his short career, London published nearly two hundred short stories. A large number are set in the Yukon. Many others are set in Hawaii and the South Seas. Apart from *Tales of the Fish Patrol* (republished here in its entirety), London's San Francisco Bay Area stories have always been scattered across numerous collections. This anthology gathers the best of them for the first time to create a composite portrait of the Bay Area in a vanished age.

Parts I and II loosely follow the chronology of London's life in Oakland and on the Bay. Excerpts from London's ostensibly non-fictional *John Barleycorn* (1913) are interspersed with fictions. 'The Apostate' is London's often-anthologised dramatization of child servitude in factories. Although no explicit mention is made of Oakland, this story is generally believed to be inspired by London's own experiences as an exploited teenage worker. A short extract

I. YOUTH

THE APOSTATE

Now I wake me up to work;
I pray the Lord I may not shirk.
If I should die before the night,
I pray the Lord my work's all right.
                              Amen.

"If you don't git up, Johnny, I won't give you a bite to eat!"

The threat had no effect on the boy. He clung stubbornly to sleep, fighting for its oblivion as the dreamer fights for his dream. The boy's hands loosely clenched themselves, and he made feeble, spasmodic blows at the air. These blows were intended for his mother, but she betrayed practised familiarity in avoiding them as she shook him roughly by the shoulder. "Lemme 'lone!"

It was a cry that began, muffled, in the deeps of sleep, that swiftly rushed upward, like a wail, into passionate belligerence, and that died away and sank down into an inarticulate whine. It was a bestial cry, as of a soul in torment, filled with infinite protest and pain.

But she did not mind. She was a sad-eyed, tired-faced woman, and she had grown used to this task, which she repeated every day of her life. She got a grip on the bed-clothes and tried to strip them down; but the boy, ceasing his punching, clung to them desperately. In a huddle, at the foot of the bed, he still remained covered. Then she tried dragging the bedding to the floor. The boy opposed her. She braced herself. Hers was the superior weight, and the boy and bedding gave, the former instinctively following the latter in order to shelter against the chill of the room that bit into his body.

As he toppled on the edge of the bed it seemed that he must fall head-first to the floor. But consciousness fluttered up in him. He righted himself and for a moment perilously balanced. Then he struck the floor on his feet. On the instant his mother seized him by the shoulders and shook him. Again his fists struck out, this time with more force and directness. At the same time his eyes opened. She released him. He was awake.

"All right," he mumbled.

She caught up the lamp and hurried out, leaving him in darkness.

"You'll be docked," she warned back to him.

He did not mind the darkness. When he had got into his clothes, he went out into the kitchen. His tread was very heavy for so thin and light a boy. His legs dragged with their own weight, which seemed unreasonable because they were such skinny legs. He drew a broken-bottomed chair to the table.

"Johnny!" his mother called sharply.

He arose as sharply from the chair, and, without a word, went to the sink. It was a greasy, filthy sink. A smell came up from the outlet. He took no notice of it. That a sink should smell was to him part of the natural order, just as it was a part of the natural order that the soap should be grimy with dish-water and hard to lather. Nor did he try very hard to make it lather. Several splashes of the cold water from the running faucet completed the function. He did not wash his teeth. For that matter he had never seen a tooth-brush, thick with flying lint. He had coughed that first day in order to rid his lungs of the lint; and for the same reason he had coughed ever since.

The boy alongside of Johnny whimpered and sniffed. The boy's face was convulsed with hatred for the overseer who kept a threatening eye on him from a distance; but every bobbin was running full. The boy yelled terrible oaths into the whirling bobbins before him; but the sound did not carry half a dozen feet, the roaring of the room holding it in and containing it like a wall.

Of all this Johnny took no notice. He had a way of accepting things. Besides, things grow monotonous by repetition, and this particular happening he had witnessed many times. It seemed to him as useless to oppose the overseer as to defy the will of a machine. Machines were made to go in certain ways and to perform certain tasks. It was the same with the overseer.

But at eleven o'clock there was excitement in the room. In an apparently occult way the excitement instantly permeated everywhere. The one-legged boy who worked on the other side of Johnny bobbed swiftly across the floor to a bin truck that stood empty. Into this he dived out of sight, crutch and all. The superintendent of the mill was coming along, accompanied by a young man. He was well dressed and wore a starched shirt — a gentleman, in Johnny's classification of men, and also, "the Inspector."

He looked sharply at the boys as he passed along. Sometimes he stopped and asked questions. When he did so, he was compelled to shout at the top of his lungs, at which moments his face was ludicrously contorted with the strain of making himself heard. His quick eye noted the empty machine alongside of Johnny's, but he said nothing. Johnny also caught his eye, and he stopped abruptly. He caught Johnny by the arm to draw him back a step from the machine; but with an exclamation of surprise he released the arm.

"Pretty skinny," the superintendent laughed anxiously.

"Pipe stems," was the answer. "Look at those legs. The boy's got the rickets — incipient, but he's got them. If epilepsy doesn't get him in the end, it will be because tuberculosis gets him first."

Johnny listened, but did not understand. Furthermore he was not interested in future ills. There was an immediate and more serious ill that threatened him in the form of the inspector.

"Now, my boy, I want you to tell me the truth," the inspector said, or shouted, bending close to the boy's ear to make him hear. "How old are you?"

"Fourteen," Johnny lied, and he lied with the full force of his lungs. So loudly did he lie that it started him off in a dry, hacking cough that lifted the lint which had been settling in his lungs all morning.

"Looks sixteen at least," said the superintendent.

"Or sixty," snapped the inspector.

"He's always looked that way."

"How long?" asked the inspector, quickly.

"For years. Never gets a bit older."

"Or younger, I dare say. I suppose he's worked here all those years?"

"Off and on — but that was before the new law was passed," the superintendent hastened to add. "Machine idle?" the inspector asked, pointing at the unoccupied machine beside Johnny's, in which the part-filled bobbins were flying like mad.

"Looks that way." The superintendent motioned the overseer to

40

grip of sleep. Then came the meagre breakfast, the tramp through the dark, and the pale glimpse of day across the housetops as he turned his back on it and went in through the factory gate. It was another day, of all the days, and all the days were alike.

And yet there had been variety in his life — at the times he changed from one job to another, or was taken sick. When he was six, he was little mother and father to Will and the other children still younger. At seven he went into the mills — winding bobbins. When he was eight, he got work in another mill. His new job was marvellously easy. All he had to do was to sit down with a little stick in his hand and guide a stream of cloth that flowed past him. This stream of cloth came out of the maw of a machine, passed over a hot roller, and went on its way elsewhere. But he sat always in the one place, beyond the reach of daylight, a gas-jet flaring over him, himself part of the mechanism.

He was very happy at that job, in spite of the moist heat, for he was still young and in possession of dreams and illusions. And wonderful dreams he dreamed as he watched the streaming cloth streaming endlessly by. But there was no exercise about the work, no call upon his mind, and he dreamed less and less, while his mind grew torpid and drowsy. Nevertheless, he earned two dollars a week, and two dollars represented the difference between acute starvation and chronic underfeeding.

But when he was nine, he lost his job. Measles was the cause of it. After he recovered, he got work in a glass factory. The pay was better, and the work demanded skill. It was piece-work, and the more skilful he was, the bigger wages he earned. Here was incentive. And under this incentive he developed into a remarkable worker.

It was simple work, the tying of glass stoppers into small bottles. At his waist he carried a bundle of twine. He held the bottles between his knees so that he might work with both hands. Thus, in a sitting position and bending over his own knees, his narrow shoulders grew humped and his chest was contracted for ten hours each day. This was not good for the lungs, but he tied three hundred dozen bottles a day.

The superintendent was very proud of him, and brought visitors to look at him. In ten hours three hundred dozen bottles passed through his hands. This meant that he had attained machine-like perfection. All waste movements were eliminated. Every motion of his thin arms, every movement of a muscle in the thin fingers, was swift and accurate. He worked at high tension, and the result was that he grew nervous. At night his muscles twitched in his sleep, and in the daytime he could not relax and rest. He remained keyed up and his muscles continued to twitch. Also he grew sallow and his lint-cough grew worse. Then pneumonia laid hold of the feeble lungs within the contracted chest, and he lost his job in the glass-works. Now he had returned to the jute mills where he had first begun with winding bobbins. But promotion was waiting for him. He was a good worker. He would next go on the starcher, and later he would go into the loom room. There was nothing after that except increased efficiency.

The machinery ran faster than when he had first gone to work, and his mind ran slower. He no longer dreamed at all, though his earlier years had been full of dreaming. Once he had been in love. It was when he first began guiding the cloth over the hot roller, and it was with the daughter of the superintendent. She was much older than he, a young woman, and he had seen her at a distance only a movement of his hands, every twitch of his muscles, and preparations were making for a future course of action that would amaze him and all his little world.

It was in the late spring that he came home from work one night aware of unusual tiredness. There was a keen expectancy in the air as he sat down to the table, but he did not notice. He went through the meal in moody silence, mechanically eating what was before him. The children um'd and ah'd and made smacking noises with their mouths. But he was deaf to them.

"D'ye know what you're eatin'?" his mother demanded at last, desperately.

He looked vacantly at the dish before him, and vacantly at her.

"Floatin' island," she announced triumphantly.

"Oh," he said.

"Floating island!" the children chorussed loudly.

"Oh," he said. And after two or three mouthfuls, he added, "guess I ain't hungry to-night."

He dropped the spoon, shoved back his chair, and arose wearily from the table.

"An' I guess I'll go to bed."

His feet dragged more heavily than usual as he crossed the kitchen floor. Undressing was a Titan's task, a monstrous futility, and he wept weakly as he crawled into bed, one shoe still on. He was aware of a rising, swelling something inside his head that made his brain thick and fuzzy. His lean fingers felt as big as his wrist, while in the ends of them was a remoteness of sensation vague and fuzzy like his brain. The small of his back ached intolerably. All his bones ached. He ached everywhere. And in his head began the shrieking, pounding, crashing, roaring of a million looms. All space was filled with flying shuttles. They darted in and out, intricately, amongst the stars. He worked a thousand looms himself, and ever they speeded up, faster and faster, and his brain unwound, faster and faster, and became the thread that fed the thousand flying shuttles.

He did not go to work next morning. He was too busy weaving colossally on the thousand looms that ran inside his head. His mother went to work, but first she sent for the doctor. It was a severe attack of la grippe, he said. Jennie served as nurse and carried out his instructions.

It was a very severe attack, and it was a week before Johnny dressed and tottered feebly across the floor. Another week, the doctor said, and he would be fit to return to work. The foreman of the loom room visited him on Sunday afternoon, the first day of his convalescence. The best weaver in the room, the foreman told his mother. His job would be held for him. He could come back to work a week from Monday.

"Why don't you thank 'im, Johnny?" his mother asked anxiously.

"He's ben that sick he ain't himself yet," she explained apologetically to the visitor.

Johnny sat hunched up and gazing steadfastly at the floor. He sat in the same position long after the foreman had gone. It was warm outdoors, and he sat on the stoop in the afternoon. Sometimes his lips moved. He seemed lost in endless calculations.

Next morning, after the day grew warm, he took his seat on the stoop. He had pencil and paper this time with which to continue his calculations, and he calculated painfully and amazingly.

"What comes after millions?" he asked at noon, when Will came home from school. "An' how d'ye work 'em?"

He passed by a small railroad station and lay down in the grass under a tree. All afternoon he lay there. Sometimes he dozed, with muscles that twitched in his sleep. When awake, he lay without movement, watching the birds or looking up at the sky through the branches of the tree above him. Once or twice he laughed aloud, but without relevance to anything he had seen or felt.

After twilight had gone, in the first darkness of the night, a freight train rumbled into the station. When the engine was switching cars on to the side-track, Johnny crept along the side of the train. He pulled open the side-door of an empty box-car and awkwardly and laboriously climbed in. He closed the door. The engine whistled. Johnny was lying down, and in the darkness he smiled.

From *When God Laughs & Other Stories* (1911)
(First published in *Woman's Home Companion*, Vol. 33, Sept., 1906)

galleons or locking yard-arms with a French privateer, or—lots of things."

"Well — there are adventures today," I objected.

But Paul went on as though I had not spoken:

"And today we go from school to high school, and from high school to college, and then we go into the office or become doctors and things, and the only adventures we know about are the ones we read in books. Why, just as sure as I'm sitting here on the stern of the sloop *Mist*, just so sure am I that we wouldn't know what to do if a real adventure came along. Now, would we?"

"Oh, I don't know," I answered non-committally.

"Well, you wouldn't be a coward, would you?" he demanded.

I was sure I wouldn't and said so.

"But you don't have to be a coward to lose your head, do you?"

I agreed that brave men might get excited.

"Well, then," Paul summed up, with a note of regret in his voice, "the chances are that we'd spoil the adventure. So it's a shame, and that's all I can say about it."

"The adventure hasn't come yet," I answered, not caring to see him down in the mouth over nothing. You see, Paul was a peculiar fellow in some things, and I knew him pretty well. He read a good deal, and had a quick imagination, and once in a while he'd get into moods like this one. So I said, "The adventure hasn't come yet, so there's no use worrying about its being spoiled. For all we know, it might turn out splendidly."

Paul didn't say anything for some time, and I was thinking he was out of the mood, when he spoke up suddenly:

"Just imagine, Bob Kellogg, as we're sailing along now, just as we are, and never mind what for, that a boat should bear down upon us with armed men in it, what would you do to repel boarders? Think you could rise to it?"

"What would you do?" I asked pointedly. "Remember, we haven't even a single shotgun aboard."

"You would surrender, then?" he demanded angrily. "But suppose they were going to kill you?"

"I'm not saying what I'd do," I answered stiffly, beginning to get a little angry myself. "I'm asking what you'd do, without weapons of any sort?"

"I'd find something," he replied—rather shortly, I thought.

I began to chuckle. "Then the adventure wouldn't be spoiled, would it? And you've been talking rubbish."

Paul struck a match, looked at his watch, and remarked that it was nearly one o'clock—a way he had when the argument went against him. Besides, this was the nearest we ever came to quarreling now, though our share of squabbles had fallen to us in the earlier days of our friendship. I had just seen a little white light ahead when Paul spoke again.

"Anchor-light," he said. "Funny place for people to drop the hook. It may be a scow-schooner with a dinky astern, so you'd better go wide."

I eased the *Mist* several points, and, the wind puffing up, we went plowing along at a pretty fair speed, passing the light so wide that we could not make out what manner of craft it marked. Suddenly the *Mist* slacked up in a slow and easy way, as though running upon soft mud. We were both startled. The wind was blowing stronger than ever, and yet we were almost at a standstill.

"Mud-flat out here? Never heard of such a thing!"

So Paul exclaimed with a snort of unbelief, and, seizing an oar,

from *JOHN BARLEYCORN*

I was barely turned fifteen, and working long hours in a cannery. Month in and month out, the shortest day I ever worked was ten hours. When to ten hours of actual work at a machine is added the noon hour; the walking to work and walking home from work; the getting up in the morning, dressing, and eating; the eating at night, undressing, and going to bed, there remains no more than the nine hours out of the twenty-four required by a healthy youngster for sleep. Out of those nine hours, after I was in bed and ere my eyes drowsed shut, I managed to steal a little time for reading.

But many a night I did not knock off work until midnight. On occasion I worked eighteen and twenty hours on a stretch. Once I worked at my machine for thirty-six consecutive hours. And there were weeks on end when I never knocked off work earlier than eleven o'clock, got home and in bed at half after midnight, and was called at half-past five to dress, eat, walk to work, and be at my machine at seven o'clock whistle blow.

No moments here to be stolen for my beloved books. And what had John Barleycorn to do with such strenuous, Stoic toil of a lad just turned fifteen? He had everything to do with it. Let me show you. I asked myself if this were the meaning of life—to be a work-beast? I knew of no horse in the city of Oakland that worked the hours I worked. If this were living, I was entirely unenamoured of it. I remembered my skiff, lying idle and accumulating barnacles at the boat-wharf; I remembered the wind that blew every day on the bay, the sunrises and sunsets I never saw; the bite of the salt air in my nostrils, the bite of the salt water on my flesh when I plunged overside; I remembered all the beauty and the wonder and the sense-delights of the world denied me. There was only one way to escape my deadening toil. I must get out and away on the water. I must earn my bread on the water. And the way of the water led inevitably to John Barleycorn. I did not know this. And when I did learn it, I was courageous enough not to retreat back to my bestial life at the machine.

I wanted to be where the winds of adventure blew. And the winds of adventure blew the oyster pirate sloops up and down San Francisco Bay, from raided oyster-beds and fights at night on shoal and flat, to markets in the morning against city wharves, where peddlers and saloon-keepers came down to buy. Every raid on an oyster-bed was a felony. The penalty was State imprisonment, the stripes and the lockstep. And what of that? The men in stripes worked a shorter day than I at my machine. And there was vastly more romance in being an oyster pirate or a convict than in being a machine slave. And behind it all, behind all of me with youth abubble, whispered Romance, Adventure.

So I interviewed my Mammy Jennie, my old nurse at whose black breast I had suckled. She was more prosperous than my folks. She was nursing sick people at a good weekly wage. Would she lend her "white child" the money? *Would he?* What she had was mine.

Then I sought out French Frank, the oyster pirate, who wanted to sell, I had heard, his sloop, the *Razzle Dazzle*. I found him lying at anchor on the Alameda side of the estuary near the Webster Street bridge, with visitors aboard, whom he was entertaining with afternoon wine. He came on deck to talk business. He was willing to sell. But it was Sunday. Besides, he had guests. On the morrow he would make out the bill of sale and I could enter into possession. And in the meantime I must come below and meet his friends. They were two sisters, Mamie and Tess; a Mrs. Hadley, who chaperoned them; "Whisky" Bob, a youthful oyster pirate of sixteen; and "Spider" Healey, a black-whiskered wharf-rat of twenty. Mamie, who was Spider's niece, was called the Queen of the Oyster Pirates, and, on occasion, presided at their revels. French Frank was in love with her, though I did not know it at the time; and she steadfastly refused to marry him.

French Frank poured a tumbler of red wine from a big demijohn to drink to our transaction. I remembered the red wine of the Italian rancho, and shuddered inwardly. Whisky and beer were not quite so repulsive. But the Queen of the Oyster Pirates was looking at me, a part-emptied glass in her own hand. I had my pride. If I was only fifteen, at least I could not show myself any less a man than she. Besides, there were her sister, and Mrs. Hadley, and the young oyster pirate, and the whiskered wharf-rat, all with glasses in their hands. Was I a milk-and-water sop? No; a thousand times no, and a thousand glasses no. I downed the tumblerful like a man.

French Frank was elated by the sale, which I had bound with a twenty-dollar goldpiece. He poured more wine. I had learned my strong head and stomach, and I was certain I could drink with them in a temperate way and not poison myself for a week to come. I could stand as much as they; and besides, they had already been drinking for some time.

71

We got to singing. Spider sang "The Boston Burglar" and "Black Lulu." The Queen sang "Then I Wisht I Were a Little Bird." And her sister Tess sang "Oh, Treat My Daughter Kindily." The fun grew fast and furious. I found myself able to miss drinks without being noticed or called to account. Also, standing in the companionway, head and shoulders out and glass in hand, I could fling the wine overboard.

I reasoned something like this: It is a queerness of these people that they like this vile-tasting wine. Well, let them. I cannot quarrel with their tastes. My manhood, according to their queer notions, must compel me to appear to like this wine. Very well. I shall so appear. But I shall drink no more than is unavoidable.

And the Queen began to make love to me, the latest recruit to the oyster pirate fleet, and no mere hand, but a master and owner. She went upon deck to take the air, and took me with her. She knew, of course, but I never dreamed, how French Frank was raging down below. Then Tess joined us, sitting on the cabin; and Spider, and Bob; and at the last, Mrs. Hadley and French Frank. And we sat there, glasses in hand, and sang, while the big demijohn went around; and I was the only strictly sober one.

And I enjoyed it as no one of them was able to enjoy it. Here, in this atmosphere of bohemianism, I could not but contrast the scene with my scene of the day before, sitting at my machine, in the stifling, shut-in air, repeating, endlessly repeating, at top speed, my series of mechanical motions. And here I sat now, glass in hand, in warm-glowing camaraderie, with the oyster pirates, adventurers who refused to be slaves to petty routine, who flouted restrictions and the law, who carried their lives and their liberty in their hands. And it was through John Barleycorn that I came to join this glorious company of free souls, unashamed and unafraid.

And the afternoon seabreeze blew its tang into my lungs, and curled the waves in mid-channel. Before it came the scow schooners, wing-and-wing, blowing their horns for the drawbridges to open. Red-stacked tugs tore by, rocking the *Razzle Dazzle* in the waves of their wake. A sugar barque towed from the "boneyard" to sea. The sun-wash was on the crisping water, and life was big. And Spider sang:

"Oh, it's Lulu, black Lulu, my darling, Oh, it's where have you been so long? Been layin' in jail, A-waitin' for bail, Till my bully comes rollin' along."

There it was, the smack and slap of the spirit of revolt, of adventure, of romance, of the things forbidden and done defiantly and grandly. And I knew that on the morrow I would not go back to my machine at the cannery. To-morrow I would be an oyster pirate, as free a freebooter as the century and the waters of San Francisco Bay would permit. Spider had already agreed to sail with me as my crew of one, and, also, as cook while I did the deck work. We would outfit our grub and water in the morning, hoist the big mainsail (which was a bigger piece of canvas than any I had ever sailed under), and beat our way out the estuary on the first of the seabreeze and the last of the ebb. Then we would slack sheets, and on the first of the flood run down the bay to the Asparagus Islands, where we would anchor miles off shore. And at last my dream would be realised: I would sleep upon the water. And next morning I would wake upon the water; and thereafter all my days and nights would be on the water.

And the Queen asked me to row her ashore in my skiff, when at sunset French Frank prepared to take his guests ashore. Nor did I catch the significance of his abrupt change of plan when he turned the task of rowing his skiff over to Whisky Bob, himself remaining on board the sloop. Nor did I understand Spider's grinning side-remark to me: "Gee! There's nothin' slow about *you*." How could it possibly enter my boy's head that a grizzled man of fifty should be jealous of me?

*

We met by appointment, early Monday morning, to complete the deal, in Johnny Heinhold's "Last Chance"—a saloon, of course, for the transactions of men. I paid the money over, received the bill of sale, and French Frank treated. This struck me as an evident custom, and a logical one—the seller, who receives, the money, to wet a piece of it in the establishment where the trade was consummated. But, to my surprise, French Frank treated the house. He and I drank, which seemed just; but why should Johnny Heinhold, who owned the saloon and waited behind the bar, be invited to drink? I figured it immediately that he made a profit on the very drink he drank. I could, in a way, considering that they were friends and shipmates, understand Spider and Whisky Bob being asked to drink; but why should the longshoremen, Bill Kelley and Soup Kennedy, be asked?

Then there was Pat, the Queen's brother, making a total of eight of us. It was early morning, and all ordered whisky. What could I do, here in this company of big men, all drinking whisky? "Whisky," I said, with the careless air of one who had said it a thousand times. And such whisky! I tossed it down. A-r-r-r-gh! I can taste it yet.

And I was appalled at the price French Frank had paid—eighty cents. *Eighty cents*! It was an outrage to my thrifty soul. Eighty cents—the equivalent of eight long hours of my toil at the machine, gone down our throats, and gone like that, in a twinkling, leaving only a bad taste in the mouth. There was no discussion that French Frank was a waster.

I was anxious to be gone, out into the sunshine, out over the water to my glorious boat. But all hands lingered. Even Spider, my crew, lingered. No hint broke through my obtuseness of why they lingered. I have often thought since of how they must have regarded me, the newcomer being welcomed into their company standing at bar with them, and not standing for a single round of drinks.

French Frank, who, unknown to me, had swallowed his chagrin since the day before, now that the money for the *Razzle Dazzle* was in his pocket, began to behave curiously toward me. I sensed the change in his attitude, saw the forbidding glitter in his eyes, and wondered. The more I saw of men, the queerer they became. Johnny Heinhold leaned across the bar and whispered in my ear: "He's got it in for you. Watch out."

I nodded comprehension of his statement, and acquiescence in it, as a man should nod who knows all about men. But secretly I was perplexed. Heavens! How was I, who had worked hard and read books of adventure, and who was only fifteen years old, who had not dreamed of giving the Queen of the Oyster Pirates a second thought, and who did not know that French Frank was madly and Latinly in love with her—how was I to guess that I had done him shame? And how was I to guess that the story of how the Queen had thrown him down on his own boat, the moment I hove in sight, was already the gleeful gossip of the water-front? And by the same token, how was I to guess that her brother Pat's offishness with me was anything else than temperamental gloominess of spirit?

Whisky Bob got me aside a moment. "Keep your eyes open," he muttered. "Take my tip. French Frank's ugly. I'm going up river with him to get a schooner for oystering. When he gets down on the beds, watch out. He says he'll run you down. After dark, any time he's around, change your anchorage and douse your riding light. Savve?"

Oh, certainly, I savve'd. I nodded my head, and, as one man to another, thanked him for his tip; and drifted back to the group at the bar. No; I did not treat. I never dreamed that I was expected to treat. I left with Spider, and my ears burn now as I try to surmise the things they must have said about me.

I asked Spider, in an off-hand way, what was eating French Frank. "He's crazy jealous of you," was the answer. "Do you think so?" I said, and dismissed the matter as not worth thinking about.

But I leave it to any one—the swell of my fifteen-years-old manhood at learning that French Frank, the adventurer of fifty, the sailor of all the seas of all the world, was jealous of me— and jealous over a girl most romantically named the Queen of the Oyster Pirates. I had read of such things in books, and regarded them as personal probabilities of a distant maturity. Oh, I felt a rare young devil, as we hoisted the big mainsail that morning, broke out anchor, and filled away close-hauled on the three-mile beat to windward out into the bay.

Such was my escape from the killing machine-toil, and my introduction to the oyster pirates. True, the introduction had begun with drink, and the life promised to continue with drink. But was I to stay away from it for such reason? Wherever life ran free and great, there men drank. Romance and Adventure seemed always to go down the street locked arm in arm with John Barleycorn. To know the two, I must know the third. Or else I must go back to my free library books and read of the deeds of other men and do no deeds of my own save slave for ten cents an hour at a machine in a cannery.

No; I was not to be deterred from this brave life on the water by the fact that the water-dwellers had queer and expensive desires for beer and wine and whisky. What if their notions of happiness included the strange one of seeing me drink? When they persisted in buying the stuff and thrusting it upon me, why, I would drink it. It was the price I would pay for their comradeship. And I didn't have to get drunk. I had not got drunk the Sunday afternoon I arranged to buy the *Razzle Dazzle*, despite the fact that not one of the rest was sober. Well, I could go on into the future that way, drinking the stuff when it gave them pleasure that I should drink it, but carefully avoiding over-drinking.

*

Gradual as was my development as a heavy drinker among the oyster pirates, the real heavy drinking came suddenly, and was the result, not of desire for alcohol, but of an intellectual conviction.

The more I saw of the life, the more I was enamoured of it. I can never forget my thrills the first night I took part in a concerted raid, when we assembled on board the *Annie*—rough men, big and unafraid, and weazened wharf-rats, some of them ex-convicts, all of them enemies of the law and meriting jail, in sea-boots and sea-gear, talking in gruff low voices, and "Big" George with revolvers strapped about his waist to show that he meant business.

Oh, I know, looking back, that the whole thing was sordid and silly. But I was not looking back in those days when I was rubbing shoulders with John Barleycorn and beginning to accept him. The life was brave and wild, and I was living the adventure I had read so much about.

Nelson, "Young Scratch" they called him, to distinguish him from "Old Scratch," his father, sailed in the sloop *Reindeer*, partners with one "Clam." Clam was a dare-devil, but Nelson was a reckless maniac. He was twenty years old, with the body of a Hercules. When he was shot in Benicia, a couple of years later, the coroner said he was the greatest-shouldered man he had ever seen laid on a slab.

Nelson could not read or write. He had been "dragged" up by his father on San Francisco Bay, and boats were second nature with him. His strength was prodigious, and his reputation along the water-front for violence was anything but savoury. He had Berserker rages and did mad, terrible things. I made his acquaintance the first cruise of the *Razzle Dazzle*, and saw him sail the *Reindeer* in a blow and dredge oysters all around the rest of us as we lay at two anchors, troubled with fear of going ashore.

He was some man, this Nelson; and when, passing by the Last Chance saloon, he spoke to me, I felt very proud. But try to imagine my pride when he promptly asked me in to have a drink. I stood at the bar and drank a glass of beer with him, and talked manfully of oysters, and boats, and of the mystery of who had put the load of buckshot through the *Annie*'s mainsail.

We talked and lingered at the bar. It seemed to me strange that we lingered. We had had our beer. But who was I to lead the way outside when great Nelson chose to lean against the bar? After a few minutes, to my surprise, he asked me to have another drink, which I did. And still we talked, and Nelson evinced no intention of leaving the bar.

Bear with me while I explain the way of my reasoning and of my innocence. First of all, I was very proud to be in the company of Nelson, who was the most heroic figure among the oyster pirates and bay adventurers. Unfortunately for my stomach and mucous membranes, Nelson had a strange quirk of nature that made him find happiness in treating me to beer. I had no moral disinclination for beer, and just because I didn't like the taste of it and the weight of it was no reason I should forgo the honour of his company. It was his whim to drink beer, and to have me drink beer with him. Very well, I would put up with the passing discomfort.

So we continued to talk at the bar, and to drink beer ordered and paid for by Nelson. I think, now, when I look back upon it, that Nelson was curious. He wanted to find out just what kind of a gink I was. He wanted to see how many times I'd let him treat without offering to treat in return.

After I had drunk half a dozen glasses, my policy of temperateness in mind, I decided that I had had enough for that time. So I mentioned that I was going aboard the *Razzle Dazzle*, then lying at the city wharf, a hundred yards away.

I said good-bye to Nelson, and went on down the wharf. But, John Barleycorn, to the extent of six glasses, went with me. My brain tingled and was very much alive. I was uplifted by my sense of manhood. I, a truly-true oyster pirate, was going aboard my own boat after hob-nobbing in the Last Chance with Nelson, the greatest oyster pirate of us all. Strong in my brain was the vision of us

79

leaning against the bar and drinking beer. And curious it was, I decided, this whim of nature that made men happy in spending good money for beer for a fellow like me who didn't want it.

As I pondered this, I recollected that several times other men, in couples, had entered the Last Chance, and first one, then the other, had treated to drinks. I remembered, on the drunk on the *Idler*, how Scotty and the harpooner and myself had raked and scraped dimes and nickels with which to buy the whisky. Then came my boy code: when on a day a fellow gave another a "cannon-ball" or a chunk of taffy, on some other day he would expect to receive back a cannon-ball or a chunk of taffy.

That was why Nelson had lingered at the bar. Having bought a drink, he had waited for me to buy one. *I had let him buy six drinks and never once offered to treat.* And he was the great Nelson! I could feel myself blushing with shame. I sat down on the stringer-piece of the wharf and buried my face in my hands. And the heat of my shame burned up my neck and into my cheeks and forehead. I have blushed many times in my life, but never have I experienced so terrible a blush as that one.

And sitting there on the stringer-piece in my shame, I did a great deal of thinking and transvaluing of values. I had been born poor. Poor I had lived. I had gone hungry on occasion. I had never had toys nor playthings like other children. My first memories of life were pinched by poverty. The pinch of poverty had been chronic. I was eight years old when I wore my first little undershirt actually sold in a store across the counter. And then it had been only one little undershirt. When it was soiled I had to return to the awful home-made things until it was washed. I had been so proud of it that I insisted on wearing it without any outer garment. For the first time I mutinied against my mother—mutinied myself into hysteria, until she let me wear the store undershirt so all the world could see.

Only a man who has undergone famine can properly value food; only sailors and desert-dwellers know the meaning of fresh water. And only a child, with a child's imagination, can come to know the meaning of things it has been long denied. I early discovered that the only things I could have were those I got for myself. My meagre childhood developed meagreness. The first things I had been able to get for myself had been cigarette pictures, cigarette posters, and cigarette albums. I had not had the spending of the money I earned, so I traded "extra" newspapers for these treasures. I traded duplicates with the other boys, and circulating, as I did, all about town, I had greater opportunities for trading and acquiring.

It was not long before I had complete every series issued by every cigarette manufacturer—such as the Great Race Horses, Parisian Beauties, Women of All Nations, Flags of All Nations, Noted Actors, Champion Prize Fighters, etc. And each series I had three different ways: in the card from the cigarette package, in the poster, and in the album.

Then I began to accumulate duplicate sets, duplicate albums. I traded for other things that boys valued and which they usually bought with money given them by their parents. Naturally, they did not have the keen sense of values that I had, who was never given money to buy anything. I traded for postage-stamps, for minerals, for curios, for birds' eggs, for marbles (I had a more magnificent collection of agates than I have ever seen any boy possess—and the nucleus of the collection was a handful worth at least three dollars, which I had kept as security for twenty cents I loaned to a messenger-boy who was sent to reform school before he could redeem them).

I'd trade anything and everything for anything else, and turn it over in a dozen more trades until it was transmuted into something that was worth something. I was famous as a trader. I was notorious as a miser. I could even make a junkman weep when I had dealings with him. Other boys called me in to sell for them their collections of bottles, rags, old iron, grain, and gunny-sacks, and five-gallon oil-cans—aye, and gave me a commission for doing it.

And this was the thrifty, close-fisted boy, accustomed to slave at a machine for ten cents an hour, who sat on the stringer-piece and considered the matter of beer at five cents a glass and gone in a moment with nothing to show for it. I was now with men I admired. I was proud to be with them. Had all my pinching and saving brought me the equivalent of one of the many thrills which had been mine since I came among the oyster pirates? Then what was worth while—money or thrills? These men had no horror of squandering a nickel, or many nickels. They were magnificently careless of money, calling up eight men to drink whisky at ten cents a glass, as French Frank had done. Why, Nelson had just spent sixty cents on beer for the two of us.

Which was it to be? I was aware that I was making a grave decision. I was deciding between money and men, between niggardliness and romance. Either I must throw overboard all my old values of money and look upon it as something to be flung about wastefully, or I must throw overboard my comradeship with these men whose peculiar quirks made them like strong drink.

I retraced my steps up the wharf to the Last Chance, where Nelson still stood outside. "Come on and have a beer," I invited.

Again we stood at the bar and drank and talked, but this time it was I who paid ten cents! a whole hour of my labour at a machine for a drink of something I didn't want and which tasted rotten. But it wasn't difficult. I had achieved a concept. Money no longer counted. It was comradeship that counted. "Have another?" I said. And we had another, and I paid for it. Nelson, with the wisdom of the skilled drinker, said to the barkeeper, "Make mine a small one, Johnny." Johnny nodded and gave him a glass that contained only a third as much as the glasses we had been drinking. Yet the charge was the same—five cents.

By this time I was getting nicely jingled, so such extravagance didn't hurt me much. Besides, I was learning. There was more in this buying of drinks than mere quantity. I got my finger on it. There was a stage when the beer didn't count at all, but just the spirit of comradeship of drinking together. And, ha!—another thing! I, too, could call for small beers and minimise by two- thirds the detestable freightage with which comradeship burdened one.

"I had to go aboard to get some money," I remarked casually, as we drank, in the hope Nelson would take it as an explanation of why I had let him treat six consecutive times.

"Oh, well, you didn't have to do that," he answered. "Johnny'll trust a fellow like you—won't you, Johnny!"

"Sure," Johnny agreed, with a smile.

"How much you got down against me?" Nelson queried.

Johnny pulled out the book he kept behind the bar, found Nelson's page, and added up the account of several dollars. At once I became possessed with a desire to have a page in that book. Almost it seemed the final badge of manhood.

After a couple more drinks, for which I insisted on paying,

Nelson decided to go. We parted true comradely, and I wandered down the wharf to the *Razzle Dazzle*. Spider was just building the fire for supper.

"Where'd you get it?" he grinned up at me through the open companion.

"Oh, I've been with Nelson," I said carelessly, trying to hide my pride.

Then an idea came to me. Here was another one of them. Now that I had achieved my concept, I might as well practise it thoroughly. "Come on," I said, "up to Johnny's and have a drink."

Going up the wharf, we met Clam coming down. Clam was Nelson's partner, and he was a fine, brave, handsome, moustached man of thirty—everything, in short, that his nickname did not connote. "Come on," I said, "and have a drink." He came. As we turned into the Last Chance, there was Pat, the Queen's brother, coming out.

"What's your hurry?" I greeted him. "We're having a drink. Come on along." "I've just had one," he demurred. "What of it?—we're having one now," I retorted. And Pat consented to join us, and I melted my way into his good graces with a couple of glasses of beer. Oh! I was learning things that afternoon about John Barleycorn. There was more in him than the bad taste when you swallowed him. Here, at the absurd cost of ten cents, a gloomy, grouchy individual, who threatened to become an enemy, was made into a good friend. He became even genial, his looks were kindly, and our voices mellowed together as we talked water-front and oyster-bed gossip.

"Small beer for me, Johnny," I said, when the others had ordered schooners. Yes, and I said it like the accustomed drinker, carelessly, casually, as a sort of spontaneous thought that had just occurred to me. Looking back, I am confident that the only one there who guessed I was a tyro at bar-drinking was Johnny Heinhold.

"Where'd he get it?" I overheard Spider confidentially ask Johnny.

"Oh, he's been sousin' here with Nelson all afternoon," was Johnny's answer.

I never let on that I'd heard, but *proud*? Aye, even the barkeeper was giving me a recommendation as a man. "*He's been sousin' here with nelson all afternoon.*" Magic words! The accolade delivered by a barkeeper with a beer glass!

I remembered that French Frank had treated Johnny the day I bought the *Razzle Dazzle*. The glasses were filled and we were ready to drink. "Have something yourself, Johnny," I said, with an air of having intended to say it all the time, but of having been a trifle remiss because of the interesting conversation I had been holding with Clam and Pat.

Johnny looked at me with quick sharpness, divining, I am positive, the strides I was making in my education, and poured himself whisky from his private bottle. This hit me for a moment on my thrifty side. He had taken a ten-cent drink when the rest of us were drinking five-cent drinks! But the hurt was only for a moment. I dismissed it as ignoble, remembered my concept, and did not give myself away.

"You'd better put me down in the book for this," I said, when we had finished the drink. And I had the satisfaction of seeing a fresh page devoted to my name and a charge pencilled for a round of drinks amounting to thirty cents. And I glimpsed, as through a golden haze, a future wherein that page would be much charged, and crossed off, and charged again.

I treated a second time around, and then, to my amazement, Johnny redeemed himself in that matter of the ten-cent drink. He treated us around from behind the bar, and I decided that he had arithmetically evened things up handsomely.

"Let's go around to the St. Louis House," Spider suggested when we got outside. Pat, who had been shovelling coal all day, had gone home, and Clam had gone upon the *Reindeer* to cook supper.

So around Spider and I went to the St. Louis House—my first visit—a huge bar-room, where perhaps fifty men, mostly longshoremen, were congregated. And there I met Soup Kennedy for the second time, and Bill Kelley. And Smith, of the *Annie*, drifted in—he of the belt-buckled revolvers. And Nelson showed up. And I met others, including the Vigy brothers, who ran the place, and, chiefest of all, Joe Goose, with the wicked eyes, the twisted nose, and the flowered vest, who played the harmonica like a roystering angel and went on the most atrocious tears that even the Oakland water-front could conceive of and admire.

As I bought drinks—others treated as well—the thought flickered across my mind that Mammy Jennie wasn't going to be repaid much on her loan out of that week's earnings of the *Razzle Dazzle*. "But what of it?" I thought, or rather, John Barleycorn thought it for me. "You're a man and you're getting acquainted with men. Mammy Jennie doesn't need the money as promptly as all that. She isn't starving. You know that. She's got other money in the bank. Let her wait, and pay her back gradually."

And thus it was I learned another trait of John Barleycorn. He inhibits morality. Wrong conduct that it is impossible for one to do sober, is done quite easily when one is not sober. In fact, it is the only thing one can do, for John Barleycorn's inhibition rises like a wall between one's immediate desires and long-learned morality.

I dismissed my thought of debt to Mammy Jennie and proceeded to get acquainted at the trifling expense of some trifling money and a jingle that was growing unpleasant. Who took me on board and put me to bed that night I do not know, but I imagine it must have been Spider.

*

And so I won my manhood's spurs. My status on the water-front and with the oyster pirates became immediately excellent. I was looked upon as a good fellow, as well as no coward. And somehow, from the day I achieved that concept sitting on the stringer-piece of the Oakland City Wharf, I have never cared much for money. No one has ever considered me a miser since, while my carelessness of money is a source of anxiety and worry to some that know me.

So completely did I break with my parsimonious past that I sent word home to my mother to call in the boys of the neighbourhood and give to them all my collections. I never even cared to learn what boys got what collections. I was a man now, and I made a clean sweep of everything that bound me to my boyhood.

My reputation grew. When the story went around the water-front of how French Frank had tried to run me down with his schooner, and of how I had stood on the deck of the *Razzle Dazzle*, a cocked double-barrelled shotgun in my hands, steering with my feet and holding her to her course, and compelled him to put up his wheel and keep away, the water-front decided that there was something in me despite my youth. And I continued to show what was in me. There were the times I brought the *Razzle Dazzle* in with a bigger load of oysters than any other two-man craft; there was the time when we raided far down in Lower Bay, and mine was the only craft back at daylight to the anchorage off Asparagus Island; there was the Thursday night we raced for market and I brought the *Razzle Dazzle* in without a rudder, first of the fleet, and skimmed the cream of the Friday morning trade; and there was the time I brought her in from Upper Bay under a jib, when Scotty burned my mainsail. (Yes; it was Scotty of the *Idler* adventure. Irish had followed Spider on board the *Razzle Dazzle*, and Scotty, turning up, had taken Irish's place.)

But the things I did on the water only partly counted. What completed everything, and won for me the title of "Prince of the Oyster Beds," was that I was a good fellow ashore with my money, buying drinks like a man. I little dreamed that the time would come when the Oakland water-front, which had shocked me at first would be shocked and annoyed by the devilry of the things I did.

But always the life was tied up with drinking. The saloons are poor men's clubs. Saloons are congregating places. We engaged to meet one another in saloons. We celebrated our good fortune or wept our grief in saloons. We got acquainted in saloons.

Can I ever forget the afternoon I met "Old Scratch," Nelson's father? It was in the Last Chance. Johnny Heinhold introduced us. That Old Scratch was Nelson's father was noteworthy enough. But there was more in it than that. He was owner and master of the scow-schooner *Annie Mine*, and some day I might ship as a sailor with him. Still more, he was romance. He was a blue-eyed, yellow-haired, raw-boned Viking, big-bodied and strong-muscled despite his age. And he had sailed the seas in ships of all nations in the old savage sailing days.

I had heard many weird tales about him, and worshipped him from a distance. It took the saloon to bring us together. Even so, our acquaintance might have been no more than a hand-grip and a word— he was a laconic old fellow—had it not been for the drinking.

"Have a drink," I said, with promptitude, after the pause which I had learned good form in drinking dictates. Of course, while we drank our beer, which I had paid for, it was incumbent on him to listen to me and to talk to me. And Johnny, like a true host, made the tactful remarks that enabled us to find mutual topics of conversation. And of course, having drunk my beer, Captain Nelson must now buy beer in turn. This led to more talking, and Johnny drifted out of the conversation to wait on other customers.

The more beer Captain Nelson and I drank, the better we got acquainted. In me he found an appreciative listener, who, by virtue of book-reading, knew much about the sea-life he had lived. So he drifted back to his wild young days, and spun many a rare yarn for me, while we downed beer, treat by treat, all through a blessed summer afternoon. And it was only John Barleycorn that made possible that long afternoon with the old sea-dog.

It was Johnny Heinhold who secretly warned me across the bar that I was getting pickled and advised me to take small beers. But as long as Captain Nelson drank large beers, my pride forbade anything else than large beers. And not until the skipper ordered his first small beer did I order one for myself. Oh, when we came to a lingering fond farewell, I was drunk. But I had the satisfaction of seeing Old Scratch as drunk as I. My youthful modesty scarcely let me dare believe that the hardened old buccaneer was even more drunk.

And afterwards, from Spider, and Pat, and Clam, and Johnny Heinhold, and others, came the tips that Old Scratch liked me and had nothing but good words for the fine lad I was. Which was the more remarkable, because he was known as a savage, cantankerous old cuss who never liked anybody. (His very nickname, "Scratch," arose from a Berserker trick of his, in fighting, of tearing off his opponent's face.) And that I had won his friendship, all thanks were due to John Barleycorn. I have given the incident merely as an example of the multitudinous lures and draws and services by which John Barleycorn wins his followers.

1913

II. TALES OF THE FISH PATROL (1905)

Illustrations from the original edition
by George Varian

"I put my hand to my hip pocket."

WHITE AND YELLOW

San Francisco Bay is so large that often its storms are more disastrous to ocean-going craft than is the ocean itself in its violent moments. The waters of the bay contain all manner of fish, wherefore its surface is ploughed by the keels of all manner of fishing boats manned by all manner of fishermen. To protect the fish from this motley floating population many wise laws have been passed, and there is a fish patrol to see that these laws are enforced. Exciting times are the lot of the fish patrol: in its history more than one dead patrolman has marked defeat, and more often dead fishermen across their illegal nets have marked success.

Wildest among the fisher-folk may be accounted the Chinese shrimp- catchers. It is the habit of the shrimp to crawl along the bottom in vast armies till it reaches fresh water, when it turns about and crawls back again to the salt. And where the tide ebbs and flows, the Chinese sink great bag-nets to the bottom, with gaping mouths, into which the shrimp crawls and from which it is transferred to the boiling-pot. This in itself would not be bad, were it not for the small mesh of the nets, so small that the tiniest fishes, little new-hatched things not a quarter of an inch long, cannot pass through. The beautiful beaches of Points Pedro and Pablo, where are the shrimp-catchers' villages, are made fearful by the stench from myriads of decaying fish, and against this wasteful destruction it has ever been the duty of the fish patrol to act.

When I was a youngster of sixteen, a good sloop-sailor and all-round bay-waterman, my sloop, the *Reindeer*, was chartered by the Fish Commission, and I became for the time being a deputy patrolman. After a deal of work among the Greek fishermen of the Upper Bay and rivers, where knives flashed at the beginning of trouble and men permitted themselves to be made prisoners only after a revolver was thrust in their faces, we hailed with delight an expedition to the Lower Bay against the Chinese shrimp-catchers.

There were six of us, in two boats, and to avoid suspicion we ran down after dark and dropped anchor under a projecting bluff of land known as Point Pinole. As the east paled with the first light of dawn we got under way again, and hauled close on the land breeze as we slanted across the bay toward Point Pedro. The morning mists curled and clung to the water so that we could see nothing, but we busied ourselves driving the chill from our bodies with hot coffee. Also we had to devote ourselves to the miserable task of bailing, for in some incomprehensible way the *Reindeer* had sprung a generous leak. Half the night had been spent in overhauling the ballast and exploring the seams, but the labor had been without avail. The water still poured in, and perforce we doubled up in the cockpit and tossed it out again.

After coffee, three of the men withdrew to the other boat, a Columbia River salmon boat, leaving three of us in the *Reindeer*. Then the two craft proceeded in company till the sun showed over the eastern sky-line. Its fiery rays dispelled the clinging vapors, and there, before our eyes, like a picture, lay the shrimp fleet, spread out in a great half-moon, the tips of the crescent fully three miles apart, and each junk moored fast to the buoy of a shrimp-net. But there was no stir, no sign of life.

The situation dawned upon us. While waiting for slack water, in which to lift their heavy nets from the bed of the bay, the Chinese had all gone to sleep below. We were elated, and our plan of battle was swiftly formed.

"Throw each of your two men on to a junk," whispered Le Grant to me from the salmon boat. "And you make fast to a third yourself. We'll do the same, and there's no reason in the world why we shouldn't capture six junks at the least."

Then we separated. I put the *Reindeer* about on the other tack, ran up under the lee of a junk, shivered the mainsail into the wind and lost headway, and forged past the stern of the junk so slowly and so near that one of the patrolmen stepped lightly aboard. Then I kept off, filled the mainsail, and bore away for a second junk.

Up to this time there had been no noise, but from the first junk captured by the salmon boat an uproar now broke forth. There was shrill Oriental yelling, a pistol shot, and more yelling.

"It's all up. They're warning the others," said George, the remaining patrolman, as he stood beside me in the cockpit.

By this time we were in the thick of the fleet, and the alarm was spreading with incredible swiftness. The decks were beginning to swarm with half-awakened and half-naked Chinese. Cries and yells of warning and anger were flying over the quiet water, and somewhere a conch shell was being blown with great success. To the right of us I saw the captain of a junk chop away his mooring line with an axe and spring to help his crew at the hoisting of the huge, outlandish lug-sail. But to the left the first heads were popping up from below on another junk, and I rounded up the *Reindeer* alongside long enough for George to spring aboard.

The whole fleet was now under way. In addition to the sails they had gotten out long sweeps, and the bay was being ploughed in every direction by the fleeing junks. I was now alone in the *Reindeer*, seeking feverishly to capture a third prize. The first junk I took after was a clean miss, for it trimmed its sheets and shot away surprisingly into the wind. By fully half a point it outpointed the *Reindeer*, and I began to feel respect for the clumsy craft. Realizing the hopelessness of the pursuit, I filled away, threw out the main-sheet, and drove down before the wind upon the junks to leeward, where I had them at a disadvantage.

The one I had selected wavered indecisively before me, and, as I swung wide to make the boarding gentle, filled suddenly and darted away, the smart Mongols shouting a wild rhythm as they bent to the sweeps. But I had been ready for this. I luffed suddenly. Putting the tiller hard down, and holding it down with my body, I brought the main-sheet in, hand over hand, on the run, so as to retain all possible striking force. The two starboard sweeps of the junk were crumpled up, and then the two boats came together with a crash. The *Reindeer's* bowsprit, like a monstrous hand, reached over and ripped out the junk's chunky mast and towering sail.

This was met by a curdling yell of rage. A big Chinaman, remarkably evil-looking, with his head swathed in a yellow silk handkerchief and face badly pock-marked, planted a pike-pole on the *Reindeer's* bow and began to shove the entangled boats apart. Pausing long enough to let go the jib halyards, and just as the *Reindeer* cleared and began to drift astern, I leaped aboard the junk with a line and made fast. He of the yellow handkerchief and pock-marked face came toward me threateningly, but I put my hand into my hip pocket, and he hesitated. I was unarmed, but the Chinese have learned to be fastidiously careful of American hip pockets, and it was upon this that I depended to keep him and his savage crew at a distance.

I ordered him to drop the anchor at the junk's bow, to which he replied, "No sabbe." The crew responded in like fashion, and though I made my meaning plain by signs, they refused to understand. Realizing the inexpediency of discussing the matter, I went forward myself, overran the line, and let the anchor go.

"Now get aboard, four of you," I said in a loud voice, indicating with my fingers that four of them were to go with me and the fifth was to remain by the junk. The Yellow Handkerchief hesitated; but I repeated the order fiercely (much more fiercely than I felt), at the same time sending my hand to my hip. Again the Yellow Handkerchief was overawed, and with surly looks he led three of his men aboard the *Reindeer*. I cast off at once, and, leaving the jib down, steered a course for George's junk. Here it was easier, for there were two of us, and George had a pistol to fall back on if it came to the worst. And here, as with my junk, four Chinese were transferred to the sloop and one left behind to take care of things.

Four more were added to our passenger list from the third junk. By this time the salmon boat had collected its twelve prisoners and came alongside, badly overloaded. To make matters worse, as it was a small boat, the patrolmen were so jammed in with their prisoners that they would have little chance in case of trouble.

"You'll have to help us out," said Le Grant.

I looked over my prisoners, who had crowded into the cabin and on top of it. "I can take three," I answered.

"Make it four," he suggested, "and I'll take Bill with me." (Bill was the third patrolman.) "We haven't elbow room here, and in case of a scuffle one white to every two of them will be just about the right proportion."

The exchange was made, and the salmon boat got up its spritsail and headed down the bay toward the marshes off San Rafael. I ran up the jib and followed with the *Reindeer*. San Rafael, where we were to turn our catch over to the authorities, communicated with the bay by way of a long and tortuous slough, or marshland creek, which could be navigated only when the tide was in. Slack water had come, and, as the ebb was commencing, there was need for hurry if we cared to escape waiting half a day for the next tide.

But the land breeze had begun to die away with the rising sun, and now came only in failing puffs. The salmon boat got out its oars and soon left us far astern. Some of the Chinese stood in the forward part of the cockpit, near the cabin doors, and once, as I leaned over the cockpit rail to flatten down the jib-sheet a bit, I felt some one brush against my hip pocket. I made no sign, but out of the corner of my eye I saw that the Yellow Handkerchief had discovered the emptiness of the pocket which had hitherto overawed him.

To make matters serious, during all the excitement of boarding the junks the *Reindeer* had not been bailed, and the water was beginning to slush over the cockpit floor. The shrimp-catchers pointed at it and looked to me questioningly.

"Yes," I said. "Bime by, allee same dlown, velly quick, you no bail now. Sabbe?"

No, they did not "sabbe," or at least they shook their heads to that effect, though they chattered most comprehendingly to one another in their own lingo. I pulled up three or four of the bottom boards, got a couple of buckets from a locker, and by unmistakable sign-language invited them to fall to. But they laughed, and some crowded into the cabin and some climbed up on top.

Their laughter was not good laughter. There was a hint of menace in it, a maliciousness which their black looks verified. The Yellow Handkerchief, since his discovery of my empty pocket, had become most insolent in his bearing, and he wormed about among the other prisoners, talking to them with great earnestness.

Swallowing my chagrin, I stepped down into the cockpit and began throwing out the water. But hardly had I begun, when the boom swung overhead, the mainsail filled with a jerk, and the *Reindeer* heeled over. The day wind was springing up. George was the veriest of landlubbers, so I was forced to give over bailing and take the tiller. The wind was blowing directly off Point Pedro and the high mountains behind, and because of this was squally and uncertain, half the time bellying the canvas out and the other half flapping it idly.

George was about the most all-round helpless man I had ever met. Among his other disabilities, he was a consumptive, and I knew that if he attempted to bail, it might bring on a hemorrhage. Yet the rising water warned me that something must be done. Again I ordered the shrimp-catchers to lend a hand with the buckets. They laughed defiantly, and those inside the cabin, the water up to their ankles, shouted back and forth with those on top.

"You'd better get out your gun and make them bail," I said to George.

But he shook his head and showed all too plainly that he was afraid. The Chinese could see the funk he was in as well as I could, and their insolence became insufferable. Those in the cabin broke into the food lockers, and those above scrambled down and joined them in a feast on our crackers and canned goods.

"What do we care?" George said weakly.

I was fuming with helpless anger. "If they get out of hand, it will be too late to care. The best thing you can do is to get them in check right now."

The water was rising higher and higher, and the gusts, forerunners of a steady breeze, were growing stiffer and stiffer. And between the gusts, the prisoners, having gotten away with a week's grub, took to crowding first to one side and then to the other till the *Reindeer* rocked like a cockle-shell. Yellow Handkerchief approached me, and, pointing out his village on the Point Pedro beach, gave me to understand that if I turned the *Reindeer* in that direction and put them ashore, they, in turn, would go to bailing. By now the water in the cabin was up to the bunks, and the bed-clothes were sopping. It was a foot deep on the cockpit floor. Nevertheless I refused, and I could see by George's face that he was disappointed.

"If you don't show some nerve, they'll rush us and throw us overboard," I said to him. "Better give me your revolver, if you want to be safe."

"The safest thing to do," he chattered cravenly, "is to put them ashore. I, for one, don't want to be drowned for the sake of a handful of dirty Chinamen."

"And I, for another, don't care to give in to a handful of dirty Chinamen to escape drowning," I answered hotly.

"You'll sink the *Reindeer* under us all at this rate," he whined. "And what good that'll do I can't see."

"Every man to his taste," I retorted.

He made no reply, but I could see he was trembling pitifully. Between the threatening Chinese and the rising water he was beside himself with fright; and, more than the Chinese and the water, I feared him and what his fright might impel him to do. I could see him casting longing glances at the small skiff towing astern, so in the next calm I hauled the skiff alongside. As I did so his eyes brightened with hope; but before he could guess my intention, I stove the frail bottom through with a hand-axe, and the skiff filled to its gunwales.

"It's sink or float together," I said. "And if you'll give me your revolver, I'll have the *Reindeer* bailed out in a jiffy."

"They're too many for us," he whimpered. "We can't fight them all."

I turned my back on him in disgust. The salmon boat had long since passed from sight behind a little archipelago known as the Marin Islands, so no help could be looked for from that quarter. Yellow Handkerchief came up to me in a familiar manner, the water in the cockpit slushing against his legs. I did not like his looks. I felt that beneath the pleasant smile he was trying to put on his face there was an ill purpose. I ordered him back, and so sharply that he obeyed.

"Now keep your distance," I commanded, "and don't you come closer!"

"Wha' fo'?" he demanded indignantly. "I t'ink-um talkee talkee heap good."

"Talkee talkee," I answered bitterly, for I knew now that he had understood all that passed between George and me. "What for talkee talkee? You no sabbe talkee talkee."

He grinned in a sickly fashion. "Yep, I sabbe velly much. I honest Chinaman."

"All right," I answered. "You sabbe talkee talkee, then you bail water plenty plenty. After that we talkee talkee."

He shook his head, at the same time pointing over his shoulder to his comrades. "No can do. Velly bad Chinamen, heap velly bad. I t'ink-um - "

"Stand back!" I shouted, for I had noticed his hand disappear beneath his blouse and his body prepare for a spring.

Disconcerted, he went back into the cabin, to hold a council, apparently, from the way the jabbering broke forth. The *Reindeer* was very deep in the water, and her movements had grown quite loggy. In a rough sea she would have inevitably swamped; but the wind, when it did blow, was off the land, and scarcely a ripple disturbed the surface of the bay.

"I think you'd better head for the beach," George said abruptly, in a manner that told me his fear had forced him to make up his mind to some course of action.

"I think not," I answered shortly.

"I command you," he said in a bullying tone.

"I was commanded to bring these prisoners into San Rafael," was my reply.

Our voices were raised, and the sound of the altercation brought the Chinese out of the cabin.

"Now will you head for the beach?"

This from George, and I found myself looking into the muzzle of his revolver - of the revolver he dared to use on me, but was too cowardly to use on the prisoners.

My brain seemed smitten with a dazzling brightness. The whole situation, in all its bearings, was focussed sharply before me - the shame of losing the prisoners, the worthlessness and cowardice of George, the meeting with Le Grant and the other patrol men and the lame explanation; and then there was the fight I had fought so hard, victory wrenched from me just as I thought I had it within my grasp. And out of the tail of my eye I could see the Chinese crowding together by the cabin doors and leering triumphantly. It would never do.

I threw my hand up and my head down. The first act elevated the muzzle, and the second removed my head from the path of the bullet which went whistling past. One hand closed on George's wrist, the other on the revolver. Yellow Handkerchief and his gang sprang toward me. It was now or never. Putting all my strength into a sudden effort, I swung George's body forward to meet them. Then I pulled back with equal suddenness, ripping the revolver out of his fingers and jerking him off his feet. He fell against Yellow Handkerchief's knees, who stumbled over him, and the pair wallowed in the bailing hole where the cockpit floor was torn open. The next instant I was covering them with my revolver, and the wild shrimp-catchers were cowering and cringing away.

But I swiftly discovered that there was all the difference in the world between shooting men who are attacking and men who are doing nothing more than simply refusing to obey. For obey they would not when I ordered them into the bailing hole. I threatened them with the revolver, but they sat stolidly in the flooded cabin and on the roof and would not move.

Fifteen minutes passed, the *Reindeer* sinking deeper and deeper, her mainsail flapping in the calm. But from off the Point Pedro shore I saw a dark line form on the water and travel toward us. It was the steady breeze I had been expecting so long. I called to the Chinese and pointed it out. They hailed it with exclamations. Then I pointed to the sail and to the water in the *Reindeer*, and indicated by signs that when the wind reached the sail, what of the water aboard we would capsize. But they jeered defiantly, for they knew it was in my power to luff the helm and let go the main-sheet, so as to spill the wind and escape damage.

But my mind was made up. I hauled in the main-sheet a foot or two, took a turn with it, and bracing my feet, put my back against the tiller. This left me one hand for the sheet and one for the revolver. The dark line drew nearer, and I could see them looking from me to it and back again with an apprehension they could not successfully conceal. My brain and will and endurance were pitted against theirs, and the problem was which could stand the strain of imminent death the longer and not give in.

Then the wind struck us. The main-sheet tautened with a brisk rattling of the blocks, the boom uplifted, the sail bellied out, and the *Reindeer* heeled over - over, and over, till the lee-rail went under, the cabin windows went under, and the bay began to pour in over the cockpit rail. So violently had she heeled over, that the men in the cabin had been thrown on top of one another into the lee bunk, where they squirmed and twisted and were washed about, those underneath being perilously near to drowning.

The wind freshened a bit, and the *Reindeer* went over farther than ever. For the moment I thought she was gone, and I knew that another puff like that and she surely would go. While I pressed her under and debated whether I should give up or not, the Chinese cried for mercy. I think it was the sweetest sound I have ever heard. And then, and not until then, did I luff up and ease out the main-sheet. The *Reindeer* righted very slowly, and when she was on an even keel was so much awash that I doubted if she could be saved.

But the Chinese scrambled madly into the cockpit and fell to bailing with buckets, pots, pans, and everything they could lay hands on. It was a beautiful sight to see that water flying over the side! And when the *Reindeer* was high and proud on the water once more, we dashed away with the breeze on our quarter, and at the last possible moment crossed the mud flats and entered the slough.

The spirit of the Chinese was broken, and so docile did they become that ere we made San Rafael they were out with the tow-rope, Yellow Handkerchief at the head of the line. As for George, it was his last trip with the fish patrol. He did not care for that sort of thing, he explained, and he thought a clerkship ashore was good enough for him. And we thought so too.

(First published in *The Youth's Companion*, Feb. 16, 1905)

"He saw fit to laugh and sneer at us, before all the fishermen."

THE KING OF THE GREEKS

Big Alec had never been captured by the fish patrol. It was his boast that no man could take him alive, and it was his history that of the many men who had tried to take him dead none had succeeded. It was also history that at least two patrolmen who had tried to take him dead had died themselves. Further, no man violated the fish laws more systematically and deliberately than Big Alec.

He was called "Big Alec" because of his gigantic stature. His height was six feet three inches, and he was correspondingly broad-shouldered and deep-chested. He was splendidly muscled and hard as steel, and there were innumerable stories in circulation among the fisher-folk concerning his prodigious strength. He was as bold and dominant of spirit as he was strong of body, and because of this he was widely known by another name, that of "The King of the Greeks." The fishing population was largely composed of Greeks, and they looked up to him and obeyed him as their chief. And as their chief, he fought their fights for them, saw that they were protected, saved them from the law when they fell into its clutches, and made them stand by one another and himself in time of trouble.

In the old days, the fish patrol had attempted his capture many disastrous times and had finally given it over, so that when the word was out that he was coming to Benicia, I was most anxious to see him. But I did not have to hunt him up. In his usual bold way,

107

the first thing he did on arriving was to hunt us up. Charley Le Grant and I at the time were under a patrol-man named Carmintel, and the three of us were on the *Reindeer*, preparing for a trip, when Big Alec stepped aboard. Carmintel evidently knew him, for they shook hands in recognition. Big Alec took no notice of Charley or me.

"I've come down to fish sturgeon a couple of months," he said to Carmintel.

His eyes flashed with challenge as he spoke, and we noticed the patrolman's eyes drop before him.

"That's all right, Alec," Carmintel said in a low voice. "I'll not bother you. Come on into the cabin, and we'll talk things over," he added.

When they had gone inside and shut the doors after them, Charley winked with slow deliberation at me. But I was only a youngster, and new to men and the ways of some men, so I did not understand. Nor did Charley explain, though I felt there was something wrong about the business.

Leaving them to their conference, at Charley's suggestion we boarded our skiff and pulled over to the Old Steamboat Wharf, where Big Alec's ark was lying. An ark is a house-boat of small though comfortable dimensions, and is as necessary to the Upper Bay fisherman as are nets and boats. We were both curious to see Big Alec's ark, for history said that it had been the scene of more than one pitched battle, and that it was riddled with bullet-holes.

We found the holes (stopped with wooden plugs and painted over), but there were not so many as I had expected. Charley noted my look of disappointment, and laughed; and then to comfort me he gave an authentic account of one expedition which had descended upon Big Alec's floating home to capture him, alive preferably, dead if necessary. At the end of half a day's fighting, the patrolmen had drawn off in wrecked boats, with one of their number killed and three wounded. And when they returned next morning with reinforcements they found only the mooring-stakes of Big Alec's ark; the ark itself remained hidden for months in the fastnesses of the Suisun tules.

"But why was he not hanged for murder?" I demanded. "Surely the United States is powerful enough to bring such a man to justice."

"He gave himself up and stood trial," Charley answered. "It cost him fifty thousand dollars to win the case, which he did on technicalities and with the aid of the best lawyers in the state. Every Greek fisherman on the river contributed to the sum. Big Alec levied and collected the tax, for all the world like a king. The United States may be all-powerful, my lad, but the fact remains that Big Alec is a king inside the United States, with a country and subjects all his own."

"But what are you going to do about his fishing for sturgeon? He's bound to fish with a 'Chinese line.'"

Charley shrugged his shoulders. "We'll see what we will see," he said enigmatically.

Now a "Chinese line" is a cunning device invented by the people whose name it bears. By a simple system of floats, weights, and anchors, thousands of hooks, each on a separate leader, are suspended at a distance of from six inches to a foot above the bottom. The remarkable thing about such a line is the hook. It is barbless, and in place of the barb, the hook is filed long and tapering to a point as sharp as that of a needle. These hoods are only a few inches apart, and when several thousand of them are suspended just above the bottom, like a fringe, for a couple of hundred fathoms, they present a formidable obstacle to the fish that travel along the bottom.

Such a fish is the sturgeon, which goes rooting along like a pig, and indeed is often called "pig-fish." Pricked by the first hook it touches, the sturgeon gives a startled leap and comes into contact with half a dozen more hooks. Then it threshes about wildly, until it receives hook after hook in its soft flesh; and the hooks, straining from many different angles, hold the luckless fish fast until it is drowned. Because no sturgeon can pass through a Chinese line, the device is called a trap in the fish laws; and because it bids fair to exterminate the sturgeon, it is branded by the fish laws as illegal. And such a line, we were confident, Big Alec intended setting, in open and flagrant violation of the law.

Several days passed after the visit of Big Alec, during which Charley and I kept a sharp watch on him. He towed his ark around the Solano Wharf and into the big bight at Turner's Shipyard. The bight we knew to be good ground for sturgeon, and there we felt sure the King of the Greeks intended to begin operations. The tide circled like a mill-race in and out of this bight, and made it possible to raise, lower, or set a Chinese line only at slack water. So between the tides Charley and I made it a point for one or the other of us to keep a lookout from the Solano Wharf.

On the fourth day I was lying in the sun behind the stringer-piece of the wharf, when I saw a skiff leave the distant shore and pull out into the bight. In an instant the glasses were at my eyes and I was following every movement of the skiff. There were two men in it, and though it was a good mile away, I made out one of them

110

to be Big Alec; and ere the skiff returned to shore I made out enough more to know that the Greek had set his line.

"Big Alec has a Chinese line out in the bight off Turner's Shipyard," Charley Le Grant said that afternoon to Carmintel.

A fleeting expression of annoyance passed over the patrolman's face, and then he said, "Yes?" in an absent way, and that was all.

Charley bit his lip with suppressed anger and turned on his heel.

"Are you game, my lad?" he said to me later on in the evening, just as we finished washing down the *Reindeer*'s decks and were preparing to turn in.

A lump came up in my throat, and I could only nod my head.

"Well, then," and Charley's eyes glittered in a determined way, "we've got to capture Big Alec between us, you and I, and we've got to do it in spite of Carmintel. Will you lend a hand?"

"It's a hard proposition, but we can do it," he added after a pause.

"Of course we can," I supplemented enthusiastically.

And then he said, "Of course we can," and we shook hands on it and went to bed.

But it was no easy task we had set ourselves. In order to convict a man of illegal fishing, it was necessary to catch him in the act with all the evidence of the crime about him - the hooks, the lines, the fish, and the man himself. This meant that we must take Big Alec on the open water, where he could see us coming and prepare for us one of the warm receptions for which he was noted.

"There's no getting around it," Charley said one morning. "If we can only get alongside it's an even toss, and there's nothing left for us but to try and get alongside. Come on, lad."

111

We were in the Columbia River salmon boat, the one we had used against the Chinese shrimp-catchers. Slack water had come, and as we dropped around the end of the Solano Wharf we saw Big Alec at work, running his line and removing the fish.

"Change places," Charley commanded, "and steer just astern of him as though you're going into the shipyard."

I took the tiller, and Charley sat down on a thwart amidships, placing his revolver handily beside him.

"If he begins to shoot," he cautioned, "get down in the bottom and steer from there, so that nothing more than your hand will be exposed."

I nodded, and we kept silent after that, the boat slipping gently through the water and Big Alec growing nearer and nearer. We could see him quite plainly, gaffing the sturgeon and throwing them into the boat while his companion ran the line and cleared the hooks as he dropped them back into the water. Nevertheless, we were five hundred yards away when the big fisherman hailed us.

"Here! You! What do you want?" he shouted.

"Keep going," Charley whispered, "just as though you didn't hear him."

The next few moments were very anxious ones. The fisherman was studying us sharply, while we were gliding up on him every second.

"You keep off if you know what's good for you!" he called out suddenly, as though he had made up his mind as to who and what we were. "If you don't, I'll fix you!"

He brought a rifle to his shoulder and trained it on me.

"Now will you keep off?" he demanded.

I could hear Charley groan with disappointment. "Keep off," he whispered; "it's all up for this time."

I put up the tiller and eased the sheet, and the salmon boat ran off five or six points. Big Alec watched us till we were out of range, when he returned to his work.

"You'd better leave Big Alec alone," Carmintel said, rather sourly, to Charley that night.

"So he's been complaining to you, has he?" Charley said significantly.

Carmintel flushed painfully. "You'd better leave him alone, I tell you," he repeated. "He's a dangerous man, and it won't pay to fool with him."

"Yes," Charley answered softly; "I've heard that it pays better to leave him alone."

This was a direct thrust at Carmintel, and we could see by the expression of his face that it sank home. For it was common knowledge that Big Alec was as willing to bribe as to fight, and that of late years more than one patrolman had handled the fisherman's money.

"Do you mean to say - " Carmintel began, in a bullying tone.

But Charley cut him off shortly. "I mean to say nothing," he said. "You heard what I said, and if the cap fits, why - "

He shrugged his shoulders, and Carmintel glowered at him, speechless.

"What we want is imagination," Charley said to me one day, when we had attempted to creep upon Big Alec in the gray of dawn and had been shot at for our trouble.

And thereafter, and for many days, I cudgelled my brains trying to imagine some possible way by which two men, on an open stretch of water, could capture another who knew how to use a rifle and was never to be found without one. Regularly, every slack water, without slyness, boldly and openly in the broad day, Big Alec was to be seen running his line. And what made it particularly exasperating was the fact that every fisherman, from Benicia to Vallejo knew that he was successfully defying us. Carmintel also bothered us, for he kept us busy among the shad-fishers of San Pablo, so that we had little time to spare on the King of the Greeks. But Charley's wife and children lived at Benicia, and we had made the place our headquarters, so that we always returned to it.

"I'll tell you what we can do," I said, after several fruitless weeks had passed; "we can wait some slack water till Big Alec has run his line and gone ashore with the fish, and then we can go out and capture the line. It will put him to time and expense to make another, and then we'll figure to capture that too. If we can't capture him, we can discourage him, you see."

Charley saw, and said it wasn't a bad idea. We watched our chance, and the next low-water slack, after Big Alec had removed the fish from the line and returned ashore, we went out in the salmon boat. We had the bearings of the line from shore marks, and we knew we would have no difficulty in locating it. The first of the flood tide was setting in, when we ran below where we thought the line was stretched and dropped over a fishing-boat anchor. Keeping a short rope to the anchor, so that it barely touched the bottom, we dragged it slowly along until it stuck and the boat fetched up hard and fast.

"We've got it," Charley cried. "Come on and lend a hand to get it in."

Together we hove up the rope till the anchor I came in sight with the sturgeon line caught across one of the flukes. Scores of the murderous-looking hooks flashed into sight as we cleared the anchor, and we had just started to run along the line to the end where we could begin to lift it, when a sharp thud in the boat startled us. We looked about, but saw nothing and returned to our work. An instant later there was a similar sharp thud and the gunwale splintered between Charley's body and mine.

"That's remarkably like a bullet, lad," he said reflectively. "And it's a long shot Big Alec's making."

"And he's using smokeless powder," he concluded, after an examination of the mile-distant shore. "That's why we can't hear the report."

I looked at the shore, but could see no sign of Big Alec, who was undoubtedly hidden in some rocky nook with us at his mercy. A third bullet struck the water, glanced, passed singing over our heads, and struck the water again beyond.

"I guess we'd better get out of this," Charley remarked coolly. "What do you think, lad?"

I thought so, too, and said we didn't want the line anyway. Whereupon we cast off and hoisted the spritsail. The bullets ceased at once, and we sailed away, unpleasantly confident that Big Alec was laughing at our discomfiture.

And more than that, the next day on the fishing wharf, where we were inspecting nets, he saw fit to laugh and sneer at us, and this before all the fishermen. Charley's face went black with anger; but beyond promising Big Alec that in the end he would surely land him behind the bars, he controlled himself and said nothing. The King of the Greeks made his boast that no fish patrol had ever taken him or ever could take him, and the fishermen cheered him and said it was true. They grew excited, and it looked like trouble for a

115

while; but Big Alec asserted his kingship and quelled them.

Carmintel also laughed at Charley, and dropped sarcastic remarks, and made it hard for him. But Charley refused to be angered, though he told me in confidence that he intended to capture Big Alec if it took all the rest of his life to accomplish it.

"I don't know how I'll do it," he said, "but do it I will, as sure as I am Charley Le Grant. The idea will come to me at the right and proper time, never fear."

And at the right time it came, and most unexpectedly. Fully a month had passed, and we were constantly up and down the river, and down and up the bay, with no spare moments to devote to the particular fisherman who ran a Chinese line in the bight of Turner's Shipyard. We had called in at Selby's Smelter one afternoon, while on patrol work, when all unknown to us our opportunity happened along. It appeared in the guise of a helpless yacht loaded with seasick people, so we could hardly be expected to recognize it as the opportunity. It was a large sloop-yacht, and it was helpless inasmuch as the trade-wind was blowing half a gale and there were no capable sailors aboard.

From the wharf at Selby's we watched with careless interest the lubberly manoeuvre performed of bringing the yacht to anchor, and the equally lubberly manoeuvre of sending the small boat ashore. A very miserable-looking man in draggled ducks, after nearly swamping the boat in the heavy seas, passed us the painter and climbed out. He staggered about as though the wharf were rolling, and told us his troubles, which were the troubles of the yacht. The only rough-weather sailor aboard, the man on whom they all depended, had been called back to San Francisco by a telegram, and they had attempted to continue the cruise alone. The high wind and big seas of San Pablo Bay had been too much for them; all hands were sick, nobody knew anything or could do anything; and so they had run in to the smelter either to desert the yacht or to get somebody to bring it to Benicia. In short, did we know of any sailors who would bring the yacht into Benicia?

Charley looked at me. The *Reindeer* was lying in a snug place. We had nothing on hand in the way of patrol work till midnight. With the wind then blowing, we could sail the yacht into Benicia in a couple of hours, have several more hours ashore, and come back to the smelter on the evening train.

"All right, captain," Charley said to the disconsolate yachtsman, who smiled in sickly fashion at the title.

"I'm only the owner," he explained.

We rowed him aboard in much better style than he had come ashore, and saw for ourselves the helplessness of the passengers. There were a dozen men and women, and all of them too sick even to appear grateful at our coming. The yacht was rolling savagely, broad on, and no sooner had the owner's feet touched the deck than he collapsed and joined, the others. Not one was able to bear a hand, so Charley and I between us cleared the badly tangled running gear, got up sail, and hoisted anchor.

It was a rough trip, though a swift one. The Carquinez Straits were a welter of foam and smother, and we came through them wildly before the wind, the big mainsail alternately dipping and flinging its boom skyward as we tore along. But the people did not mind. They did not mind anything. Two or three, including the owner, sprawled in the cockpit, shuddering when the yacht lifted and raced and sank dizzily into the trough, and between-whiles regarding the shore with yearning eyes. The rest were huddled on the cabin floor among the cushions. Now and again some one groaned, but for the most part they were as limp as so many dead persons.

As the bight at Turner's Shipyard opened out, Charley edged into it to get the smoother water. Benicia was in view, and we were bowling along over comparatively easy water, when a speck of a boat danced up ahead of us, directly in our course. It was low-water slack. Charley and I looked at each other. No word was spoken, but at once the yacht began a most astonishing performance, veering and yawing as though the greenest of amateurs was at the wheel. It was a sight for sailormen to see. To all appearances, a runaway yacht was careering madly over the bight, and now and again yielding a little bit to control in a desperate effort to make Benicia.

The owner forgot his seasickness long enough to look anxious. The speck of a boat grew larger and larger, till we could see Big Alec and his partner, with a turn of the sturgeon line around a cleat, resting from their labor to laugh at us. Charley pulled his sou'wester over his eyes, and I followed his example, though I could not guess the idea he evidently had in mind and intended to carry into execution.

We came foaming down abreast of the skiff, so close that we could hear above the wind the voices of Big Alec and his mate as they shouted at us with all the scorn that professional watermen feel for amateurs, especially when amateurs are making fools of themselves.

We thundered on past the fishermen, and nothing had happened. Charley grinned at the disappointment he saw in my face, and then shouted:

"Stand by the main-sheet to jibe!"

He put the wheel hard over, and the yacht whirled around obediently. The main-sheet slacked and dipped, then shot over our heads after the boom and tautened with a crash on the traveller. The yacht heeled over almost on her beam ends, and a great wail went up from the seasick passengers as they swept across the cabin floor in a tangled mass and piled into a heap in the starboard bunks.

But we had no time for them. The yacht, completing the manoeuvre, headed into the wind with slatting canvas, and righted to an even keel. We were still plunging ahead, and directly in our path was the skiff. I saw Big Alec dive overboard and his mate leap for our bowsprit. Then came the crash as we struck the boat, and a series of grinding bumps as it passed under our bottom.

"That fixes his rifle," I heard Charley mutter, as he sprang upon the deck to look for Big Alec somewhere astern.

The wind and sea quickly stopped our forward movement, and we began to drift backward over the spot where the skiff had been. Big Alec's black head and swarthy face popped up within arm's reach; and all unsuspecting and very angry with what he took to be the clumsiness of amateur sailors, he was hauled aboard. Also he was out of breath, for he had dived deep and stayed down long to escape our keel.

The next instant, to the perplexity and consternation of the owner, Charley was on top of Big Alec in the cockpit, and I was helping bind him with gaskets. The owner was dancing excitedly about and demanding an explanation, but by that time Big Alec's partner had crawled aft from the bowsprit and was peering apprehensively over the rail into the cockpit. Charley's arm shot around his neck and the man landed on his back beside Big Alec.

"More gaskets!" Charley shouted, and I made haste to supply

them.

The wrecked skiff was rolling sluggishly a short distance to windward, and I trimmed the sheets while Charley took the wheel and steered for it.

"These two men are old offenders," he explained to the angry owner; "and they are most persistent violators of the fish and game laws. You have seen them caught in the act, and you may expect to be subpoenaed as witness for the state when the trial comes off."

As he spoke he rounded alongside the skiff. It had been torn from the line, a section of which was dragging to it. He hauled in forty or fifty feet with a young sturgeon still fast in a tangle of barbless hooks, slashed that much of the line free with his knife, and tossed it into the cockpit beside the prisoners.

"And there's the evidence, Exhibit A, for the people," Charley continued. "Look it over carefully so that you may identify it in the court-room with the time and place of capture."

And then, in triumph, with no more veering and yawing, we sailed into Benicia, the King of the Greeks bound hard and fast in the cockpit, and for the first time in his life a prisoner of the fish patrol.

(First published in *The Youth's Companion*, Mar. 2, 1905)

"The Centipede and the Porpoise doubled up on the cabin
in paroxysms of laughter."

A RAID ON THE OYSTER PIRATES

Of the fish patrolmen under whom we served at various times, Charley Le Grant and I were agreed, I think, that Neil Partington was the best. He was neither dishonest nor cowardly; and while he demanded strict obedience when we were under his orders, at the same time our relations were those of easy comradeship, and he permitted us a freedom to which we were ordinarily unaccustomed, as the present story will show.

Neil's family lived in Oakland, which is on the Lower Bay, not more than six miles across the water from San Francisco. One day, while scouting among the Chinese shrimp-catchers of Point Pedro, he received word that his wife was very ill; and within the hour the *Reindeer* was bowling along for Oakland, with a stiff northwest breeze astern. We ran up the Oakland Estuary and came to anchor, and in the days that followed, while Neil was ashore, we tightened up the *Reindeer's* rigging, overhauled the ballast, scraped down, and put the sloop into thorough shape.

This done, time hung heavy on our hands. Neil's wife was dangerously ill, and the outlook was a week's lie-over, awaiting the crisis. Charley and I roamed the docks, wondering what we should do, and so came upon the oyster fleet lying at the Oakland City Wharf. In the main they were trim, natty boats, made for speed and bad weather, and we sat down on the stringer-piece of the dock to study them.

"A good catch, I guess," Charley said, pointing to the heaps of oysters, assorted in three sizes, which lay upon their decks.

Pedlers were backing their wagons to the edge of the wharf, and from the bargaining and chaffering that went on, I managed to learn the selling price of the oysters.

"That boat must have at least two hundred dollars' worth aboard," I calculated. "I wonder how long it took to get the load?"

"Three or four days," Charley answered. "Not bad wages for two men - twenty-five dollars a day apiece."

The boat we were discussing, the *Ghost*, lay directly beneath us. Two men composed its crew. One was a squat, broad-shouldered fellow with remarkably long and gorilla-like arms, while the other was tall and well proportioned, with clear blue eyes and a mat of straight black hair. So unusual and striking was this combination of hair and eyes that Charley and I remained somewhat longer than we intended.

And it was well that we did. A stout, elderly man, with the dress and carriage of a successful merchant, came up and stood beside us, looking down upon the deck of the *Ghost*. He appeared angry, and the longer he looked the angrier he grew.

"Those are my oysters," he said at last. "I know they are my oysters. You raided my beds last night and robbed me of them."

The tall man and the short man on the *Ghost* looked up.

"Hello, Taft," the short man said, with insolent familiarity. (Among the bayfarers he had gained the nickname of "The Centipede" on account of his long arms.) "Hello, Taft," he repeated, with the same touch of insolence. "Wot 'r you growling about now?"

"Those are my oysters - that's what I said. You've stolen them from my beds."

"Yer mighty wise, ain't ye?" was the Centipede's sneering reply. "S'pose you can tell your oysters wherever you see 'em?"

"Now, in my experience," broke in the tall man, "oysters is oysters wherever you find 'em, an' they're pretty much alike all the Bay over, and the world over, too, for that matter. We're not wantin' to quarrel with you, Mr. Taft, but we jes' wish you wouldn't insinuate that them oysters is yours an' that we're thieves an' robbers till you can prove the goods."

"I know they're mine; I'd stake my life on it!" Mr. Taft snorted.

"Prove it," challenged the tall man, who we afterward learned was known as "The Porpoise" because of his wonderful swimming abilities.

Mr. Taft shrugged his shoulders helplessly. Of course he could not prove the oysters to be his, no matter how certain he might be.

"I'd give a thousand dollars to have you men behind the bars!" he cried. "I'll give fifty dollars a head for your arrest and conviction, all of you!"

A roar of laughter went up from the different boats, for the rest of the pirates had been listening to the discussion.

"There's more money in oysters," the Porpoise remarked dryly.

Mr. Taft turned impatiently on his heel and walked away. From out of the corner of his eye, Charley noted the way he went. Several minutes later, when he had disappeared around a corner, Charley rose lazily to his feet. I followed him, and we sauntered off in the opposite direction to that taken by Mr. Taft.

"Come on! Lively!" Charley whispered, when we passed from the view of the oyster fleet.

Our course was changed at once, and we dodged around corners and raced up and down side-streets till Mr. Taft's generous form loomed up ahead of us.

"I'm going to interview him about that reward," Charley explained, as we rapidly over-hauled the oyster-bed owner. "Neil will be delayed here for a week, and you and I might as well be doing something in the meantime. What do you say?"

"Of course, of course," Mr. Taft said, when Charley had introduced himself and explained his errand. "Those thieves are robbing me of thousands of dollars every year, and I shall be glad to break them up at any price, - yes, sir, at any price. As I said, I'll give fifty dollars a head, and call it cheap at that. They've robbed my beds, torn down my signs, terrorized my watchmen, and last year killed one of them. Couldn't prove it. All done in the blackness of night. All I had was a dead watchman and no evidence. The detectives could do nothing. Nobody has been able to do anything with those men. We have never succeeded in arresting one of them. So I say, Mr. — What did you say your name was?"

"Le Grant," Charley answered.

"So I say, Mr. Le Grant, I am deeply obliged to you for the assistance you offer. And I shall be glad, most glad, sir, to co-operate with you in every way. My watchmen and boats are at your disposal. Come and see me at the San Francisco offices any time, or telephone at my expense. And don't be afraid of spending money. I'll foot your expenses, whatever they are, so long as they are within reason. The situation is growing desperate, and something must be done to determine whether I or that band of ruffians own those oyster beds."

"Now we'll see Neil," Charley said, when he had seen Mr. Taft upon his train to San Francisco.

Not only did Neil Partington interpose no obstacle to our

adventure, but he proved to be of the greatest assistance. Charley and I knew nothing of the oyster industry, while his head was an encyclopaedia of facts concerning it. Also, within an hour or so, he was able to bring to us a Greek boy of seventeen or eighteen who knew thoroughly well the ins and outs of oyster piracy.

At this point I may as well explain that we of the fish patrol were free lances in a way. While Neil Partington, who was a patrolman proper, received a regular salary, Charley and I, being merely deputies, received only what we earned - that is to say, a certain percentage of the fines imposed on convicted violators of the fish laws. Also, any rewards that chanced our way were ours. We offered to share with Partington whatever we should get from Mr. Taft, but the patrolman would not hear of it. He was only too happy, he said, to do a good turn for us, who had done so many for him.

We held a long council of war, and mapped out the following line of action. Our faces were unfamiliar on the Lower Bay, but as the *Reindeer* was well known as a fish-patrol sloop, the Greek boy, whose name was Nicholas, and I were to sail some innocent-looking craft down to Asparagus Island and join the oyster pirates' fleet. Here, according to Nicholas's description of the beds and the manner of raiding, it was possible for us to catch the pirates in the act of stealing oysters, and at the same time to get them in our power. Charley was to be on the shore, with Mr. Taft's watchmen and a posse of constables, to help us at the right time.

"I know just the boat," Neil said, at the conclusion of the discussion, "a crazy old sloop that's lying over at Tiburon. You and Nicholas can go over by the ferry, charter it for a song, and sail direct for the beds."

"Good luck be with you, boys," he said at parting, two days later. "Remember, they are dangerous men, so be careful."

Nicholas and I succeeded in chartering the sloop very cheaply; and between laughs, while getting up sail, we agreed that she was even crazier and older than she had been described. She was a big, flat-bottomed, square-sterned craft, sloop-rigged, with a sprung mast, slack rigging, dilapidated sails, and rotten running-gear, clumsy to handle and uncertain in bringing about, and she smelled vilely of coal tar, with which strange stuff she had been smeared from stem to stern and from cabin-roof to centreboard. And to cap it all, *Coal Tar Maggie* was printed in great white letters the whole length of either side.

It was an uneventful though laughable run from Tiburon to Asparagus Island, where we arrived in the afternoon of the following day. The oyster pirates, a fleet of a dozen sloops, were lying at anchor on what was known as the "Deserted Beds." The *Coal Tar Maggie* came sloshing into their midst with a light breeze astern, and they crowded on deck to see us. Nicholas and I had caught the spirit of the crazy craft, and we handled her in most lubberly fashion.

"Wot is it?" some one called.

"Name it 'n' ye kin have it!" called another.

"I swan naow, ef it ain't the old Ark itself!" mimicked the Centipede from the deck of the *Ghost*.

"Hey! Ahoy there, clipper ship!" another wag shouted. "Wot's yer port?"

We took no notice of the joking, but acted, after the manner of greenhorns, as though the *Coal Tar Maggie* required our undivided attention. I rounded her well to windward of the *Ghost*, and

Nicholas ran for'ard to drop the anchor. To all appearances it was a bungle, the way the chain tangled and kept the anchor from reaching the bottom. And to all appearances Nicholas and I were terribly excited as we strove to clear it. At any rate, we quite deceived the pirates, who took huge delight in our predicament.

But the chain remained tangled, and amid all kinds of mocking advice we drifted down upon and fouled the *Ghost*, whose bowsprit poked square through our mainsail and ripped a hole in it as big as a barn door. The Centipede and the Porpoise doubled up on the cabin in paroxysms of laughter, and left us to get clear as best we could. This, with much unseaman-like performance, we succeeded in doing, and likewise in clearing the anchor-chain, of which we let out about three hundred feet. With only ten feet of water under us, this would permit the *Coal Tar Maggie* to swing in a circle six hundred feet in diameter, in which circle she would be able to foul at least half the fleet.

The oyster pirates lay snugly together at short hawsers, the weather being fine, and they protested loudly at our ignorance in putting out such an unwarranted length of anchor-chain. And not only did they protest, for they made us heave it in again, all but thirty feet.

Having sufficiently impressed them with our general lubberliness, Nicholas and I went below to congratulate ourselves and to cook supper. Hardly had we finished the meal and washed the dishes, when a skiff ground against the *Coal Tar Maggie's* side, and heavy feet trampled on deck. Then the Centipede's brutal face appeared in the companionway, and he descended into the cabin, followed by the Porpoise. Before they could seat themselves on a bunk, another skiff came alongside, and another, and another, till the whole fleet was represented by the gathering in the cabin.

"Where'd you swipe the old tub?" asked a squat and hairy man, with cruel eyes and Mexican features.

"Didn't swipe it," Nicholas answered, meeting them on their own ground and encouraging the idea that we had stolen the *Coal Tar Maggie*. "And if we did, what of it?"

"Well, I don't admire your taste, that's all," sneered he of the Mexican features. "I'd rot on the beach first before I'd take a tub that couldn't get out of its own way."

"How were we to know till we tried her?" Nicholas asked, so innocently as to cause a laugh. "And how do you get the oysters?" he hurried on. "We want a load of them; that's what we came for, a load of oysters."

"What d'ye want 'em for?" demanded the Porpoise.

"Oh, to give away to our friends, of course," Nicholas retorted. "That's what you do with yours, I suppose."

This started another laugh, and as our visitors grew more genial we could see that they had not the slightest suspicion of our identity or purpose.

"Didn't I see you on the dock in Oakland the other day?" the Centipede asked suddenly of me.

"Yep," I answered boldly, taking the bull by the horns. "I was watching you fellows and figuring out whether we'd go oystering or not. It's a pretty good business, I calculate, and so we're going in for it. That is," I hastened to add, "if you fellows don't mind."

"I'll tell you one thing, which ain't two things," he replied, "and that is you'll have to hump yerself an' get a better boat. We won't stand to be disgraced by any such box as this. Understand?"

"Sure," I said. "Soon as we sell some oysters we'll outfit in style."

"And if you show yerself square an' the right sort," he went on, "why, you kin run with us. But if you don't" (here his voice became stern and menacing), "why, it'll be the sickest day of yer life. Understand?"

"Sure," I said.

After that and more warning and advice of similar nature, the conversation became general, and we learned that the beds were to be raided that very night. As they got into their boats, after an hour's stay, we were invited to join them in the raid with the assurance of "the more the merrier."

"Did you notice that short, Mexican-looking chap?" Nicholas asked, when they had departed to their various sloops. "He's Barchi, of the Sporting Life Gang, and the fellow that came with him is Skilling. They're both out now on five thousand dollars' bail."

I had heard of the Sporting Life Gang before, a crowd of hoodlums and criminals that terrorized the lower quarters of Oakland, and two-thirds of which were usually to be found in state's prison for crimes that ranged from perjury and ballot-box stuffing to murder.

"They are not regular oyster pirates," Nicholas continued. "They've just come down for the lark and to make a few dollars. But we'll have to watch out for them."

We sat in the cockpit and discussed the details of our plan till eleven o'clock had passed, when we heard the rattle of an oar in a boat from the direction of the *Ghost*. We hauled up our own skiff, tossed in a few sacks, and rowed over. There we found all the skiffs assembling, it being the intention to raid the beds in a body.

To my surprise, I found barely a foot of water where we had dropped anchor in ten feet. It was the big June run-out of the full moon, and as the ebb had yet an hour and a half to run, I knew that our anchorage would be dry ground before slack water.

Mr. Taft's beds were three miles away, and for a long time we rowed silently in the wake of the other boats, once in a while grounding and our oar blades constantly striking bottom. At last we came upon soft mud covered with not more than two inches of water - not enough to float the boats. But the pirates at once were over the side, and by pushing and pulling on the flat-bottomed skiffs, we moved steadily along.

The full moon was partly obscured by high-flying clouds, but the pirates went their way with the familiarity born of long practice. After half a mile of the mud, we came upon a deep channel, up which we rowed, with dead oyster shoals looming high and dry on either side. At last we reached the picking grounds. Two men, on one of the shoals, hailed us and warned us off. But the Centipede, the Porpoise, Barchi, and Skilling took the lead, and followed by the rest of us, at least thirty men in half as many boats, rowed right up to the watchmen.

"You'd better slide outa this here," Barchi said threateningly, "or we'll fill you so full of holes you wouldn't float in molasses."

The watchmen wisely retreated before so overwhelming a force, and rowed their boat along the channel toward where the shore should be. Besides, it was in the plan for them to retreat.

We hauled the noses of the boats up on the shore side of a big shoal, and all hands, with sacks, spread out and began picking. Every now and again the clouds thinned before the face of the moon, and we could see the big oysters quite distinctly. In almost no time sacks were filled and carried back to the boats, where fresh ones were obtained. Nicholas and I returned often and anxiously to the boats with our little loads, but always found some one of the pirates coming or going.

"Never mind," he said; "no hurry. As they pick farther and farther away, it will take too long to carry to the boats. Then they'll stand the full sacks on end and pick them up when the tide comes in and the skiffs will float to them."

Fully half an hour went by, and the tide had begun to flood, when this came to pass. Leaving the pirates at their work, we stole back to the boats. One by one, and noiselessly, we shoved them off and made them fast in an awkward flotilla. Just as we were shoving off the last skiff, our own, one of the men came upon us. It was Barchi. His quick eye took in the situation at a glance, and he sprang for us; but we went clear with a mighty shove, and he was left floundering in the water over his head. As soon as he got back to the shoal he raised his voice and gave the alarm.

We rowed with all our strength, but it was slow going with so many boats in tow. A pistol cracked from the shoal, a second, and a third; then a regular fusillade began. The bullets spat and spat all about us; but thick clouds had covered the moon, and in the dim darkness it was no more than random firing. It was only by chance that we could be hit.

"Wish we had a little steam launch," I panted.

"I'd just as soon the moon stayed hidden," Nicholas panted back.

It was slow work, but every stroke carried us farther away from the shoal and nearer the shore, till at last the shooting died down, and when the moon did come out we were too far away to be in danger. Not long afterward we answered a shoreward hail, and two Whitehall boats, each pulled by three pairs of oars, darted up to us. Charley's welcome face bent over to us, and he gripped us by the hands while he cried, "Oh, you joys! You joys! Both of you!"

When the flotilla had been landed, Nicholas and I and a watchman rowed out in one of the Whitehalls, with Charley in the stern- sheets. Two other Whitehalls followed us, and as the moon now shone brightly, we easily made out the oyster pirates on their lonely shoal. As we drew closer, they fired a rattling volley from their revolvers, and we promptly retreated beyond range.

"Lot of time," Charley said. "The flood is setting in fast, and by the time it's up to their necks there won't be any fight left in them."

So we lay on our oars and waited for the tide to do its work. This was the predicament of the pirates: because of the big run-out, the tide was now rushing back like a mill-race, and it was impossible for the strongest swimmer in the world to make against it the three miles to the sloops. Between the pirates and the shore were we, precluding escape in that direction. On the other hand, the water was rising rapidly over the shoals, and it was only a question of a few hours when it would be over their heads.

It was beautifully calm, and in the brilliant white moonlight we watched them through our night glasses and told Charley of the voyage of the *Coal Tar Maggie*. One o'clock came, and two o'clock, and the pirates were clustering on the highest shoal, waist-deep in water.

"Now this illustrates the value of imagination," Charley was saying. "Taft has been trying for years to get them, but he went at it with bull strength and failed. Now we used our heads . . ."

Just then I heard a scarcely audible gurgle of water, and holding up my hand for silence, I turned and pointed to a ripple slowly widening out in a growing circle. It was not more than fifty feet from us. We kept perfectly quiet and waited. After a minute the

134

water broke six feet away, and a black head and white shoulder showed in the moonlight. With a snort of surprise and of suddenly expelled breath, the head and shoulder went down.

We pulled ahead several strokes and drifted with the current. Four pairs of eyes searched the surface of the water, but never another ripple showed, and never another glimpse did we catch of the black head and white shoulder.

"It's the Porpoise," Nicholas said. "It would take broad daylight for us to catch him."

At a quarter to three the pirates gave their first sign of weakening. We heard cries for help, in the unmistakable voice of the Centipede, and this time, on rowing closer, we were not fired upon. The Centipede was in a truly perilous plight. Only the heads and shoulders of his fellow-marauders showed above the water as they braced themselves against the current, while his feet were off the bottom and they were supporting him.

"Now, lads," Charley said briskly, "we have got you, and you can't get away. If you cut up rough, we'll have to leave you alone and the water will finish you. But if you're good we'll take you aboard, one man at a time, and you'll all be saved. What do you say?"

"Ay," they chorused hoarsely between their chattering teeth.

"Then one man at a time, and the short men first."

The Centipede was the first to be pulled aboard, and he came willingly, though he objected when the constable put the handcuffs on him. Barchi was next hauled in, quite meek and resigned from his soaking. When we had ten in, our boat we drew back, and the second Whitehall was loaded. The third Whitehall received nine prisoners only - a catch of twenty-nine in all.

"You didn't get the Porpoise," the Centipede said exultantly, as though his escape materially diminished our success.

Charley laughed. "But we saw him just the same, a-snorting for shore like a puffing pig."

It was a mild and shivering band of pirates that we marched up the beach to the oyster house. In answer to Charley's knock, the door was flung open, and a pleasant wave of warm air rushed out upon us.

"You can dry your clothes here, lads, and get some hot coffee," Charley announced, as they filed in.

And there, sitting ruefully by the fire, with a steaming mug in his hand, was the Porpoise. With one accord Nicholas and I looked at Charley. He laughed gleefully.

"That comes of imagination," he said. "When you see a thing, you've got to see it all around, or what's the good of seeing it at all? I saw the beach, so I left a couple of constables behind to keep an eye on it. That's all."

(First published in *The Youth's Companion*, Mar. 16, 1905)

"I suddenly arose and threw the grappling iron."

THE SIEGE OF THE 'LANCASHIRE QUEEN'

Possibly our most exasperating experience on the fish patrol was when Charley Le Grant and I laid a two weeks' siege to a big four-masted English ship. Before we had finished with the affair, it became a pretty mathematical problem, and it was by the merest chance that we came into possession of the instrument that brought it to a successful termination.

After our raid on the oyster pirates we had returned to Oakland, where two more weeks passed before Neil Partington's wife was out of danger and on the highroad to recovery. So it was after an absence of a month, all told, that we turned the *Reindeer's* nose toward Benicia. When the cat's away the mice will play, and in these four weeks the fishermen had become very bold in violating the law. When we passed Point Pedro we noticed many signs of activity among the shrimp-catchers, and, well into San Pablo Bay, we observed a widely scattered fleet of Upper Bay fishing-boats hastily pulling in their nets and getting up sail.

This was suspicious enough to warrant investigation, and the first and only boat we succeeded in boarding proved to have an illegal net. The law permitted no smaller mesh for catching shad than one that measured seven and one-half inches inside the knots, while the mesh of this particular net measured only three inches. It was a flagrant breach of the rules, and the two fishermen were forthwith put under arrest. Neil Partington took one of them with him to help manage the *Reindeer*, while Charley and I went on ahead with the other in the captured boat.

But the shad fleet had headed over toward the Petaluma shore in wild flight, and for the rest of the run through San Pablo Bay we saw no more fishermen at all. Our prisoner, a bronzed and bearded Greek, sat sullenly on his net while we sailed his craft. It was a new Columbia River salmon boat, evidently on its first trip, and it handled splendidly. Even when Charley praised it, our prisoner refused to speak or to notice us, and we soon gave him up as a most unsociable fellow.

We ran up the Carquinez Straits and edged into the bight at Turner's Shipyard for smoother water. Here were lying several English steel sailing ships, waiting for the wheat harvest; and here, most unexpectedly, in the precise place where we had captured Big Alec, we came upon two Italians in a skiff that was loaded with a complete "Chinese" sturgeon line. The surprise was mutual, and we were on top of them before either they or we were aware. Charley had barely time to luff into the wind and run up to them. I ran forward and tossed them a line with orders to make it fast. One of the Italians took a turn with it over a cleat, while I hastened to lower our big spritsail. This accomplished, the salmon boat dropped astern, dragging heavily on the skiff.

Charley came forward to board the prize, but when I proceeded to haul alongside by means of the line, the Italians cast it off. We at once began drifting to leeward, while they got out two pairs of oars and rowed their light craft directly into the wind. This manoeuvre for the moment disconcerted us, for in our large and heavily loaded boat we could not hope to catch them with the oars. But our prisoner came unexpectedly to our aid. His black eyes were flashing eagerly, and his face was flushed with suppressed excitement, as he dropped the centre-board, sprang forward with a single leap, and put up the sail.

"I've always heard that Greeks don't like Italians," Charley laughed, as he ran aft to the tiller.

And never in my experience have I seen a man so anxious for the capture of another as was our prisoner in the chase that followed. His eyes fairly snapped, and his nostrils quivered and dilated in a most extraordinary way. Charley steered while he tended the sheet; and though Charley was as quick and alert as a cat, the Greek could hardly control his impatience.

The Italians were cut off from the shore, which was fully a mile away at its nearest point. Did they attempt to make it, we could haul after them with the wind abeam, and overtake them before they had covered an eighth of the distance. But they were too wise to attempt it, contenting themselves with rowing lustily to windward along the starboard side of a big ship, the *Lancashire Queen*. But beyond the ship lay an open stretch of fully two miles to the shore in that direction. This, also, they dared not attempt, for we were bound to catch them before they could cover it. So, when they reached the bow of the *Lancashire Queen*, nothing remained but to pass around and row down her port side toward the stern, which meant rowing to leeward and giving us the advantage.

We in the salmon boat, sailing close on the wind, tacked about and crossed the ship's bow. Then Charley put up the tiller and headed down the port side of the ship, the Greek letting out the sheet and grinning with delight. The Italians were already half-way down the ship's length; but the stiff breeze at our back drove us after them far faster than they could row. Closer and closer we

141

came, and I, lying down forward, was just reaching out to grasp the skiff, when it ducked under the great stern of the *Lancashire Queen*.

The chase was virtually where it had begun. The Italians were rowing up the starboard side of the ship, and we were hauled close on the wind and slowly edging out from the ship as we worked to windward. Then they darted around her bow and began the row down her port side, and we tacked about, crossed her bow, and went plunging down the wind hot after them. And again, just as I was reaching for the skiff, it ducked under the ship's stern and out of danger. And so it went, around and around, the skiff each time just barely ducking into safety.

By this time the ship's crew had become aware of what was taking place, and we could see their heads in a long row as they looked at us over the bulwarks. Each time we missed the skiff at the stern, they set up a wild cheer and dashed across to the other side of the *Lancashire Queen* to see the chase to wind-ward. They showered us and the Italians with jokes and advice, and made our Greek so angry that at least once on each circuit he raised his fist and shook it at them in a rage. They came to look for this, and at each display greeted it with uproarious mirth.

"Wot a circus!" cried one.

"Tork about yer marine hippodromes, - if this ain't one, I'd like to know!" affirmed another.

"Six-days-go-as-yer-please," announced a third. "Who says the dagoes won't win?"

On the next tack to windward the Greek offered to change places with Charley.

"Let-a me sail-a de boat," he demanded. "I fix-a them, I catch-a them, sure."

This was a stroke at Charley's professional pride, for pride himself he did upon his boat-sailing abilities; but he yielded the tiller to the prisoner and took his place at the sheet. Three times again we made the circuit, and the Greek found that he could get no more speed out of the salmon boat than Charley had.

"Better give it up," one of the sailors advised from above.

The Greek scowled ferociously and shook his fist in his customary fashion. In the meanwhile my mind had not been idle, and I had finally evolved an idea.

"Keep going, Charley, one time more," I said.

And as we laid out on the next tack to wind-ward, I bent a piece of line to a small grappling hook I had seen lying in the bail-hole. The end of the line I made fast to the ring-bolt in the bow, and with the hook out of sight I waited for the next opportunity to use it. Once more they made their leeward pull down the port side of the *Lancashire Queen*, and once more we churned down after them before the wind. Nearer and nearer we drew, and I was making believe to reach for them as before. The stern of the skiff was not six feet away, and they were laughing at me derisively as they ducked under the ship's stern. At that instant I suddenly arose and threw the grappling iron. It caught fairly and squarely on the rail of the skiff, which was jerked backward out of safety as the rope tautened and the salmon boat ploughed on.

A groan went up from the row of sailors above, which quickly changed to a cheer as one of the Italians whipped out a long sheath-knife and cut the rope. But we had drawn them out of safety, and Charley, from his place in the stern-sheets, reached over and clutched the stern of the skiff. The whole thing happened in a second of time, for the first Italian was cutting the rope and Charley was clutching the skiff when the second Italian dealt him a rap over the head with an oar, Charley released his hold and collapsed, stunned, into the bottom of the salmon boat, and the Italians bent to their oars and escaped back under the ship's stern.

The Greek took both tiller and sheet and continued the chase around the *Lancashire Queen*, while I attended to Charley, on whose head a nasty lump was rapidly rising. Our sailor audience was wild with delight, and to a man encouraged the fleeing Italians. Charley sat up, with one hand on his head, and gazed about him sheepishly.

"It will never do to let them escape now," he said, at the same time drawing his revolver.

On our next circuit, he threatened the Italians with the weapon; but they rowed on stolidly, keeping splendid stroke and utterly disregarding him.

"If you don't stop, I'll shoot," Charley said menacingly.

But this had no effect, nor were they to be frightened into surrendering even when he fired several shots dangerously close to them. It was too much to expect him to shoot unarmed men, and this they knew as well as we did; so they continued to pull doggedly round and round the ship.

"We'll run them down, then!" Charley exclaimed. "We'll wear them out and wind them!"

So the chase continued. Twenty times more we ran them around the *Lancashire Queen*, and at last we could see that even their iron muscles were giving out. They were nearly exhausted, and it was only a matter of a few more circuits, when the game took on a new feature. On the row to windward they always gained on us, so that they were half-way down the ship's side on the row to leeward when we were passing the bow. But this last time, as we passed the bow, we saw them escaping up the ship's gangway, which had been suddenly lowered. It was an organized move on the part of the sailors, evidently countenanced by the captain; for by the time we arrived where the gangway had been, it was being hoisted up, and the skiff, slung in the ship's davits, was likewise flying aloft out of reach.

The parley that followed with the captain was short and snappy. He absolutely forbade us to board the *Lancashire Queen*, and as absolutely refused to give up the two men. By this time Charley was as enraged as the Greek. Not only had he been foiled in a long and ridiculous chase, but he had been knocked senseless into the bottom of his boat by the men who had escaped him.

"Knock off my head with little apples," he declared emphatically, striking the fist of one hand into the palm of the other, "if those two men ever escape me! I'll stay here to get them if it takes the rest of my natural life, and if I don't get them, then I promise you I'll live unnaturally long or until I do get them, or my name's not Charley Le Grant!"

And then began the siege of the *Lancashire Queen*, a siege memorable in the annals of both fishermen and fish patrol. When the *Reindeer* came along, after a fruitless pursuit of the shad fleet, Charley instructed Neil Partington to send out his own salmon boat, with blankets, provisions, and a fisherman's charcoal stove. By sunset this exchange of boats was made, and we said good-by to our Greek, who perforce had to go into Benicia and be locked up for his own violation of the law. After supper, Charley and I kept alternate four-hour watches till day-light. The fishermen made no attempt to escape that night, though the ship sent out a boat for scouting purposes to find if the coast were clear.

By the next day we saw that a steady siege was in order, and we perfected our plans with an eye to our own comfort. A dock, known as the Solano Wharf, which ran out from the Benicia shore, helped us in this. It happened that the *Lancashire Queen*, the shore at Turner's Shipyard, and the Solano Wharf were the corners of a big equilateral triangle. From ship to shore, the side of the triangle along which the Italians had to escape, was a distance equal to that from the Solano Wharf to the shore, the side of the triangle along which we had to travel to get to the shore before the Italians. But as we could sail much faster than they could row, we could permit them to travel about half their side of the triangle before we darted out along our side. If we allowed them to get more than half-way, they were certain to beat us to shore; while if we started before they were half-way, they were equally certain to beat us back to the ship.

We found that an imaginary line, drawn from the end of the wharf to a windmill farther along the shore, cut precisely in half the line of the triangle along which the Italians must escape to reach the land. This line made it easy for us to determine how far to let them run away before we bestirred ourselves in pursuit. Day after day we would watch them through our glasses as they rowed leisurely along toward the half-way point; and as they drew close into line with the windmill, we would leap into the boat and get up sail. At sight of our preparation, they would turn and row slowly back to the *Lancashire Queen*, secure in the knowledge that we could not overtake them.

To guard against calms - when our salmon boat would be useless - we also had in readiness a light rowing skiff equipped with spoon- oars. But at such times, when the wind failed us, we were forced to row out from the wharf as soon as they rowed from the ship. In the night-time, on the other hand, we were compelled to patrol the immediate vicinity of the ship; which we did, Charley and I standing four-hour watches turn and turn about. The Italians, however, preferred the daytime in which to escape, and so our long night vigils were without result.

"What makes me mad," said Charley, "is our being kept from our honest beds while those rascally lawbreakers are sleeping soundly every night. But much good may it do them," he threatened. "I'll keep them on that ship till the captain charges them board, as sure as a sturgeon's not a catfish!"

It was a tantalizing problem that confronted us. As long as we were vigilant, they could not escape; and as long as they were careful, we would be unable to catch them. Charley cudgelled his brains continually, but for once his imagination failed him. It was a problem apparently without other solution than that of patience. It was a waiting game, and whichever waited the longer was bound to win. To add to our irritation, friends of the Italians established a code of signals with them from the shore, so that we never dared relax the siege for a moment. And besides this, there were always one or two suspicious-looking fishermen hanging around the Solano Wharf and keeping watch on our actions. We could do nothing but "grin and bear it," as Charley said, while it took up all our time and prevented us from doing other work.

The days went by, and there was no change in the situation. Not that no attempts were made to change it. One night friends from the shore came out in a skiff and attempted to confuse us while the two Italians escaped. That they did not succeed was due to the lack of a little oil on the ship's davits. For we were drawn back from the pursuit of the strange boat by the creaking of the davits, and arrived at the *Lancashire Queen* just as the Italians were lowering their skiff. Another night, fully half a dozen skiffs rowed around us in the darkness, but we held on like a leech to the side of the ship and frustrated their plan till they grew angry and showered us with abuse. Charley laughed to himself in the bottom of the boat.

"It's a good sign, lad," he said to me. "When men begin to abuse, make sure they're losing patience; and shortly after they lose patience, they lose their heads. Mark my words, if we only hold out, they'll get careless some fine day, and then we'll get them."

But they did not grow careless, and Charley confessed that this was one of the times when all signs failed. Their patience seemed equal to ours, and the second week of the siege dragged monotonously along. Then Charley's lagging imagination quickened sufficiently to suggest a ruse. Peter Boyelen, a new patrolman and one unknown to the fisher-folk, happened to arrive in Benicia and we took him into our plan. We were as secret as possible about it, but in some unfathomable way the friends ashore got word to the beleaguered Italians to keep their eyes open.

On the night we were to put our ruse into effect, Charley and I took up our usual station in our rowing skiff alongside the *Lancashire Queen*. After it was thoroughly dark, Peter Boyelen came out in a crazy duck boat, the kind you can pick up and carry away under one arm. When we heard him coming along, paddling noisily, we slipped away a short distance into the darkness, and rested on our oars. Opposite the gangway, having jovially hailed the anchor- watch of the *Lancashire Queen* and asked the direction of the Scottish Chiefs, another wheat ship, he awkwardly capsized himself. The man who was standing the anchor-watch ran down the gangway and hauled him out of the water. This was what he wanted, to get aboard the ship; and the next thing he expected was to be taken on deck and then below to warm up and dry out. But the captain inhospitably kept him perched on the lowest gang-way step, shivering miserably and with his feet dangling in the water, till we, out of very pity, rowed in from the darkness and took him off. The jokes and gibes of the awakened crew sounded anything but sweet in our ears, and even the two Italians climbed up on the rail and laughed down at us long and maliciously.

"That's all right," Charley said in a low voice, which I only could hear. "I'm mighty glad it's not us that's laughing first. We'll save our laugh to the end, eh, lad?"

He clapped a hand on my shoulder as he finished, but it seemed to me that there was more determination than hope in his voice.

It would have been possible for us to secure the aid of United States marshals and board the English ship, backed by Government authority. But the instructions of the Fish Commission were to the effect that the patrolmen should avoid complications, and this one, did we call on the higher powers, might well end in a pretty international tangle.

The second week of the siege drew to its close, and there was no sign of change in the situation. On the morning of the fourteenth day the change came, and it came in a guise as unexpected and startling to us as it was to the men we were striving to capture.

Charley and I, after our customary night vigil by the side of the _Lancashire Queen_, rowed into the Solana Wharf.

"Hello!" cried Charley, in surprise. "In the name of reason and common sense, what is that? Of all unmannerly craft did you ever see the like?"

Well might he exclaim, for there, tied up to the dock, lay the strangest looking launch I had ever seen. Not that it could be called a launch, either, but it seemed to resemble a launch more than any other kind of boat. It was seventy feet long, but so narrow was it, and so bare of superstructure, that it appeared much smaller than it really was. It was built wholly of steel, and was painted black. Three smokestacks, a good distance apart and raking well aft, arose in single file amidships; while the bow, long and lean and sharp as a knife, plainly advertised that the boat was made for speed. Passing under the stern, we read *Streak*, painted in small white letters.

Charley and I were consumed with curiosity. In a few minutes we were on board and talking with an engineer who was watching the sunrise from the deck. He was quite willing to satisfy our curiosity, and in a few minutes we learned that the *Streak* had come in after dark from San Francisco; that this was what might be called the trial trip; and that she was the property of Silas Tate, a young mining millionaire of California, whose fad was high-speed yachts. There was some talk about turbine engines, direct application of steam, and the absence of pistons, rods, and cranks, - all of which was beyond me, for I was familiar only with sailing craft; but I did understand the last words of the engineer.

"Four thousand horse-power and forty-five miles an hour, though you wouldn't think it," he concluded proudly.

"Say it again, man! Say it again!" Charley exclaimed in an excited voice.

"Four thousand horse-power and forty-five miles an hour," the engineer repeated, grinning good-naturedly.

"Where's the owner?" was Charley's next question. "Is there any way I can speak to him?"

The engineer shook his head. "No, I'm afraid not. He's asleep, you see."

At that moment a young man in blue uniform came on deck farther aft and stood regarding the sunrise.

"There he is, that's him, that's Mr. Tate," said the engineer.

Charley walked aft and spoke to him, and while he talked earnestly the young man listened with an amused expression on his face. He must have inquired about the depth of water close in to the shore at Turner's Shipyard, for I could see Charley making gestures and explaining. A few minutes later he came back in high glee.

"Come on lad," he said. "On to the dock with you. We've got them!"

It was our good fortune to leave the *Streak* when we did, for a little later one of the spy fishermen appeared. Charley and I took up our accustomed places, on the stringer-piece, a little ahead of the *Streak* and over our own boat, where we could comfortably watch the *Lancashire Queen*. Nothing occurred till about nine o'clock, when we saw the two Italians leave the ship and pull along their side of the triangle toward the shore. Charley looked as unconcerned as could be, but before they had covered a quarter of the distance, he whispered to me:

"Forty-five miles an hour . . . nothing can save them . . . they are ours!"

Slowly the two men rowed along till they were nearly in line with the windmill. This was the point where we always jumped into our salmon boat and got up the sail, and the two men, evidently expecting it, seemed surprised when we gave no sign.

When they were directly in line with the windmill, as near to the shore as to the ship, and nearer the shore than we had ever allowed them before, they grew suspicious. We followed them through the glasses, and saw them standing up in the skiff and trying to find out what we were doing. The spy fisherman, sitting beside us on the stringer-piece was likewise puzzled. He could not understand our inactivity. The men in the skiff rowed nearer the shore, but stood up again and scanned it, as if they thought we might be in hiding there. But a man came out on the beach and waved a handkerchief to indicate that the coast was clear. That settled them. They bent to the oars to make a dash for it. Still Charley waited. Not until they had covered three-quarters of the distance from the *Lancashire Queen*, which left them hardly more than a quarter of a mile to gain the shore, did Charley slap me on the shoulder and cry:

"They're ours! They're ours!"

We ran the few steps to the side of the *Streak* and jumped aboard. Stern and bow lines were cast off in a jiffy. The *Streak* shot ahead and away from the wharf. The spy fisherman we had left behind on the stringer-piece pulled out a revolver and fired five shots into the air in rapid succession. The men in the skiff gave instant heed to the warning, for we could see them pulling away like mad.

But if they pulled like mad, I wonder how our progress can be described? We fairly flew. So frightful was the speed with which we displaced the water, that a wave rose up on either side our bow and foamed aft in a series of three stiff, up-standing waves, while astern a great crested billow pursued us hungrily, as though at each moment it would fall aboard and destroy us. The *Streak* was pulsing and vibrating and roaring like a thing alive. The wind of our progress was like a gale - a forty-five-mile gale. We could not face it and draw breath without choking and strangling. It blew the smoke straight back from the mouths of the smoke-stacks at a direct right angle to the perpendicular. In fact, we were travelling as fast as an express train. "We just *streaked* it," was the way Charley told it afterward, and I think his description comes nearer than any I can give.

As for the Italians in the skiff - hardly had we started, it seemed to me, when we were on top of them. Naturally, we had to slow down long before we got to them; but even then we shot past like a whirlwind and were compelled to circle back between them and the shore. They had rowed steadily, rising from the thwarts at every stroke, up to the moment we passed them, when they recognized Charley and me. That took the last bit of fight out of them. They hauled in their oars, and sullenly submitted to arrest.

"Well, Charley," Neil Partington said, as we discussed it on the wharf afterward, "I fail to see where your boasted imagination came into play this time."

But Charley was true to his hobby. "Imagination?" he demanded, pointing to the *Streak*. "Look at that! just look at it! If the invention of that isn't imagination, I should like to know what is."

"Of course," he added, "it's the other fellow's imagination, but it did the work all the same."

(First published in *The Youth's Companion*, Mar. 30, 1905)

"The consternation we spread among the fishermen was
tremendous."

CHARLEY'S COUP

Perhaps our most laughable exploit on the fish patrol, and at the same time our most dangerous one, was when we rounded in, at a single haul, an even score of wrathful fishermen. Charley called it a "coop," having heard Neil Partington use the term; but I think he misunderstood the word, and thought it meant "coop," to catch, to trap. The fishermen, however, coup or coop, must have called it a Waterloo, for it was the severest stroke ever dealt them by the fish patrol, while they had invited it by open and impudent defiance of the law.

During what is called the "open season" the fishermen might catch as many salmon as their luck allowed and their boats could hold. But there was one important restriction. From sun-down Saturday night to sun-up Monday morning, they were not permitted to set a net. This was a wise provision on the part of the Fish Commission, for it was necessary to give the spawning salmon some opportunity to ascend the river and lay their eggs. And this law, with only an occasional violation, had been obediently observed by the Greek fishermen who caught salmon for the canneries and the market.

One Sunday morning, Charley received a telephone call from a friend in Collinsville, who told him that the full force of fishermen was out with its nets. Charley and I jumped into our salmon boat and started for the scene of the trouble. With a light favoring wind at our back we went through the Carquinez Straits, crossed Suisun Bay, passed the Ship Island Light, and came upon the whole fleet at work.

But first let me describe the method by which they worked. The net used is what is known as a gill-net. It has a simple diamond-shaped mesh which measures at least seven and one-half inches between the knots. From five to seven and even eight hundred feet in length, these nets are only a few feet wide. They are not stationary, but float with the current, the upper edge supported on the surface by floats, the lower edge sunk by means of leaden weights,

This arrangement keeps the net upright in the current and effectually prevents all but the smaller fish from ascending the river. The salmon, swimming near the surface, as is their custom, run their heads through these meshes, and are prevented from going on through by their larger girth of body, and from going back because of their gills, which catch in the mesh. It requires two fishermen to set such a net, - one to row the boat, while the other, standing in the stern, carefully pays out the net. When it is all out, stretching directly across the stream, the men make their boat fast to one end of the net and drift along with it.

As we came upon the fleet of law-breaking fishermen, each boat two or three hundred yards from its neighbors, and boats and nets dotting the river as far as we could see, Charley said:

"I've only one regret, lad, and that is that I have'nt a thousand arms so as to be able to catch them all. As it is, we'll only be able to catch one boat, for while we are tackling that one it will be up nets and away with the rest."

As we drew closer, we observed none of the usual flurry and

excitement which our appearance invariably produced. Instead, each boat lay quietly by its net, while the fishermen favored us with not the slightest attention.

"It's curious," Charley muttered. "Can it be they don't recognize us?"

I said that it was impossible, and Charley agreed; yet there was a whole fleet, manned by men who knew us only too well, and who took no more notice of us than if we were a hay scow or a pleasure yacht.

This did not continue to be the case, however, for as we bore down upon the nearest net, the men to whom it belonged detached their boat and rowed slowly toward the shore. The rest of the boats showed no, sign of uneasiness.

"That's funny," was Charley's remark. "But we can confiscate the net, at any rate."

We lowered sail, picked up one end of the net, and began to heave it into the boat. But at the first heave we heard a bullet zip-zipping past us on the water, followed by the faint report of a rifle. The men who had rowed ashore were shooting at us. At the next heave a second bullet went zipping past, perilously near. Charley took a turn around a pin and sat down. There were no more shots. But as soon as he began to heave in, the shooting recommenced.

"That settles it," he said, flinging the end of the net overboard. "You fellows want it worse than we do, and you can have it."

We rowed over toward the next net, for Charley was intent on finding out whether or not we were face to face with an organized defiance. As we approached, the two fishermen proceeded to cast off from their net and row ashore, while the first two rowed back and made fast to the net we had abandoned. And at the second net we were greeted by rifle shots till we desisted and went on to the third, where the manoeuvre was again repeated.

Then we gave it up, completely routed, and hoisted sail and started on the long windward beat back to Benicia. A number of Sundays went by, on each of which the law was persistently violated. Yet, short of an armed force of soldiers, we could do nothing. The fishermen had hit upon a new idea and were using it for all it was worth, while there seemed no way by which we could get the better of them.

About this time Neil Partington happened along from the Lower Bay, where he had been for a number of weeks. With him was Nicholas, the Greek boy who had helped us in our raid on the oyster pirates, and the pair of them took a hand. We made our arrangements carefully. It was planned that while Charley and I tackled the nets, they were to be hidden ashore so as to ambush the fishermen who landed to shoot at us.

It was a pretty plan. Even Charley said it was. But we reckoned not half so well as the Greeks. They forestalled us by ambushing Neil and Nicholas and taking them prisoners, while, as of old, bullets whistled about our ears when Charley and I attempted to take possession of the nets. When we were again beaten off, Neil Partington and Nicholas were released. They were rather shamefaced when they put in an appearance, and Charley chaffed them unmercifully. But Neil chaffed back, demanding to know why Charley's imagination had not long since overcome the difficulty.

"Just you wait; the idea'll come all right," Charley promised.

"Most probably," Neil agreed. "But I'm afraid the salmon will be exterminated first, and then there will be no need for it when it does come."

Neil Partington, highly disgusted with his adventure, departed for the Lower Bay, taking Nicholas with him, and Charley and I were left to our own resources. This meant that the Sunday fishing would be left to itself, too, until such time as Charley's idea happened along. I puzzled my head a good deal to find out some way of checkmating the Greeks, as also did Charley, and we broached a thousand expedients which on discussion proved worthless.

The fishermen, on the other hand, were in high feather, and their boasts went up and down the river to add to our discomfiture. Among all classes of them we became aware of a growing insubordination. We were beaten, and they were losing respect for us. With the loss of respect, contempt began to arise. Charley began to be spoken of as the "olda woman," and I received my rating as the "pee-wee kid." The situation was fast becoming unbearable, and we knew that we should have to deliver a stunning stroke at the Greeks in order to regain the old-time respect in which we had stood.

Then one morning the idea came. We were down on Steamboat Wharf, where the river steamers made their landings, and where we found a group of amused long-shoremen and loafers listening to the hard- luck tale of a sleepy-eyed young fellow in long sea-boots. He was a sort of amateur fisherman, he said, fishing for the local market of Berkeley. Now Berkeley was on the Lower Bay, thirty miles away. On the previous night, he said, he had set his net and dozed off to sleep in the bottom of the boat.

The next he knew it was morning, and he opened his eyes to find his boat rubbing softly against the piles of Steamboat Wharf at Benicia. Also he saw the river steamer *Apache* lying ahead of him, and a couple of deck-hands disentangling the shreds of his net from the paddle-wheel. In short, after he had gone to sleep, his fisherman's riding light had gone out, and the *Apache* had run over his net. Though torn pretty well to pieces, the net in some way still remained foul, and he had had a thirty-mile tow out of his course.

Charley nudged me with his elbow. I grasped his thought on the instant, but objected:

"We can't charter a steamboat."

"Don't intend to," he rejoined. "But let's run over to Turner's Shipyard. I've something in my mind there that may be of use to us."

And over we went to the shipyard, where Charley led the way to the *Mary Rebecca*, lying hauled out on the ways, where she was being cleaned and overhauled. She was a scow-schooner we both knew well, carrying a cargo of one hundred and forty tons and a spread of canvas greater than other schooner on the bay.

"How d'ye do, Ole," Charley greeted a big blue-shirted Swede who was greasing the jaws of the main gaff with a piece of pork rind.

Ole grunted, puffed away at his pipe, and went on greasing. The captain of a bay schooner is supposed to work with his hands just as well as the men.

Ole Ericsen verified Charley's conjecture that the *Mary Rebecca*, as soon as launched, would run up the San Joaquin River nearly to Stockton for a load of wheat. Then Charley made his proposition, and Ole Ericsen shook his head.

"Just a hook, one good-sized hook," Charley pleaded.

"No, Ay tank not," said Ole Ericsen. "Der *Mary Rebecca* yust hang up on efery mud-bank with that hook. Ay don't want to lose der *Mary Rebecca*. She's all Ay got."

"No, no," Charley hurried to explain. "We can put the end of the hook through the bottom from the outside, and fasten it on the inside with a nut. After it's done its work, why, all we have to do is to go down into the hold, unscrew the nut, and out drops the hook. Then drive a wooden peg into the hole, and the *Mary Rebecca* will be all right again."

Ole Ericsen was obstinate for a long time; but in the end, after we had had dinner with him, he was brought round to consent.

"Ay do it, by Yupiter!" he said, striking one huge fist into the palm of the other hand. "But yust hurry you up wid der hook. Der *Mary Rebecca* slides into der water to-night."

It was Saturday, and Charley had need to hurry. We headed for the shipyard blacksmith shop, where, under Charley's directions, a most generously curved book of heavy steel was made. Back we hastened to the *Mary Rebecca*. Aft of the great centre-board case, through what was properly her keel, a hole was bored. The end of the hook was inserted from the outside, and Charley, on the inside, screwed the nut on tightly. As it stood complete, the hook projected over a foot beneath the bottom of the schooner. Its curve was something like the curve of a sickle, but deeper.

In the late afternoon the *Mary Rebecca* was launched, and preparations were finished for the start up-river next morning. Charley and Ole intently studied the evening sky for signs of wind, for without a good breeze our project was doomed to failure. They agreed that there were all the signs of a stiff westerly wind - not the ordinary afternoon sea-breeze, but a half-gale, which even then was springing up.

Next morning found their predictions verified. The sun was shining brightly, but something more than a half-gale was shrieking up the Carquinez Straits, and the *Mary Rebecca* got under way with two reefs in her mainsail and one in her foresail. We found it quite rough in the Straits and in Suisun Bay; but as the water grew more land-locked it became calm, though without let-up in the wind.

Off Ship Island Light the reefs were shaken out, and at Charley's suggestion a big fisherman's staysail was made all ready for hoisting, and the maintopsail, bunched into a cap at the masthead, was overhauled so that it could be set on an instant's notice.

We were tearing along, wing-and-wing, before the wind, foresail to starboard and mainsail to port, as we came upon the salmon fleet. There they were, boats and nets, as on that first Sunday when they had bested us, strung out evenly over the river as far as we could see. A narrow space on the right-hand side of the channel was left clear for steamboats, but the rest of the river was covered with the wide-stretching nets. The narrow space was our logical course, but Charley, at the wheel, steered the *Mary Rebecca* straight for the nets. This did not cause any alarm among the fishermen, because up-river sailing craft are always provided with "shoes" on the ends of their keels, which permit them to slip over the nets without fouling them.

"Now she takes it!" Charley cried, as we dashed across the middle of a line of floats which marked a net. At one end of this line was a small barrel buoy, at the other the two fishermen in their boat. Buoy and boat at once began to draw together, and the fishermen to cry out, as they were jerked after us. A couple of minutes later we hooked a second net, and then a third, and in this fashion we tore straight up through the centre of the fleet.

The consternation we spread among the fishermen was tremendous. As fast as we hooked a net the two ends of it, buoy and boat, came together as they dragged out astern; and so many buoys and boats, coming together at such breakneck speed, kept the fishermen on the jump to avoid smashing into one another. Also, they shouted at us like mad to heave to into the wind, for they took it as some drunken prank on the part of scow-sailors, little dreaming that we were the fish patrol.

The drag of a single net is very heavy, and Charley and Ole Ericsen decided that even in such a wind ten nets were all the *Mary Rebecca* could take along with her. So when we had hooked ten nets, with ten boats containing twenty men streaming along behind us, we veered to the left out of the fleet and headed toward Collinsville.

We were all jubilant. Charley was handling the wheel as though he were steering the winning yacht home in a race. The two sailors who made up the crew of the *Mary Rebecca*, were grinning and joking. Ole Ericsen was rubbing his huge hands in child-like glee.

"Ay tank you fish patrol fallers never ban so lucky as when you sail with Ole Ericsen," he was saying, when a rifle cracked sharply astern, and a bullet gouged along the newly painted cabin, glanced on a nail, and sang shrilly onward into space.

This was too much for Ole Ericsen. At sight of his beloved paintwork thus defaced, he jumped up and shook his fist at the fishermen; but a second bullet smashed into the cabin not six inches from his head, and he dropped down to the deck under cover of the rail.

All the fishermen had rifles, and they now opened a general fusillade. We were all driven to cover - even Charley, who was compelled to desert the wheel. Had it not been for the heavy drag of the nets, we would inevitably have broached to at the mercy of the enraged fishermen. But the nets, fastened to the bottom of the *Mary*

Rebecca well aft, held her stern into the wind, and she continued to plough on, though somewhat erratically.

Charley, lying on the deck, could just manage to reach the lower spokes of the wheel; but while he could steer after a fashion, it was very awkward. Ole Ericsen bethought himself of a large piece of sheet steel in the empty hold.

It was in fact a plate from the side of the *New Jersey*, a steamer which had recently been wrecked outside the Golden Gate, and in the salving of which the *Mary Rebecca* had taken part.

Crawling carefully along the deck, the two sailors, Ole, and myself got the heavy plate on deck and aft, where we reared it as a shield between the wheel and the fishermen. The bullets whanged and banged against it till it rang like a bull's-eye, but Charley grinned in its shelter, and coolly went on steering.

So we raced along, behind us a howling, screaming bedlam of wrathful Greeks, Collinsville ahead, and bullets spat-spatting all around us.

"Ole," Charley said in a faint voice, "I don't know what we're going to do."

Ole Ericsen, lying on his back close to the rail and grinning upward at the sky, turned over on his side and looked at him. "Ay tank we go into Collinsville yust der same," he said.

"But we can't stop," Charley groaned. "I never thought of it, but we can't stop."

A look of consternation slowly overspread Ole Ericsen's broad face. It was only too true. We had a hornet's nest on our hands, and to stop at Collinsville would be to have it about our ears.

"Every man Jack of them has a gun," one of the sailors remarked cheerfully.

164

"Yes, and a knife, too," the other sailor added.

It was Ole Ericsen's turn to groan. "What for a Svaidish faller like me monkey with none of my biziness, I don't know," he soliloquized.

A bullet glanced on the stern and sang off to starboard like a spiteful bee. "There's nothing to do but plump the *Mary Rebecca* ashore and run for it," was the verdict of the first cheerful sailor.

"And leaf der *Mary Rebecca*?" Ole demanded, with unspeakable horror in his voice.

"Not unless you want to," was the response. "But I don't want to be within a thousand miles of her when those fellers come aboard" - indicating the bedlam of excited Greeks towing behind.

We were right in at Collinsville then, and went foaming by within biscuit-toss of the wharf.

"I only hope the wind holds out," Charley said, stealing a glance at our prisoners.

"What of der wind?" Ole demanded disconsolately. "Der river will not hold out, and then . . . and then . . ."

"It's head for tall timber, and the Greeks take the hindermost," adjudged the cheerful sailor, while Ole was stuttering over what would happen when we came to the end of the river.

We had now reached a dividing of the ways. To the left was the mouth of the Sacramento River, to the right the mouth of the San Joaquin. The cheerful sailor crept forward and jibed over the foresail as Charley put the helm to starboard and we swerved to the right into the San Joaquin. The wind, from which we had been running away on an even keel, now caught us on our beam, and the *Mary Rebecca* was pressed down on her port side as if she were about to capsize.

Still we dashed on, and still the fishermen dashed on behind. The value of their nets was greater than the fines they would have to pay for violating the fish laws; so to cast off from their nets and escape, which they could easily do, would profit them nothing. Further, they remained by their nets instinctively, as a sailor remains by his ship. And still further, the desire for vengeance was roused, and we could depend upon it that they would follow us to the ends of the earth, if we undertook to tow them that far.

The rifle-firing had ceased, and we looked astern to see what our prisoners were doing. The boats were strung along at unequal distances apart, and we saw the four nearest ones bunching together. This was done by the boat ahead trailing a small rope astern to the one behind. When this was caught, they would cast off from their net and heave in on the line till they were brought up to the boat in front. So great was the speed at which we were travelling, however, that this was very slow work. Sometimes the men would strain to their utmost and fail to get in an inch of the rope; at other times they came ahead more rapidly.

When the four boats were near enough together for a man to pass from one to another, one Greek from each of three got into the nearest boat to us, taking his rifle with him. This made five in the foremost boat, and it was plain that their intention was to board us. This they undertook to do, by main strength and sweat, running hand over hand the float-line of a net. And though it was slow, and they stopped frequently to rest, they gradually drew nearer.

Charley smiled at their efforts, and said, "Give her the topsail, Ole."

The cap at the mainmast head was broken out, and sheet and downhaul pulled flat, amid a scattering rifle fire from the boats; and the *Mary Rebecca* lay over and sprang ahead faster than ever.

But the Greeks were undaunted. Unable, at the increased speed, to draw themselves nearer by means of their hands, they rigged from the blocks of their boat sail what sailors call a "watch-tackle." One of them, held by the legs by his mates, would lean far over the bow and make the tackle fast to the float-line. Then they would heave in on the tackle till the blocks were together, when the manoeuvre would be repeated.

"Have to give her the staysail," Charley said.

Ole Ericsen looked at the straining *Mary Rebecca* and shook his head. "It will take der masts out of her," he said.

"And we'll be taken out of her if you don't," Charley replied.

Ole shot an anxious glance at his masts, another at the boat load of armed Greeks, and consented.

The five men were in the bow of the boat - a bad place when a craft is towing. I was watching the behavior of their boat as the great fisherman's staysail, far, far larger than the top-sail and used only in light breezes, was broken out. As the *Mary Rebecca* lurched forward with a tremendous jerk, the nose of the boat ducked down into the water, and the men tumbled over one another in a wild rush into the stern to save the boat from being dragged sheer under water.

"That settles them!" Charley remarked, though he was anxiously studying the behavior of the *Mary Rebecca*, which was being driven under far more canvas than she was rightly able to carry.

"Next stop is Antioch!" announced the cheerful sailor, after the manner of a railway conductor. "And next comes Merryweather!"

"Come here, quick," Charley said to me.

I crawled across the deck and stood upright beside him in the shelter of the sheet steel.

"Feel in my inside pocket," he commanded, "and get my notebook. That's right. Tear out a blank page and write what I tell you."

And this is what I wrote:

Telephone to Merryweather, to the sheriff, the constable, or the judge. Tell them we are coming and to turn out the town. Arm everybody. Have them down on the wharf to meet us or we are gone gooses.

Now make it good and fast to that marlin-spike, and stand by to toss it ashore."

I did as he directed. By then we were close to Antioch. The wind was shouting through our rigging, the *Mary Rebecca* was half over on her side and rushing ahead like an ocean greyhound. The seafaring folk of Antioch had seen us breaking out topsail and staysail, a most reckless performance in such weather, and had hurried to the wharf-ends in little groups to find out what was the matter.

Straight down the water front we boomed, Charley edging in till a man could almost leap ashore. When he gave the signal I tossed the marlinspike. It struck the planking of the wharf a resounding smash, bounced along fifteen or twenty feet, and was pounced upon by the amazed onlookers.

It all happened in a flash, for the next minute Antioch was behind and we were heeling it up the San Joaquin toward Merryweather, six miles away. The river straightened out here into its general easterly course, and we squared away before the wind, wing-and-wing once more, the foresail bellying out to starboard.

Ole Ericsen seemed sunk into a state of stolid despair. Charley and the two sailors were looking hopeful, as they had good reason to be. Merryweather was a coal-mining town, and, it being Sunday, it was reasonable to expect the men to be in town. Further, the coal-miners had never lost any love for the Greek fishermen, and were pretty certain to render us hearty assistance.

We strained our eyes for a glimpse of the town, and the first sight we caught of it gave us immense relief. The wharves were black with men. As we came closer, we could see them still arriving, stringing down the main street, guns in their hands and on the run. Charley glanced astern at the fishermen with a look of ownership in his eye which till then had been missing. The Greeks were plainly overawed by the display of armed strength and were putting their own rifles away.

We took in topsail and staysail, dropped the main peak, and as we got abreast of the principal wharf jibed the mainsail. The *Mary Rebecca* shot around into the wind, the captive fishermen describing a great arc behind her, and forged ahead till she lost way, when lines we're flung ashore and she was made fast. This was accomplished under a hurricane of cheers from the delighted miners.

Ole Ericsen heaved a great sigh. "Ay never tank Ay see my wife never again," he confessed.

"Why, we were never in any danger," said Charley.

Ole looked at him incredulously.

"Sure, I mean it," Charley went on. "All we had to do, any time, was to let go our end - as I am going to do now, so that those Greeks can untangle their nets."

He went below with a monkey-wrench, unscrewed the nut, and let the hook drop off. When the Greeks had hauled their nets into their boats and made everything shipshape, a posse of citizens took them off our hands and led them away to jail.

"Ay tank Ay ban a great big fool," said Ole Ericsen. But he changed his mind when the admiring townspeople crowded aboard to shake hands with him, and a couple of enterprising newspaper men took photographs of the *Mary Rebecca* and her captain.

(First published in *The Youth's Companion*, Feb. 16, 1905)

"There, in the stern, sat Demetrios Contos."

DEMETRIOS CONTOS

It must not be thought, from what I have told of the Greek fishermen, that they were altogether bad. Far from it. But they were rough men, gathered together in isolated communities and fighting with the elements for a livelihood. They lived far away from the law and its workings, did not understand it, and thought it tyranny. Especially did the fish laws seem tyrannical. And because of this, they looked upon the men of the fish patrol as their natural enemies.

We menaced their lives, or their living, which is the same thing, in many ways. We confiscated illegal traps and nets, the materials of which had cost them considerable sums and the making of which required weeks of labor. We prevented them from catching fish at many times and seasons, which was equivalent to preventing them from making as good a living as they might have made had we not been in existence. And when we captured them, they were brought into the courts of law, where heavy cash fines were collected from them. As a result, they hated us vindictively. As the dog is the natural enemy of the cat, the snake of man, so were we of the fish patrol the natural enemies of the fishermen.

But it is to show that they could act generously as well as hate bitterly that this story of Demetrios Contos is told. Demetrios Contos lived in Vallejo. Next to Big Alec, he was the largest, bravest, and most influential man among the Greeks. He had given us no trouble, and I doubt if he would ever have clashed with us had he not invested in a new salmon boat. This boat was the cause of all the trouble. He had had it built upon his own model, in which the lines of the general salmon boat were somewhat modified.

To his high elation he found his new boat very fast - in fact, faster than any other boat on the bay or rivers. Forthwith he grew proud and boastful: and, our raid with the *Mary Rebecca* on the Sunday salmon fishers having wrought fear in their hearts, he sent a challenge up to Benicia. One of the local fishermen conveyed it to us; it was to the effect that Demetrios Contos would sail up from Vallejo on the following Sunday, and in the plain sight of Benicia set his net and catch salmon, and that Charley Le Grant, patrolman, might come and get him if he could. Of course Charley and I had heard nothing of the new boat. Our own boat was pretty fast, and we were not afraid to have a brush with any other that happened along.

Sunday came. The challenge had been bruited abroad, and the fishermen and seafaring folk of Benicia turned out to a man, crowding Steamboat Wharf till it looked like the grand stand at a football match. Charley and I had been sceptical, but the fact of the crowd convinced us that there was something in Demetrios Contos's dare.

In the afternoon, when the sea-breeze had picked up in strength, his sail hove into view as he bowled along before the wind. He tacked a score of feet from the wharf, waved his hand theatrically, like a knight about to enter the lists, received a hearty cheer in return, and stood away into the Straits for a couple of hundred yards. Then he lowered sail, and, drifting the boat sidewise by means of the wind, proceeded to set his net. He did not set much of it, possibly fifty feet; yet Charley and I were thunderstruck at the man's effrontery. We did not know at the time, but we learned afterward, that the net he used was old and worthless. It *could* catch fish, true; but a catch of any size would have torn it to pieces.

Charley shook his head and said:

"I confess, it puzzles me. What if he has out only fifty feet? He could never get it in if we once started for him. And why does he come here anyway, flaunting his law-breaking in our faces? Right in our home town, too."

Charley's voice took on an aggrieved tone, and he continued for some minutes to inveigh against the brazenness of Demetrios Contos.

In the meantime, the man in question was lolling in the stern of his boat and watching the net floats. When a large fish is meshed in a gill-net, the floats by their agitation advertise the fact. And they evidently advertised it to Demetrios, for he pulled in about a dozen feet of net, and held aloft for a moment, before he flung it into the bottom of the boat, a big, glistening salmon. It was greeted by the audience on the wharf with round after round of cheers. This was more than Charley could stand.

"Come on, lad," he called to me; and we lost no time jumping into our salmon boat and getting up sail.

The crowd shouted warning to Demetrios, and as we darted out from the wharf we saw him slash his worthless net clear with a long knife. His sail was all ready to go up, and a moment later it fluttered in the sunshine. He ran aft, drew in the sheet, and filled on the long tack toward the Contra Costa Hills.

By this time we were not more than thirty feet astern. Charley was jubilant. He knew our boat was fast, and he knew, further, that in fine sailing few men were his equals. He was confident that we should surely catch Demetrios, and I shared his confidence. But somehow we did not seem to gain.

It was a pretty sailing breeze. We were gliding sleekly through the water, but Demetrios was slowly sliding away from us. And not only was he going faster, but he was eating into the wind a fraction of a point closer than we. This was sharply impressed upon us when he went about under the Contra Costa Hills and passed us on the other tack fully one hundred feet dead to windward.

"Whew!" Charley exclaimed. "Either that boat is a daisy, or we've got a five-gallon coal-oil can fast to our keel!"

It certainly looked it one way or the other. And by the time Demetrios made the Sonoma Hills, on the other side of the Straits, we were so hopelessly outdistanced that Charley told me to slack off the sheet, and we squared away for Benicia. The fishermen on Steamboat Wharf showered us with ridicule when we returned and tied up. Charley and I got out and walked away, feeling rather sheepish, for it is a sore stroke to one's pride when he thinks he has a good boat and knows how to sail it, and another man comes along and beats him.

Charley mooned over it for a couple of days; then word was brought to us, as before, that on the next Sunday Demetrios Contos would repeat his performance. Charley roused himself. He had our boat out of the water, cleaned and repainted its bottom, made a trifling alteration about the centre-board, overhauled the running gear, and sat up nearly all of Saturday night sewing on a new and much larger sail. So large did he make it, in fact, that additional ballast was imperative, and we stowed away nearly five hundred extra pounds of old railroad iron in the bottom of the boat.

Sunday came, and with it came Demetrios Contos, to break the law defiantly in open day. Again we had the afternoon sea-breeze, and again Demetrios cut loose some forty or more feet of his rotten net, and got up sail and under way under our very noses. But he had anticipated Charley's move, and his own sail peaked higher than ever, while a whole extra cloth had been added to the after leech.

It was nip and tuck across to the Contra Costa Hills, neither of us seeming to gain or to lose. But by the time we had made the return tack to the Sonoma Hills, we could see that, while we footed it at about equal speed, Demetrios had eaten into the wind the least bit more than we. Yet Charley was sailing our boat as finely and delicately as it was possible to sail it, and getting more out of it than he ever had before.

Of course, he could have drawn his revolver and fired at Demetrios; but we had long since found it contrary to our natures to shoot at a fleeing man guilty of only a petty offence. Also a sort of tacit agreement seemed to have been reached between the patrolmen and the fishermen. If we did not shoot while they ran away, they, in turn, did not fight if we once laid hands on them. Thus Demetrios Contos ran away from us, and we did no more than try our best to overtake him; and, in turn, if our boat proved faster than his, or was sailed better, he would, we knew, make no resistance when we caught up with him.

With our large sails and the healthy breeze romping up the Carquinez Straits, we found that our sailing was what is called "ticklish." We had to be constantly on the alert to avoid a capsize, and while Charley steered I held the main-sheet in my hand with but a single turn round a pin, ready to let go at any moment.

177

Demetrios, we could see, sailing his boat alone, had his hands full.

But it was a vain undertaking for us to attempt to catch him. Out of his inner consciousness he had evolved a boat that was better than ours. And though Charley sailed fully as well, if not the least bit better, the boat he sailed was not so good as the Greek's.

"Slack away the sheet," Charley commanded; and as our boat fell off before the wind, Demetrios's mocking laugh floated down to us.

Charley shook his head, saying, "It's no use. Demetrios has the better boat. If he tries his performance again, we must meet it with some new scheme."

This time it was my imagination that came to the rescue.

"What's the matter," I suggested, on the Wednesday following, "with my chasing Demetrios in the boat next Sunday, while you wait for him on the wharf at Vallejo when he arrives?"

Charley considered it a moment and slapped his knee.

"A good idea! You're beginning to use that head of yours. A credit to your teacher, I must say."

"But you mustn't chase him too far," he went on, the next moment, "or he'll head out into San Pablo Bay instead of running home to Vallejo, and there I'll be, standing lonely on the wharf and waiting in vain for him to arrive."

On Thursday Charley registered an objection to my plan.

"Everybody'll know I've gone to Vallejo, and you can depend upon it that Demetrios will know, too. I'm afraid we'll have to give up the idea."

This objection was only too valid, and for the rest of the day I struggled under my disappointment. But that night a new way seemed to open to me, and in my eagerness I awoke Charley from a sound sleep.

"Well," he grunted, "what's the matter? House afire?"

"No," I replied, "but my head is. Listen to this. On Sunday you and I will be around Benicia up to the very moment Demetrios's sail heaves into sight. This will lull everybody's suspicions. Then, when Demetrios's sail does heave in sight, do you stroll leisurely away and up-town. All the fishermen will think you're beaten and that you know you're beaten."

"So far, so good," Charley commented, while I paused to catch breath.

"And very good indeed," I continued proudly. "You stroll carelessly up-town, but when you're once out of sight you leg it for all you're worth for Dan Maloney's. Take the little mare of his, and strike out on the country road for Vallejo. The road's in fine condition, and you can make it in quicker time than Demetrios can beat all the way down against the wind."

"And I'll arrange right away for the mare, first thing in the morning," Charley said, accepting the modified plan without hesitation.

"But, I say," he said, a little later, this time waking *me* out of a sound sleep.

I could hear him chuckling in the dark.

"I say, lad, isn't it rather a novelty for the fish patrol to be taking to horseback?"

"Imagination," I answered. "It's what you're always preaching - 'keep thinking one thought ahead of the other fellow, and you're bound to win out.'"

"He! he!" he chuckled. "And if one thought ahead, including a mare, doesn't take the other fellow's breath away this time, I'm not your humble servant, Charley Le Grant."

179

"But can you manage the boat alone?" he asked, on Friday. "Remember, we've a ripping big sail on her."

I argued my proficiency so well that he did not refer to the matter again till Saturday, when he suggested removing one whole cloth from the after leech. I guess it was the disappointment written on my face that made him desist; for I, also, had a pride in my boat-sailing abilities, and I was almost wild to get out alone with the big sail and go tearing down the Carquinez Straits in the wake of the flying Greek.

As usual, Sunday and Demetrios Contos arrived together. It had become the regular thing for the fishermen to assemble on Steamboat Wharf to greet his arrival and to laugh at our discomfiture. He lowered sail a couple of hundred yards out and set his customary fifty feet of rotten net.

"I suppose this nonsense will keep up as long as his old net holds out," Charley grumbled, with intention, in the hearing of several of the Greeks.

"Den I give-a heem my old-a net-a," one of them spoke up, promptly and maliciously.

"I don't care," Charley answered. "I've got some old net myself he can have - if he'll come around and ask for it."

They all laughed at this, for they could afford to be sweet-tempered with a man so badly outwitted as Charley was.

"Well, so long, lad," Charley called to me a moment later. "I think I'll go up-town to Maloney's."

"Let me take the boat out?" I asked.

"If you want to," was his answer, as he turned on his heel and walked slowly away.

Demetrios pulled two large salmon out of his net, and I jumped into the boat. The fishermen crowded around in a spirit of fun, and when I started to get up sail overwhelmed me with all sorts of jocular advice. They even offered extravagant bets to one another that I would surely catch Demetrios, and two of them, styling themselves the committee of judges, gravely asked permission to come along with me to see how I did it.

But I was in no hurry. I waited to give Charley all the time I could, and I pretended dissatisfaction with the stretch of the sail and slightly shifted the small tackle by which the huge sprit forces up the peak. It was not until I was sure that Charley had reached Dan Maloney's and was on the little mare's back, that I cast off from the wharf and gave the big sail to the wind. A stout puff filled it and suddenly pressed the lee gunwale down till a couple of buckets of water came inboard. A little thing like this will happen to the best small-boat sailors, and yet, though I instantly let go the sheet and righted, I was cheered sarcastically, as though I had been guilty of a very awkward blunder.

When Demetrios saw only one person in the fish patrol boat, and that one a boy, he proceeded to play with me. Making a short tack out, with me not thirty feet behind, he returned, with his sheet a little free, to Steamboat Wharf. And there he made short tacks, and turned and twisted and ducked around, to the great delight of his sympathetic audience. I was right behind him all the time, and I dared to do whatever he did, even when he squared away before the wind and jibed his big sail over - a most dangerous trick with such a sail in such a wind.

He depended upon the brisk sea breeze and the strong ebb-tide, which together kicked up a nasty sea, to bring me to grief. But I was on my mettle, and never in all my life did I sail a boat better than on that day. I was keyed up to concert pitch, my brain was working smoothly and quickly, my hands never fumbled once, and it seemed that I almost divined the thousand little things which a small-boat sailor must be taking into consideration every second.

It was Demetrios who came to grief instead. Something went wrong with his centre-board, so that it jammed in the case and would not go all the way down. In a moment's breathing space, which he had gained from me by a clever trick, I saw him working impatiently with the centre-board, trying to force it down. I gave him little time, and he was compelled quickly to return to the tiller and sheet.

The centre-board made him anxious. He gave over playing with me, and started on the long beat to Vallejo. To my joy, on the first long tack across, I found that I could eat into the wind just a little bit closer than he. Here was where another man in the boat would have been of value to him; for, with me but a few feet astern, he did not dare let go the tiller and run amidships to try to force down the centre-board.

Unable to hang on as close in the eye of the wind as formerly, he proceeded to slack his sheet a trifle and to ease off a bit, in order to outfoot me. This I permitted him to do till I had worked to windward, when I bore down upon him. As I drew close, he feinted at coming about. This led me to shoot into the wind to forestall him. But it was only a feint, cleverly executed, and he held back to his course while I hurried to make up lost ground.

He was undeniably smarter than I when it came to manoeuvring. Time after time I all but had him, and each time he tricked me and escaped. Besides, the wind was freshening, constantly, and each of us had his hands full to avoid capsizing. As for my boat, it could not have been kept afloat but for the extra ballast. I sat cocked over the weather gunwale, tiller in one hand and sheet in the other; and the sheet, with a single turn around a pin, I was very often forced to let go in the severer puffs. This allowed the sail to spill the wind, which was equivalent to taking off so much driving power, and of course I lost ground. My consolation was that Demetrios was as often compelled to do the same thing.

The strong ebb-tide, racing down the Straits in the teeth of the wind, caused an unusually heavy and spiteful sea, which dashed aboard continually. I was dripping wet, and even the sail was wet half-way up the after leech. Once I did succeed in outmanoeuvring Demetrios, so that my bow bumped into him amidships. Here was where I should have had another man. Before I could run forward and leap aboard, he shoved the boats apart with an oar, laughing mockingly in my face as he did so.

We were now at the mouth of the Straits, in a bad stretch of water. Here the Vallejo Straits and the Carquinez Straits rushed directly at each other. Through the first flowed all the water of Napa River and the great tide-lands; through the second flowed all the water of Suisun Bay and the Sacramento and San Joaquin rivers. And where such immense bodies of water, flowing swiftly, clashed together, a terrible tide-rip was produced. To make it worse, the wind howled up San Pablo Bay for fifteen miles and drove in a tremendous sea upon the tide-rip.

Conflicting currents tore about in all directions, colliding, forming whirlpools, sucks, and boils, and shooting up spitefully into hollow waves which fell aboard as often from leeward as from windward. And through it all, confused, driven into a madness of motion, thundered the great smoking seas from San Pablo Bay.

I was as wildly excited as the water. The boat was behaving splendidly, leaping and lurching through the welter like a race-horse. I could hardly contain myself with the joy of it. The huge sail, the howling wind, the driving seas, the plunging boat - I, a pygmy, a mere speck in the midst of it, was mastering the elemental strife, flying through it and over it, triumphant and victorious.

And just then, as I roared along like a conquering hero, the boat received a frightful smash and came instantly to a dead stop. I was flung forward and into the bottom. As I sprang up I caught a fleeting glimpse of a greenish, barnacle-covered object, and knew it at once for what it was, that terror of navigation, a sunken pile. No man may guard against such a thing. Water-logged and floating just beneath the surface, it was impossible to sight it in the troubled water in time to escape.

The whole bow of the boat must have been crushed in, for in a few seconds the boat was half full. Then a couple of seas filled it, and it sank straight down, dragged to bottom by the heavy ballast. So quickly did it all happen that I was entangled in the sail and drawn under. When I fought my way to the surface, suffocating, my lungs almost bursting, I could see nothing of the oars. They must have been swept away by the chaotic currents. I saw Demetrios Contos looking back from his boat, and heard the vindictive and mocking tones of his voice as he shouted exultantly. He held steadily on his course, leaving me to perish.

There was nothing to do but to swim for it, which, in that wild confusion, was at the best a matter of but a few moments. Holding my breath and working with my hands, I managed to get off my heavy sea-boots and my jacket. Yet there was very little breath I could catch to hold, and I swiftly discovered that it was not so much a matter of swimming as of breathing.

I was beaten and buffeted, smashed under by the great San Pablo whitecaps, and strangled by the hollow tide-rip waves which flung themselves into my eyes, nose, and mouth. Then the strange sucks would grip my legs and drag me under, to spout me up in some fierce boiling, where, even as I tried to catch my breath, a great whitecap would crash down upon my head.

It was impossible to survive any length of time. I was breathing more water than air, and drowning all the time. My senses began to leave me, my head to whirl around. I struggled on, spasmodically, instinctively, and was barely half conscious when I felt myself caught by the shoulders and hauled over the gunwale of a boat.

For some time I lay across a seat where I had been flung, face downward, and with the water running out of my mouth. After a while, still weak and faint, I turned around to see who was my rescuer. And there, in the stern, sheet in one hand and tiller in the other, grinning and nodding good-naturedly, sat Demetrios Contos. He had intended to leave me to drown, - he said so afterward, - but his better self had fought the battle, conquered, and sent him back to me.

"You all-a right?" he asked.

I managed to shape a "yes" on my lips, though I could not yet speak.

"You sail-a de boat verr-a good-a," he said. "So good-a as a man."

A compliment from Demetrios Contos was a compliment indeed, and I keenly appreciated it, though I could only nod my head in acknowledgment.

We held no more conversation, for I was busy recovering and he was busy with the boat. He ran in to the wharf at Vallejo, made the boat fast, and helped me out. Then it was, as we both stood on the wharf, that Charley stepped out from behind a net-rack and put his hand on Demetrios Contos's arm.

"He saved my life, Charley," I protested; "and I don't think he ought to be arrested."

A puzzled expression came into Charley's face, which cleared immediately after, in a way it had when he made up his mind.

"I can't help it, lad," he said kindly. "I can't go back on my duty, and it's plain duty to arrest him. To-day is Sunday; there are two salmon in his boat which he caught to-day. What else can I do?"

"But he saved my life," I persisted, unable to make any other argument.

Demetrios Contos's face went black with rage when he learned Charley's judgment. He had a sense of being unfairly treated. The better part of his nature had triumphed, he had performed a generous act and saved a helpless enemy, and in return the enemy was taking him to jail.

Charley and I were out of sorts with each other when we went back to Benicia. I stood for the spirit of the law and not the letter; but by the letter Charley made his stand. As far as he could see, there was nothing else for him to do. The law said distinctly that no salmon should be caught on Sunday. He was a patrolman, and it was his duty to enforce that law. That was all there was to it. He had done his duty, and his conscience was clear. Nevertheless, the whole thing seemed unjust to me, and I felt very sorry for Demetrios Contos.

Two days later we went down to Vallejo to the trial. I had to go along as a witness, and it was the most hateful task that I ever performed in my life when I testified on the witness stand to seeing

Demetrios catch the two salmon Charley had captured him with.

Demetrios had engaged a lawyer, but his case was hopeless. The jury was out only fifteen minutes, and returned a verdict of guilty. The judge sentenced Demetrios to pay a fine of one hundred dollars or go to jail for fifty days.

Charley stepped up to the clerk of the court. "I want to pay that fine," he said, at the same time placing five twenty-dollar gold pieces on the desk. "It - it was the only way out of it, lad," he stammered, turning to me.

The moisture rushed into my eyes as I seized his hand. "I want to pay - " I began.

"To pay your half?" he interrupted. "I certainly shall expect you to pay it."

In the meantime Demetrios had been informed by his lawyer that his fee likewise had been paid by Charley.

Demetrios came over to shake Charley's hand, and all his warm Southern blood flamed in his face. Then, not to be outdone in generosity, he insisted on paying his fine and lawyer's fee himself, and flew half-way into a passion because Charley refused to let him.

More than anything else we ever did, I think, this action of Charley's impressed upon the fishermen the deeper significance of the law. Also Charley was raised high in their esteem, while I came in for a little share of praise as a boy who knew how to sail a boat. Demetrios Contos not only never broke the law again, but he became a very good friend of ours, and on more than one occasion he ran up to Benicia to have a gossip with us.

(First published in *The Youth's Companion*, Apr. 27, 1905)

" I went aft and took charge of the prize."

YELLOW HANDKERCHIEF

"I'm not wanting to dictate to you, lad," Charley said; "but I'm very much against your making a last raid. You've gone safely through rough times with rough men, and it would be a shame to have something happen to you at the very end."

"But how can I get out of making a last raid?" I demanded, with the cocksureness of youth. "There always has to be a last, you know, to anything."

Charley crossed his legs, leaned back, and considered the problem. "Very true. But why not call the capture of Demetrios Contos the last? You're back from it safe and sound and hearty, for all your good wetting, and - and - " His voice broke and he could not speak for a moment. "And I could never forgive myself if anything happened to you now."

I laughed at Charley's fears while I gave in to the claims of his affection, and agreed to consider the last raid already performed. We had been together for two years, and now I was leaving the fish patrol in order to go back and finish my education. I had earned and saved money to put me through three years at the high school, and though the beginning of the term was several months away, I intended doing a lot of studying for the entrance examinations.

My belongings were packed snugly in a sea-chest, and I was all ready to buy my ticket and ride down on the train to Oakland, when Neil Partington arrived in Benicia. The *Reindeer* was needed immediately for work far down on the Lower Bay, and Neil said he intended to run straight for Oakland. As that was his home and as I was to live with his family while going to school, he saw no reason, he said, why I should not put my chest aboard and come along.

So the chest went aboard, and in the middle of the afternoon we hoisted the *Reindeer's* big mainsail and cast off. It was tantalizing fall weather. The sea-breeze, which had blown steadily all summer, was gone, and in its place were capricious winds and murky skies which made the time of arriving anywhere extremely problematical. We started on the first of the ebb, and as we slipped down the Carquinez Straits, I looked my last for some time upon Benicia and the bight at Turner's Shipyard, where we had besieged the *Lancashire Queen*, and had captured Big Alec, the King of the Greeks. And at the mouth of the Straits I looked with not a little interest upon the spot where a few days before I should have drowned but for the good that was in the nature of Demetrios Contos.

A great wall of fog advanced across San Pablo Bay to meet us, and in a few minutes the *Reindeer* was running blindly through the damp obscurity. Charley, who was steering, seemed to have an instinct for that kind of work. How he did it, he himself confessed that he did not know; but he had a way of calculating winds, currents, distance, time, drift, and sailing speed that was truly marvellous.

"It looks as though it were lifting," Neil Partington said, a couple of hours after we had entered the fog. "Where do you say we are, Charley?"

Charley looked at his watch, "Six o'clock, and three hours more of ebb," he remarked casually.

"But where do you say we are?" Neil insisted.

Charley pondered a moment, and then answered, "The tide has edged us over a bit out of our course, but if the fog lifts right now, as it is going to lift, you'll find we're not more than a thousand miles off McNear's Landing."

"You might be a little more definite by a few miles, anyway," Neil grumbled, showing by his tone that he disagreed.

"All right, then," Charley said, conclusively, "not less than a quarter of a mile, not more than a half."

The wind freshened with a couple of little puffs, and the fog thinned perceptibly.

"McNear's is right off there," Charley said, pointing directly into the fog on our weather beam.

The three of us were peering intently in that direction, when the *Reindeer* struck with a dull crash and came to a standstill. We ran forward, and found her bowsprit entangled in the tanned rigging of a short, chunky mast. She had collided, head on, with a Chinese junk lying at anchor.

At the moment we arrived forward, five Chinese, like so many bees, came swarming out of the little 'tween-decks cabin, the sleep still in their eyes.

Leading them came a big, muscular man, conspicuous for his pock- marked face and the yellow silk handkerchief swathed about his head. It was Yellow Handkerchief, the Chinaman whom we had arrested for illegal shrimp-fishing the year before, and who, at that time, had nearly sunk the *Reindeer*, as he had nearly sunk it now by violating the rules of navigation.

"What d'ye mean, you yellow-faced heathen, lying here in a fairway without a horn a-going?" Charley cried hotly.

"Mean?" Neil calmly answered. "Just take a look - that's what he means."

Our eyes followed the direction indicated by Neil's finger, and we saw the open amidships of the junk, half filled, as we found on closer examination, with fresh-caught shrimps. Mingled with the shrimps were myriads of small fish, from a quarter of an inch upward in size.

Yellow Handkerchief had lifted the trap-net at high-water slack, and, taking advantage of the concealment offered by the fog, had boldly been lying by, waiting to lift the net again at low-water slack.

"Well," Neil hummed and hawed, "in all my varied and extensive experience as a fish patrolman, I must say this is the easiest capture I ever made. What'll we do with them, Charley?"

"Tow the junk into San Rafael, of course," came the answer. Charley turned to me. "You stand by the junk, lad, and I'll pass you a towing line. If the wind doesn't fail us, we'll make the creek before the tide gets too low, sleep at San Rafael, and arrive in Oakland to-morrow by midday."

So saying, Charley and Neil returned to the *Reindeer* and got under way, the junk towing astern. I went aft and took charge of the prize, steering by means of an antiquated tiller and a rudder with large, diamond-shaped holes, through which the water rushed back and forth.

By now the last of the fog had vanished, and Charley's estimate of our position was confirmed by the sight of McNear's Landing a short half-mile away. Following along the west shore, we rounded Point Pedro in plain view of the Chinese shrimp villages, and a great to- do was raised when they saw one of their junks towing behind the familiar fish patrol sloop.

The wind, coming off the land, was rather puffy and uncertain, and it would have been more to our advantage had it been stronger. San Rafael Creek, up which we had to go to reach the town and turn over our prisoners to the authorities, ran through wide-stretching marshes, and was difficult to navigate on a falling tide, while at low tide it was impossible to navigate at all. So, with the tide already half-ebbed, it was necessary for us to make time. This the heavy junk prevented, lumbering along behind and holding the *Reindeer* back by just so much dead weight.

"Tell those coolies to get up that sail," Charley finally called to me. "We don't want to hang up on the mud flats for the rest of the night."

I repeated the order to Yellow Handkerchief, who mumbled it huskily to his men. He was suffering from a bad cold, which doubled him up in convulsive coughing spells and made his eyes heavy and bloodshot. This made him more evil-looking than ever, and when he glared viciously at me I remembered with a shiver the close shave I had had with him at the time of his previous arrest.

His crew sullenly tailed on to the halyards, and the strange, outlandish sail, lateen in rig and dyed a warm brown, rose in the air. We were sailing on the wind, and when Yellow Handkerchief flattened down the sheet the junk forged ahead and the tow-line went slack. Fast as the *Reindeer* could sail, the junk outsailed her; and to avoid running her down I hauled a little closer on the wind. But the junk likewise outpointed, and in a couple of minutes I was abreast of the *Reindeer* and to windward. The tow-line had now tautened, at right angles to the two boats, and the predicament was laughable.

"Cast off!" I shouted.

Charley hesitated.

"It's all right," I added. "Nothing can happen. We'll make the creek on this tack, and you'll be right behind me all the way up to San Rafael."

At this Charley cast off, and Yellow Handkerchief sent one of his men forward to haul in the line. In the gathering darkness I could just make out the mouth of San Rafael Creek, and by the time we entered it I could barely see its banks. The *Reindeer* was fully five minutes astern, and we continued to leave her astern as we beat up the narrow, winding channel. With Charley behind us, it seemed I had little to fear from my five prisoners; but the darkness prevented my keeping a sharp eye on them, so I transferred my revolver from my trousers pocket to the side pocket of my coat, where I could more quickly put my hand on it.

Yellow Handkerchief was the one I feared, and that he knew it and made use of it, subsequent events will show. He was sitting a few feet away from me, on what then happened to be the weather side of the junk. I could scarcely see the outlines of his form, but I soon became convinced that he was slowly, very slowly, edging closer to me. I watched him carefully. Steering with my left hand, I slipped my right into my pocket and got hold of the revolver.

I saw him shift along for a couple of inches, and I was just about to order him back - the words were trembling on the tip of my tongue - when I was struck with great force by a heavy figure that had leaped through the air upon me from the lee side. It was one of the crew. He pinioned my right arm so that I could not withdraw my hand from my pocket, and at the same time clapped his other hand over my mouth. Of course, I could have struggled away from him and freed my hand or gotten my mouth clear so that I might cry an alarm, but in a trice Yellow Handkerchief was on top of me.

I struggled around to no purpose in the bottom of the junk, while my legs and arms were tied and my mouth securely bound in what I afterward found to be a cotton shirt. Then I was left lying in the bottom. Yellow Handkerchief took the tiller, issuing his orders in whispers; and from our position at the time, and from the alteration of the sail, which I could dimly make out above me as a blot against the stars, I knew the junk was being headed into the mouth of a small slough which emptied at that point into San Rafael Creek.

In a couple of minutes we ran softly alongside the bank, and the sail was silently lowered. The Chinese kept very quiet. Yellow Handkerchief sat down in the bottom alongside of me, and I could feel him straining to repress his raspy, hacking cough. Possibly seven or eight minutes later I heard Charley's voice as the *Reindeer* went past the mouth of the slough.

"I can't tell you how relieved I am," I could plainly hear him saying to Neil, "that the lad has finished with the fish patrol without accident."

Here Neil said something which I could not catch, and then Charley's voice went on:

"The youngster takes naturally to the water, and if, when he finishes high school, he takes a course in navigation and goes deep sea, I see no reason why he shouldn't rise to be master of the finest and biggest ship afloat."

It was all very flattering to me, but lying there, bound and gagged by my own prisoners, with the voices growing faint and fainter as the *Reindeer* slipped on through the darkness toward San Rafael, I must say I was not in quite the proper situation to enjoy my smiling future. With the *Reindeer* went my last hope. What was to happen next I could not imagine, for the Chinese were a different race from mine, and from what I knew I was confident that fair play was no part of their make-up.

After waiting a few minutes longer, the crew hoisted the lateen sail, and Yellow Handkerchief steered down toward the mouth of San Rafael Creek. The tide was getting lower, and he had difficulty in escaping the mud-banks. I was hoping he would run aground, but he succeeded in making the Bay without accident.

As we passed out of the creek a noisy discussion arose, which I knew related to me. Yellow Handkerchief was vehement, but the other four as vehemently opposed him. It was very evident that he advocated doing away with me and that they were afraid of the consequences. I was familiar enough with the Chinese character to know that fear alone restrained them. But what plan they offered in place of Yellow Handkerchief's murderous one, I could not make out.

My feelings, as my fate hung in the balance, may be guessed. The discussion developed into a quarrel, in the midst of which Yellow Handkerchief unshipped the heavy tiller and sprang toward me. But his four companions threw themselves between, and a clumsy struggle took place for possession of the tiller. In the end Yellow Handkerchief was overcome, and sullenly returned to the steering, while they soundly berated him for his rashness.

Not long after, the sail was run down and the junk slowly urged forward by means of the sweeps. I felt it ground gently on the soft mud. Three of the Chinese - they all wore long sea-boots - got over the side, and the other two passed me across the rail. With Yellow Handkerchief at my legs and his two companions at my shoulders, they began to flounder along through the mud. After some time their feet struck firmer footing, and I knew they were carrying me up some beach. The location of this beach was not doubtful in my mind. It could be none other than one of the Marin Islands, a group of rocky islets which lay off the Marin County shore.

When they reached the firm sand that marked high tide, I was dropped, and none too gently. Yellow Handkerchief kicked me spitefully in the ribs, and then the trio floundered back through the mud to the junk. A moment later I heard the sail go up and slat in the wind as they drew in the sheet. Then silence fell, and I was left to my own devices for getting free.

I remembered having seen tricksters writhe and squirm out of ropes with which they were bound, but though I writhed and squirmed like a good fellow, the knots remained as hard as ever, and there was no appreciable slack. In the course of my squirming, however, I rolled over upon a heap of clam-shells - the remains, evidently, of some yachting party's clam-bake. This gave me an idea. My hands were tied behind my back; and, clutching a shell in them, I rolled over and over, up the beach, till I came to the rocks I knew to be there.

Rolling around and searching, I finally discovered a narrow crevice, into which I shoved the shell. The edge of it was sharp, and across the sharp edge I proceeded to saw the rope that bound my wrists. The edge of the shell was also brittle, and I broke it by bearing too heavily upon it. Then I rolled back to the heap and returned with as many shells as I could carry in both hands. I broke many shells, cut my hands a number of times, and got cramps in my legs from my strained position and my exertions.

While I was suffering from the cramps, and resting, I heard a familiar halloo drift across the water. It was Charley, searching for me. The gag in my mouth prevented me from replying, and I could only lie there, helplessly fuming, while he rowed past the island and his voice slowly lost itself in the distance.

I returned to the sawing process, and at the end of half an hour succeeded in severing the rope. The rest was easy. My hands once free, it was a matter of minutes to loosen my legs and to take the gag out of my mouth. I ran around the island to make sure it was an island and not by any chance a portion of the mainland. An island it certainly was, one of the Marin group, fringed with a sandy beach and surrounded by a sea of mud. Nothing remained but to wait till daylight and to keep warm; for it was a cold, raw night for California, with just enough wind to pierce the skin and cause one to shiver.

To keep up the circulation, I ran around the island a dozen times or so, and clambered across its rocky backbone as many times more - all of which was of greater service to me, as I afterward discovered, than merely to warm me up. In the midst of this exercise I wondered if I had lost anything out of my pockets while rolling over and over in the sand. A search showed the absence of my revolver and pocket-knife. The first Yellow Handkerchief had taken; but the knife had been lost in the sand.

I was hunting for it when the sound of rowlocks came to my ears. At first, of course, I thought of Charley; but on second thought I knew Charley would be calling out as he rowed along. A sudden premonition of danger seized me. The Marin Islands are lonely places; chance visitors in the dead of night are hardly to be expected. What if it were Yellow Handkerchief? The sound made by the rowlocks grew more distinct. I crouched in the sand and listened intently. The boat, which I judged a small skiff from the quick stroke of the oars, was landing in the mud about fifty yards up the beach. I heard a raspy, hacking cough, and my heart stood still. It was Yellow Handkerchief. Not to be robbed of his revenge by his more cautious companions, he had stolen away from the village and come back alone.

I did some swift thinking. I was unarmed and helpless on a tiny islet, and a yellow barbarian, whom I had reason to fear, was coming after me. Any place was safer than the island, and I turned instinctively to the water, or rather to the mud. As he began to flounder ashore through the mud, I started to flounder out into it, going over the same course which the Chinese had taken in landing me and in returning to the junk.

Yellow Handkerchief, believing me to be lying tightly bound, exercised no care, but came ashore noisily. This helped me, for, under the shield of his noise and making no more myself than necessary, I managed to cover fifty feet by the time he had made the beach. Here I lay down in the mud. It was cold and clammy, and made me shiver, but I did not care to stand up and run the risk of being discovered by his sharp eyes.

He walked down the beach straight to where he had left me lying, and I had a fleeting feeling of regret at not being able to see his surprise when he did not find me. But it was a very fleeting regret, for my teeth were chattering with the cold.

What his movements were after that I had largely to deduce from the facts of the situation, for I could scarcely see him in the dim starlight. But I was sure that the first thing he did was to make the circuit of the beach to learn if landings had been made by other boats. This he would have known at once by the tracks through the mud.

Convinced that no boat had removed me from the island, he next started to find out what had become of me. Beginning at the pile of clamshells, he lighted matches to trace my tracks in the sand. At such times I could see his villanous face plainly, and, when the sulphur from the matches irritated his lungs, between the raspy cough that followed and the clammy mud in which I was lying, I confess I shivered harder than ever.

The multiplicity of my footprints puzzled him. Then the idea that I might be out in the mud must have struck him, for he waded out a few yards in my direction, and, stooping, with his eyes searched the dim surface long and carefully. He could not have been more than fifteen feet from me, and had he lighted a match he would surely have discovered me.

He returned to the beach and clambered about, over the rocky backbone, again hunting for me with lighted matches, The closeness of the shave impelled me to further flight. Not daring to wade upright, on account of the noise made by floundering and by the suck of the mud, I remained lying down in the mud and propelled myself over its surface by means of my hands. Still keeping the trail made by the Chinese in going from and to the junk, I held on until I reached the water. Into this I waded to a depth of three feet, and then I turned off to the side on a line parallel with the beach.

The thought came to me of going toward Yellow Handkerchief's skiff and escaping in it, but at that very moment he returned to the beach, and, as though fearing the very thing I had in mind, he slushed out through the mud to assure himself that the skiff was safe. This turned me in the opposite direction. Half swimming, half wading, with my head just out of water and avoiding splashing, I succeeded in putting about a hundred feet between myself and the spot where the Chinese had begun to wade ashore from the junk. I drew myself out on the mud and remained lying flat.

Again Yellow Handkerchief returned to the beach and made a search of the island, and again he returned to the heap of clam-shells. I knew what was running in his mind as well as he did himself. No one could leave or land without making tracks in the mud. The only tracks to be seen were those leading from his skiff and from where the junk had been. I was not on the island. I must have left it by one or the other of those two tracks. He had just been over the one to his skiff, and was certain I had not left that way. Therefore I could have left the island only by going over the tracks of the junk landing. This he proceeded to verify by wading out over them himself, lighting matches as he came along.

When he arrived at the point where I had first lain, I knew, by the matches he burned and the time he took, that he had discovered the marks left by my body. These he followed straight to the water and into it, but in three feet of water he could no longer see them. On the other hand, as the tide was still falling, he could easily make out the impression made by the junk's bow, and could have likewise made out the impression of any other boat if it had landed at that particular spot. But there was no such mark; and I knew that he was absolutely convinced that I was hiding somewhere in the mud.

But to hunt on a dark night for a boy in a sea of mud would be like hunting for a needle in a haystack, and he did not attempt it. Instead he went back to the beach and prowled around for some time. I was hoping he would give me up and go, for by this time I was suffering severely from the cold. At last he waded out to his skiff and rowed away. What if this departure of Yellow

Handkerchief's were a sham? What if he had done it merely to entice me ashore?

The more I thought of it the more certain I became that he had made a little too much noise with his oars as he rowed away. So I remained, lying in the mud and shivering. I shivered till the muscles of the small of my back ached and pained me as badly as the cold, and I had need of all my self-control to force myself to remain in my miserable situation.

It was well that I did, however, for, possibly an hour later, I thought I could make out something moving on the beach. I watched intently, but my ears were rewarded first, by a raspy cough I knew only too well. Yellow Handkerchief had sneaked back, landed on the other side of the island, and crept around to surprise me if I had returned.

After that, though hours passed without sign of him, I was afraid to return to the island at all. On the other hand, I was almost equally afraid that I should die of the exposure I was undergoing. I had never dreamed one could suffer so. I grew so cold and numb, finally, that I ceased to shiver. But my muscles and bones began to ache in a way that was agony. The tide had long since begun to rise, and, foot by foot, it drove me in toward the beach. High water came at three o'clock, and at three o'clock I drew myself up on the beach, more dead than alive, and too helpless to have offered any resistance had Yellow Handkerchief swooped down upon me.

But no Yellow Handkerchief appeared. He had given me up and gone back to Point Pedro. Nevertheless, I was in a deplorable, not to say dangerous, condition. I could not stand upon my feet, much less walk. My clammy, muddy garments clung to me like sheets of ice. I thought I should never get them off. So numb and lifeless were my fingers, and so weak was I, that it seemed to take an hour to get off my shoes. I had not the strength to break the porpoise- hide laces, and the knots defied me. I repeatedly beat my hands upon the rocks to get some sort of life into them. Sometimes I felt sure I was going to die.

But in the end, - after several centuries, it seemed to me, - I got off the last of my clothes. The water was now close at hand, and I crawled painfully into it and washed the mud from my naked body. Still, I could not get on my feet and walk and I was afraid to lie still. Nothing remained but to crawl weakly, like a snail, and at the cost of constant pain, up and down the sand. I kept this up as long as possible, but as the east paled with the coming of dawn I began to succumb. The sky grew rosy-red, and the golden rim of the sun, showing above the horizon, found me lying helpless and motionless among the clam-shells.

As in a dream, I saw the familiar mainsail of the *Reindeer* as she slipped out of San Rafael Creek on a light puff of morning air. This dream was very much broken. There are intervals I can never recollect on looking back over it. Three things, however, I distinctly remember: the first sight of the *Reindeer's* mainsail; her lying at anchor a few hundred feet away and a small boat leaving her side; and the cabin stove roaring red-hot, myself swathed all over with blankets, except on the chest and shoulders, which Charley was pounding and mauling unmercifully, and my mouth and throat burning with the coffee which Neil Partington was pouring down a trifle too hot.

But burn or no burn, I tell you it felt good. By the time we arrived in Oakland I was as limber and strong as ever, - though Charlie and Neil Partington were afraid I was going to have pneumonia, and Mrs. Partington, for my first six months of school, kept an anxious eye upon me to discover the first symptoms of consumption.

Time flies. It seems but yesterday that I was a lad of sixteen on the fish patrol. Yet I know that I arrived this very morning from China, with a quick passage to my credit, and master of the barkentine *Harvester*. And I know that to-morrow morning I shall run over to Oakland to see Neil Partington and his wife and family, and later on up to Benicia to see Charley Le Grant and talk over old times. No; I shall not go to Benicia, now that I think about it. I expect to be a highly interested party to a wedding, shortly to take place. Her name is Alice Partington, and, since Charley has promised to be best man, he will have to come down to Oakland instead.

(First published in *The Youth's Companion*, May 11, 1905)

III. THE BAY AREA

THE BANKS OF THE SACRAMENTO

"And it's blow, ye winds, heigh-ho,
For Cal-i-for-ni-o;
For there's plenty of gold so I've been told,
On the banks of the Sacramento!"

It was only a little boy, singing in a shrill treble the sea chantey which seamen sing the wide world over when they man the capstan bars and break the anchors out for "Frisco" port. It was only a little boy who had never seen the sea, but two hundred feet beneath him rolled the Sacramento. "Young" Jerry he was called, after "Old" Jerry, his father, from whom he had learned the song, as well as received his shock of bright-red hair, his blue, dancing eyes, and his fair and inevitably freckled skin.

For Old Jerry had been a sailor, and had followed the sea till middle life, haunted always by the words of the ringing chantey. Then one day he had sung the song in earnest, in an Asiatic port, swinging and thrilling round the capstan-circle with twenty others. And at San Francisco he turned his back upon his ship and upon the sea, and went to behold with his own eyes the banks of the Sacramento.

He beheld the gold, too, for he found employment at the Yellow Dream mine, and proved of utmost usefulness in rigging the great ore- cables across the river and two hundred feet above its surface.

After that he took charge of the cables and kept them in repair, and ran them and loved them, and became himself an indispensable fixture of the Yellow Dream mine. Then he loved pretty Margaret Kelly; but she had left him and Young Jerry, the latter barely toddling, to take up be, last long sleep in the little graveyard among the great sober pines.

Old Jerry never went back to the sea. He remained by his cables, and lavished upon them and Young Jerry all the love of his nature. When evil days came to the Yellow Dream, he still remained in the employ of the company as watchman over the all but abandoned property.

But this morning he was not visible. Young Jerry only was to be seen, sitting on the cabin step and singing the ancient chantey. He had cooked and eaten his breakfast all by himself, and had just come out to take a look at the world. Twenty feet before him stood the steel drum round which the endless cable worked. By the drum, snug and fast, was the ore-car. Following with his eyes the dizzy flight of the cables to the farther bank, he could see the other drum and the other car.

The contrivance was worked by gravity, the loaded car crossing the river by virtue of its own weight, and at the same time dragging the empty car back. The loaded car being emptied, and the empty car being loaded with more ore, the performance could be repeated- a performance which had been repeated tens of thousands of times since the day Old Jerry became the keeper of the cables.

Young Jerry broke off his song at the sound of approaching footsteps. A tall, blue-skirted man, a rifle across the hollow of his arm, came out from the gloom of the pine-trees. It was Hall, watchman of the Yellow Dragon mine, the cables of which spanned the Sacramento a mile farther up.

"Hello, younker!" was his greeting. "What you doin' here by your lonesome?"

"Oh, bachin'," Jerry tried to answer unconcernedly, as if it were a very ordinary sort of thing. "Dad's away, you see."

"Where's he gone?" the man asked.

"San Francisco. Went last night. His brother's dead in the old country, and he's gone down to see the lawyers. Won't be back till tomorrow night."

So spoke Jerry, and with pride, because of the responsibility which had fallen to him of keeping an eye on the property of the Yellow Dream, and the glorious adventure of living alone on the cliff above the river and of cooking his own meals.

Well, take care of yourself," Hall said, "and don't monkey with the cables. I'm goin' to see if I can't pick up a deer in the Cripple Cow Canon."

"It's goin' to rain, I think," Jerry said, with mature deliberation.

"And it's little I mind a wettin'," Hall laughed, as he strode away among the trees.

Jerry's prediction concerning rain was more than fulfilled. By ten o'clock the pines were swaying and moaning, the cabin windows rattling, and the rain driving by in fierce squalls. At half past eleven he kindled a fire, and promptly at the stroke of twelve sat down to his dinner.

No out-of-doors for him that day, he decided, when he had washed the few dishes and put them neatly away; and he wondered how wet Hall was and whether he had succeeded in picking up a deer.

At one o'clock there came a knock at the door, and when he

opened it a man and a woman staggered in on the breast of a great gust of wind. They were Mr. and Mrs. Spillane, ranchers, who lived in a lonely valley a dozen miles back from the river.

"Where's Hall?" was Spillane's opening speech, and he spoke sharply and quickly.

Jerry noted that he was nervous and abrupt in his movements, and that Mrs. Spillane seemed laboring under some strong anxiety. She was a thin, washed-out, worked-out woman, whose life of dreary and unending toil had stamped itself harshly upon her face. It was the same life that had bowed her husband's shoulders and gnarled his hands and turned his hair to a dry and dusty gray.

"He's gone hunting up Cripple Cow," Jerry answered. "Did you want to cross?"

The woman began to weep quietly, while Spillane dropped a troubled exclamation and strode to the window. Jerry joined him in gazing out to where the cables lost themselves in the thick downpour.

It was the custom of the backwoods people in that section of country to cross the Sacramento on the Yellow Dragon cable. For this service a small toll was charged, which tolls the Yellow Dragon Company applied to the payment of Hall's wages.

"We've got to get across, Jerry," Spillane said, at the same time jerking his thumb over his shoulder in the direction of his wife. "Her father's hurt at the Clover Leaf. Powder explosion. Not expected to live. We just got word."

Jerry felt himself fluttering inwardly. He knew that Spillane wanted to cross on the Yellow Dream cable, and in the absence of his father he felt that he dared not assume such a responsibility, for the cable had never been used for passengers; in fact, had not been

210

used at all for a long time.

"Maybe Hall will be back soon;" he said.

Spillane shook his head, and demanded, "Where's your father?"

"San Francisco," Jerry answered, briefly.

Spillane groaned, and fiercely drove his clenched fist into the palm of the other hand. His wife was crying more audibly, and Jerry could hear her murmuring, "And daddy's dyin', dyin'!"

The tears welled up in his own eyes, and he stood irresolute, not knowing what he should do. But the man decided for him.

"Look here, kid," he said, with determination, "the wife and me are goin' over on this here cable of yours! Will you run it for us?"

Jerry backed slightly away. He did it unconsciously, as if recoiling instinctively from something unwelcome.

"Better see if Hall's back," he suggested.

"And if he ain't?"

Again Jerry hesitated.

"I'll stand for the risk," Spillane added. "Don't you see, kid, we've simply got to cross!"

Jerry nodded his head reluctantly.

"And there ain't no use waitin' for Hall," Spillane went on. "You know as well as me he ain't back from Cripple Cow this time of day! So come along and let's get started."

No wonder that Mrs. Spillane seemed terrified as they helped her into the ore-car — so Jerry thought, as he gazed into the apparently fathomless gulf beneath her. For it was so filled with rain and cloud, hurtling and curling in the fierce blast, that the other shore, seven hundred feet away, was invisible, while the cliff at their feet dropped sheer down and lost itself in the swirling vapor. By all appearances it might be a mile to bottom instead of two hundred feet.

"All ready?" he asked.

"Let her go!" Spillane shouted, to make himself heard above the roar of the wind.

He had clambered in beside his wife, and was holding one of her hands in his.

Jerry looked upon this with disapproval. "You'll need all your hands for holdin' on, the way the wind's yowlin'."

The man and the woman shifted their hands accordingly, tightly gripping the sides of the car, and Jerry slowly and carefully released the brake. The drum began to revolve as the endless cable passed round it, and the car slid slowly out into the chasm, its trolley wheels rolling on the stationary cable overhead, to which it was suspended.

It was not the first time Jerry had worked the cable, but it was the first time he had done so away from the supervising eye of his father. By means of the brake he regulated the speed of the car. It needed regulating, for at times, caught by the stronger gusts of wind, it swayed violently back and forth; and once, just before it was swallowed up in a rain squall, it seemed about to spill out its human contents.

After that Jerry had no way of knowing where the car was except by means of the cable. This he watched keenly as it glided around the drum. "Three hundred feet," he breathed to himself, as the cable markings went by, "three hundred and fifty, four hundred; four hundred and—"

The cable had stopped. Jerry threw off the brake, but it did not move. He caught the cable with his hands and tried to start it by tugging smartly. Something had gone wrong. What? He could not

212

guess; he could not see. Looking up, he could vaguely make out the empty car, which had been crossing from the opposite cliff at a speed equal to that of the loaded car. It was about two hundred and fifty feet away. That meant, he knew, that somewhere in the gray obscurity, two hundred feet above the river and two hundred and fifty feet from the other bank, Spillane and his wife were suspended and stationary.

Three times Jerry shouted with all the shrill force of his lungs, but no answering cry came out of the storm. It was impossible for him to hear them or to make himself heard. As he stood for a moment, thinking rapidly, the flying clouds seemed to thin and lift. He caught a brief glimpse of the swollen Sacramento beneath, and a briefer glimpse of the car and the man and woman. Then the clouds descended thicker than ever.

The boy examined the drum closely, and found nothing the matter with it. Evidently it was the drum on the other side that had gone wrong. He was appalled at thought of the man and woman out there in the midst of the storm, hanging over the abyss, rocking back and forth in the frail car and ignorant of what was taking place on shore. And he did not like to think of their hanging there while he went round by the Yellow Dragon cable to the other drum.

But he remembered a block and tackle in the tool-house, and ran and brought it. They were double blocks, and he murmured aloud, "A purchase of four," as he made the tackle fast to the endless cable. Then he heaved upon it, heaved until it seemed that his arms were being drawn out from their sockets and that his shoulder muscles would be ripped asunder. Yet the cable did not budge. Nothing remained but to cross over to the other side.

He was already soaking wet, so he did not mind the rain as he ran over the trail to the Yellow Dragon. The storm was with him, and it was easy going, although there was no Hall at the other end of it to man the brake for him and regulate the speed of the car. This he did for himself, however, by means of a stout rope, which he passed, with a turn, round the stationary cable.

As the full force of the wind struck him in mid-air, swaying the cable and whistling and roaring past it, and rocking and careening the car, he appreciated more fully what must be the condition of mind of Spillane and his wife. And this appreciation gave strength to him, as, safely across, he fought his way up the other bank, in the teeth of the gale, to the Yellow Dream cable.

To his consternation, he found the drum in thorough working order. Everything was running smoothly at both ends. Where was the hitch? In the middle, without a doubt.

From this side, the car containing Spillane was only two hundred and fifty feet away. He could make out the man and woman through the whirling vapor, crouching in the bottom of the car and exposed to the pelting rain and the full fury of the wind. In a lull between the squalls he shouted to Spillane to examine the trolley of the car.

Spillane heard, for he saw him rise up cautiously on his knees, and with his hands go over both trolley-wheels. Then he turned his face toward the bank.

"She's all right, kid!"

Jerry heard the words, faint and far, as from a remote distance. Then what was the matter? Nothing remained but the other and empty car, which he could not see, but which he knew to be there, somewhere in that terrible gulf two hundred feet beyond Spillane's car.

214

His mind was made up on the instant. He was only fourteen years old, slightly and wirily built; but his life had been lived among the mountains, his father had taught him no small measure of "sailoring," and he was not particularly afraid of heights.

In the tool-box by the drum he found an old monkey-wrench and a short bar of iron, also a coil of fairly new Manila rope. He looked in vain for a piece of board with which to rig a "boatswain's chair." There was nothing at hand but large planks, which he had no means of sawing, so he was compelled to do without the more comfortable form of saddle.

The saddle he rigged was very simple. With the rope he made merely a large loop round the stationary cable, to which hung the empty car. When he sat in the loop his hands could just reach the cable conveniently, and where the rope was likely to fray against the cable he lashed his coat, in lieu of the old sack he would have used had he been able to find one.

These preparations swiftly completed, he swung out over the chasm, sitting in the rope saddle and pulling himself along the cable by his hands. With him he carried the monkey-wrench and short iron bar and a few spare feet of rope. It was a slightly up-hill pull, but this he did not mind so much as the wind. When the furious gusts hurled him back and forth, sometimes half twisting him about, and he gazed down into the gray depths, he was aware that he was afraid. It was an old cable. What if it should break under his weight and the pressure of the wind?

It was fear he was experiencing, honest fear, and he knew that there was a "gone" feeling in the pit of his stomach, and a trembling of the knees which he could not quell.

But he held himself bravely to the task. The cable was old and

215

worn, sharp pieces of wire projected from it, and his hands were cut and bleeding by the time he took his first rest, and held a shouted conversation with Spillane. The car was directly beneath him and only a few feet away, so he was able to explain the condition of affairs and his errand.

"Wish I could help you," Spillane shouted at him as he started on, "but the wife's gone all to pieces! Anyway, kid, take care of yourself! I got myself in this fix, but it's up to you to get me out!"

"Oh, I'll do it!" Jerry shouted back. "Tell Mrs. Spillane that she'll be ashore now in a jiffy!"

In the midst of pelting rain, which half-blinded him, swinging from side to side like a rapid and erratic pendulum, his torn hands paining him severely and his lungs panting from his exertions and panting from the very air which the wind sometimes blew into his mouth with strangling force, he finally arrived at the empty car.

A single glance showed him that he had not made the dangerous journey in vain. The front trolley-wheel, loose from long wear, had jumped the cable, and the cable was now jammed tightly between the wheel and the sheave-block.

One thing was clear — the wheel must be removed from the block. A second thing was equally clear — while the wheel was being removed the car would have to be fastened to the cable by the rope he had brought.

At the end of a quarter of an hour, beyond making the car secure, he had accomplished nothing. The key which bound the wheel on its axle was rusted and jammed. He hammered at it with one hand and held on the best he could with the other, but the wind persisted in swinging and twisting his body, and made his blows miss more often than not. Nine-tenths of the strength he expended was in trying to hold himself steady. For fear that he might drop the monkey-wrench he made it fast to his wrist with his handkerchief.

At the end of half an hour Jerry had hammered the key clear, but he could not draw it out. A dozen times it seemed that he must give up in despair, that all the danger and toil he had gone through were for nothing. Then an idea came to him, and he went through his pockets with feverish haste, and found what he sought — a ten-penny nail.

But for that nail, put in his pocket he knew not when or why, he would have had to make another trip over the cable and back. Thrusting the nail through the looped head of the key, he at last had a grip, and in no time the key was out.

Then came punching and prying with the iron bar to get the wheel itself free from where it was jammed by the cable against the side of the block. After that Jerry replaced the wheel, and by means of the rope, heaved up on the car till the trolley once more rested properly on the cable.

All this took time. More than an hour and a half had elapsed since his arrival at the empty car. And now, for the first time, he dropped out of his saddle and down into the car. He removed the detaining ropes, and the trolley-wheels began slowly to revolve. The car was moving, and he knew that somewhere beyond, although he could not see, the car of Spillane was likewise moving, and in the opposite direction.

There was no need for a brake, for his weight sufficiently counterbalanced the weight in the other car; and soon he saw the cliff rising out of the cloud depths and the old familiar drum going round and round.

Jerry climbed out and made the car securely fast. He did it

217

deliberately and carefully, and then, quite unhero-like, he sank down by the drum, regardless of the pelting storm, and burst out sobbing.

There were many reasons why he sobbed — partly from the pain of his hands, which was excruciating; partly from exhaustion; partly from relief and release from the nerve-tension he had been under for so long; and in a large measure from thankfulness that the man and woman were saved.

They were not there to thank him; but somewhere beyond that howling, storm-driven gulf he knew they were hurrying over the trail toward the Clover Leaf.

Jerry staggered to the cabin, and his hand left the white knob red with blood as he opened the door, but he took no notice of it.

He was too proudly contented with himself, for he was certain that he had done well, and he was honest enough to admit to himself that he had done well. But a small regret arose and persisted in his thoughts — if his father had only been there to see!

From *Dutch Courage and Other Stories* (1922)
(First published in *The Youth's Companion*,
v. 78, March 17, 1904: 129-130)

AN ADVENTURE IN THE UPPER SEA

I am a retired captain of the upper sea. That is to say, when I was a younger man (which is not so long ago) I was an aeronaut and navigated that aerial ocean which is all around about us and above us. Naturally it is a hazardous profession, and naturally I have had many thrilling experiences, the most thrilling, or at least the most nerve-racking, being the one I am about to relate.

It happened before I went in for hydrogen gas balloons, all of varnished silk, doubled and lined, and all that, and fit for voyages of days instead of mere hours. The Little Nassau (named after the Great Nassau of many years back) was the balloon I was making ascents in at the time. It was a fair-sized, hot-air affair, of single thickness, good for an hour's flight or so and capable of attaining an altitude of a mile or more. It answered my purpose, for my act at the time was making half-mile parachute jumps at recreation parks and country fairs. I was in Oakland, a California town, filling a summer's engagement with a street railway company. The company owned a large park outside the city, and of course it was to its interest to provide attractions which would send the townspeople over its line when they went out to get a whiff of country air. My contract called for two ascensions weekly, and my act was an especially taking feature, for it was on my days that the largest crowds were drawn.

Before you can understand what happened, I must first explain a bit about the nature of the hot air balloon which is used for parachute jumping. If you have ever witnessed such a jump, you will remember that directly the parachute was cut loose the balloon turned upside down, emptied itself of its smoke and heated air, flattened out and fell straight down, beating the parachute to the ground. Thus there is no chasing a big deserted bag for miles and miles across the country, and much time, as well as trouble, is thereby saved. This maneuver is accomplished by attaching a weight, at the end of a long rope, to the top of the balloon. The aeronaut, with his parachute and trapeze, hangs to the bottom of the balloon, and, weighing more, keeps it right side down. But when he lets go, the weight attached to the top immediately drags the top down, and the bottom, which is the open mouth, goes up, the heated air pouring out. The weight used for this purpose on the Little Nassau was a bag of sand.

On the particular day I have in mind there was an unusually large crowd in attendance, and the police had their hands full keeping the people back. There was much pushing and shoving, and the ropes were bulging with the pressure of men, women and children. As I came down from the dressing room I noticed two girls outside the ropes, of about fourteen and sixteen, and inside the rope a youngster of eight or nine. They were holding him by the hands, and he was struggling, excitedly and half in laughter, to get away from them. I thought nothing of it at the time—just a bit of childish play, no more; and it was only in the light of after events that the scene was impressed vividly upon me.

"Keep them cleared out, George!" I called to my assistant. "We don't want any accidents."

"Ay," he answered, "that I will, Charley."

George Guppy had helped me in no end of ascents, and because of his coolness, judgment and absolute reliability I had come to trust my life in his hands with the utmost confidence. His business it was to overlook the inflating of the balloon, and to see that everything about the parachute was in perfect working order.

The Little Nassau was already filled and straining at the guys. The parachute lay flat along the ground and beyond it the trapeze. I tossed aside my overcoat, took my position, and gave the signal to let go. As you know, the first rush upward from the earth is very sudden, and this time the balloon, when it first caught the wind, heeled violently over and was longer than usual in righting. I looked down at the old familiar sight of the world rushing away from me. And there were the thousands of people, every face silently upturned. And the silence startled me, for, as crowds went, this was the time for them to catch their first breath and send up a roar of applause. But there was no hand-clapping, whistling, cheering-only silence. And instead, clear as a bell and distinct, without the slightest shake or quaver, came George's voice through the megaphone:

"Ride her down, Charley! Ride the balloon down!"

What had happened? I waved my hand to show that I had heard, and began to think. Had something gone wrong with the parachute? Why should I ride the balloon down instead of making the jump which thousands were waiting to see? What was the matter? And as I puzzled, I received another start. The earth was a thousand feet beneath, and yet I heard a child crying softly, and seemingly very close to hand. And though the Little Nassau was shooting skyward like a rocket, the crying did not grow fainter and fainter and die away. I confess I was almost on the edge of a funk, when, unconsciously following up the noise with my eyes, I looked above me and saw a boy astride the sandbag which was to bring the Little Nassau to earth. And it was the same little boy I had seen struggling with the two girls—his sisters, as I afterward learned.

There he was, astride the sandbag and holding on to the rope for dear life. A puff of wind heeled the balloon slightly, and he swung out into space for ten or a dozen feet, and back again, fetching up against the tight canvas with a thud which even shook me, thirty feet or more beneath. I thought to see him dashed loose, but he clung on and whimpered. They told me afterward, how, at the moment they were casting off the balloon, the little fellow had torn away from his sisters, ducked under the rope, and deliberately jumped astride the sandbag. It has always been a wonder to me that he was not jerked off in the first rush.

Well, I felt sick all over as I looked at him there, and I understood why the balloon had taken longer to right itself, and why George had called after me to ride her down. Should I cut loose with the parachute, the bag would at once turn upside down, empty itself, and begin its swift descent. The only hope lay in my riding her down and in the boy holding on. There was no possible way for me to reach him. No man could climb the slim, closed parachute; and even if a man could, and made the mouth of the balloon, what could he do? Straight out, and fifteen feet away, trailed the boy on his ticklish perch, and those fifteen feet were empty space.

I thought far more quickly than it takes to tell all this, and realized on the instant that the boy's attention must be called away from his terrible danger. Exercising all the self-control I possessed, and striving to make myself very calm, I said cheerily:

"Hello, up there, who are you?"

He looked down at me, choking back his tears and brightening up, but just then the balloon ran into a cross-current, turned half around and lay over. This set him swinging back and forth, and he fetched the canvas another bump. Then he began to cry again.

"Isn't it great?" I asked heartily, as though it was the most enjoyable thing in the world; and, without waiting for him to answer: "What's your name?"

"Tommy Dermott," he answered.

"Glad to make your acquaintance, Tommy Dermott," I went on. "But I'd like to know who said you could ride up with me?"

He laughed and said he just thought he'd ride up for the fun of it. And so we went on, I sick with fear for him, and cudgeling my brains to keep up the conversation. I knew that it was all I could do, and that his life depended upon my ability to keep his mind off his danger. I pointed out to him the great panorama spreading away to the horizon and four thousand feet beneath us. There lay San Francisco Bay like a great placid lake, the haze of smoke over the city, the Golden Gate, the ocean fog-rim beyond, and Mount Tamalpais over all, clear-cut and sharp against the sky. Directly below us I could see a buggy, apparently crawling, but I knew from experience that the men in it were lashing the horses on our trail.

But he grew tired of looking around, and I could see he was beginning to get frightened.

"How would you like to go in for the business?" I asked.

He cheered up at once and asked "Do you get good pay?"

But the Little Nassau, beginning to cool, had started on its long descent, and ran into counter currents which bobbed it roughly about. This swung the boy around pretty lively, smashing him into the bag once quite severely. His lip began to tremble at this, and he was crying again. I tried to joke and laugh, but it was no use. His pluck was oozing out, and at any moment I was prepared to see him go shooting past me.

I was in despair. Then, suddenly, I remembered how one fright could destroy another fright, and I frowned up at him and shouted sternly:

"You just hold on to that rope! If you don't I'll thrash you within an inch of your life when I get you down on the ground! Understand?"

"Ye-ye-yes, sir," he whimpered, and I saw that the thing had worked. I was nearer to him than the earth, and he was more afraid of me than of falling.

"Why, you've got a snap up there on that soft bag," I rattled on.

"Yes;" I assured him, "this bar down here is hard and narrow, and it hurts to sit on it."

Then a thought struck him, and he forgot all about his aching fingers.

"When are you going to jump?" he asked. "That's what I came up to see."

I was sorry to disappoint him, but I wasn't going to make any jump.

But he objected to that. "It said so in the papers," he said.

"I don't care," I answered. "I'm feeling sort of lazy today, and I'm just going to ride down the balloon. It's my balloon and I guess I can do as I please about it. And, anyway, we're almost down now."

And we were, too, and sinking fast. And right there and then that youngster began to argue with me as to whether it was right for me to disappoint the people, and to urge their claims upon me. And it was with a happy heart that I held up my end of it, justifying myself in a thousand different ways, till we shot over a grove of eucalyptus trees and dipped to meet the earth.

"Hold on tight!" I shouted, swinging down from the trapeze by my hands in order to make a landing on my feet.

We skimmed past a barn, missed a mesh of clothesline, frightened the barnyard chickens into a panic, and rose up again clear over a haystack-all this almost quicker than it takes to tell. Then we came down in an orchard, and when my feet had touched the ground I fetched up the balloon by a couple of turns of the trapeze around an apple tree.

I have had my balloon catch fire in mid air, I have hung on the cornice of a ten-story house, I have dropped like a bullet for six hundred feet when a parachute was slow in opening; but never have I felt so weak and faint and sick as when I staggered toward the unscratched boy and gripped him by the arm.

"Tommy Dermott," I said, when I had got my nerves back somewhat. "Tommy Dermott, I'm going to lay you across my knee and give you the greatest thrashing a boy ever got in the world's history."

"No, you don't," he answered, squirming around. "You said you wouldn't if I held on tight."

"That's all right," I said, "but I'm going to, just the same. The fellows who go up in balloons are bad, unprincipled men, and I'm going to give you a lesson right now to make you stay away from them, and from balloons, too."

And then I gave it to him, and if it wasn't the greatest thrashing in the world, it was the greatest he ever got.

But it took all the grit out of me, left me nerve-broken, that experience. I canceled the engagement with the street railway company, and later on went in for gas. Gas is much the safer, anyway.

From *Dutch Courage and Other Stories* (1922)
(First published in *The Independent*,
(New York) v.54, May 29, 1902: 1290-1292)

.

WINGED BLACKMAIL

Peter Winn lay back comfortably in a library chair, with closed eyes, deep in the cogitation of a scheme of campaign destined in the near future to make a certain coterie of hostile financiers sit up. The central idea had come to him the night before, and he was now reveling in the planning of the remoter, minor details. By obtaining control of a certain up-country bank, two general stores, and several logging camps, he could come into control of a certain dinky jerkwater line which shall here be nameless, but which, in his hands, would prove the key to a vastly larger situation involving more main-line mileage almost than there were spikes in the aforesaid dinky jerkwater. It was so simple that he had almost laughed aloud when it came to him. No wonder those astute and ancient enemies of his had passed it by.

The library door opened, and a slender, middle-aged man, weak-eyed and eye glassed, entered. In his hands was an envelope and an open letter. As Peter Winn's secretary it was his task to weed out, sort, and classify his employer's mail.

"This came in the morning post," he ventured apologetically and with the hint of a titter. "Of course it doesn't amount to anything, but I thought you would like to see it."

"Read it," Peter Winn commanded, without opening his eyes.

The secretary cleared his throat.

"It is dated July seventeenth, but is without address. Postmark San Francisco. It is also quite illiterate. The spelling is atrocious.

227

Here it is:

Mr. Peter Winn,

SIR: I send you respectfully by express a pigeon worth good money. She's a loo-loo—

"What is a loo-loo?" Peter Winn interrupted.

The secretary tittered.

"I'm sure I don't know, except that it must be a superlative of some sort. The letter continues:

Please freight it with a couple of thousand-dollar bills and let it go. If you do I wont never annoy you no more. If you dont you will be sorry.

"That is all. It is unsigned. I thought it would amuse you."

"Has the pigeon come?" Peter Winn demanded.

"I'm sure I never thought to enquire."

"Then do so."

In five minutes the secretary was back.

"Yes, sir. It came this morning."

"Then bring it in."

The secretary was inclined to take the affair as a practical joke, but Peter Winn, after an examination of the pigeon, thought otherwise.

"Look at it," he said, stroking and handling it. "See the length of the body and that elongated neck. A proper carrier. I doubt if I've ever seen a finer specimen. Powerfully winged and muscled. As our unknown correspondent remarked, she is a loo-loo. It's a temptation to keep her."

The secretary tittered.

"Why not? Surely you will not let it go back to the writer of that letter."

Peter Winn shook his head.

"I'll answer. No man can threaten me, even anonymously or in foolery."

On a slip of paper he wrote the succinct message, "Go to hell," signed it, and placed it in the carrying apparatus with which the bird had been thoughtfully supplied.

"Now we'll let her loose. Where's my son? I'd like him to see the flight."

"He's down in the workshop. He slept there last night, and had his breakfast sent down this morning."

"He'll break his neck yet," Peter Winn remarked, half-fiercely, half-proudly, as he led the way to the veranda.

Standing at the head of the broad steps, he tossed the pretty creature outward and upward. She caught herself with a quick beat of wings, fluttered about undecidedly for a space, then rose in the air.

Again, high up, there seemed indecision; then, apparently getting her bearings, she headed east, over the oak-trees that dotted the park-like grounds.

"Beautiful, beautiful," Peter Winn murmured. "I almost wish I had her back."

But Peter Winn was a very busy man, with such large plans in his head and with so many reins in his hands that he quickly forgot the incident. Three nights later the left wing of his country house was blown up. It was not a heavy explosion, and nobody was hurt, though the wing itself was ruined. Most of the windows of the rest

229

of the house were broken, and there was a deal of general damage. By the first ferry boat of the morning half a dozen San Francisco detectives arrived, and several hours later the secretary, in high excitement, erupted on Peter Winn.

"It's come!" the secretary gasped, the sweat beading his forehead and his eyes bulging behind their glasses.

"What has come?" Peter demanded. "It—the—the loo-loo bird."

Then the financier understood.

"Have you gone over the mail yet?"

"I was just going over it, sir."

"Then continue, and see if you can find another letter from our mysterious friend, the pigeon fancier."

The letter came to light. It read:

Mr. Peter Winn,

HONORABLE SIR: Now dont be a fool. If youd came through, your shack would not have blew up—I beg to inform you respectfully, am sending same pigeon. Take good care of same, thank you. Put five one thousand dollar bills on her and let her go. Dont feed her. Dont try to follow bird. She is wise to the way now and makes better time. If you dont come through, watch out.

Peter Winn was genuinely angry. This time he indited no message for the pigeon to carry. Instead, he called in the detectives, and, under their advice, weighted the pigeon heavily with shot. Her previous flight having been eastward toward the bay, the fastest motor-boat in Tiburon was commissioned to take up the chase if it led out over the water.

But too much shot had been put on the carrier, and she was exhausted before the shore was reached. Then the mistake was made of putting too little shot on her, and she rose high in the air, got her bearings and started eastward across San Francisco Bay. She flew straight over Angel Island, and here the motor-boat lost her, for it had to go around the island.

That night, armed guards patrolled the grounds. But there was no explosion. Yet, in the early morning Peter Winn learned by telephone that his sister's home in Alameda had been burned to the ground.

Two days later the pigeon was back again, coming this time by freight in what had seemed a barrel of potatoes. Also came another letter:

Mr. Peter Winn,

RESPECTABLE SIR: It was me that fixed yr sisters house. You have raised hell, aint you. Send ten thousand now. Going up all the time. Dont put any more handicap weights on that bird. You sure cant follow her, and its cruelty to animals.

Peter Winn was ready to acknowledge himself beaten. The detectives were powerless, and Peter did not know where next the man would strike—perhaps at the lives of those near and dear to him. He even telephoned to San Francisco for ten thousand dollars in bills of large denomination. But Peter had a son, Peter Winn, Junior, with the same firm-set jaw as his fathers,, and the same knitted, brooding determination in his eyes. He was only twenty-six, but he was all man, a secret terror and delight to the financier, who alternated between pride in his son's aeroplane feats and fear for an untimely and terrible end.

"Hold on, father, don't send that money," said Peter Winn, Junior. "Number Eight is ready, and I know I've at last got that reefing down fine. It will work, and it will revolutionize flying. Speed—that's what's needed, and so are the large sustaining surfaces for getting started and for altitude. I've got them both. Once I'm up I reef down. There it is. The smaller the sustaining surface, the higher the speed. That was the law discovered by Langley. And I've applied it. I can rise when the air is calm and full of holes, and I can rise when its boiling, and by my control of my plane areas I can come pretty close to making any speed I want. Especially with that new Sangster-Endholm engine."

"You'll come pretty close to breaking your neck one of these days," was his father's encouraging remark.

"Dad, I'll tell you what I'll come pretty close to-ninety miles an hour—Yes, and a hundred. Now listen! I was going to make a trial tomorrow. But it won't take two hours to start today. I'll tackle it this afternoon. Keep that money. Give me the pigeon and I'll follow her to her loft where ever it is. Hold on, let me talk to the mechanics."

He called up the workshop, and in crisp, terse sentences gave his orders in a way that went to the older man's heart. Truly, his one son was a chip off the old block, and Peter Winn had no meek notions concerning the intrinsic value of said old block.

Timed to the minute, the young man, two hours later, was ready for the start. In a holster at his hip, for instant use, cocked and with the safety on, was a large-caliber automatic pistol. With a final inspection and overhauling he took his seat in the aeroplane. He started the engine, and with a wild burr of gas explosions the beautiful fabric darted down the launching ways and lifted into the air. Circling, as he rose, to the west, he wheeled about and jockeyed and maneuvered for the real start of the race.

This start depended on the pigeon. Peter Winn held it. Nor was it weighted with shot this time. Instead, half a yard of bright ribbon was firmly attached to its leg—this the more easily to enable its flight being followed. Peter Winn released it, and it arose easily enough despite the slight drag of the ribbon. There was no uncertainty about its movements. This was the third time it had made particular homing passage, and it knew the course.

At an altitude of several hundred feet it straightened out and went due east. The aeroplane swerved into a straight course from its last curve and followed. The race was on. Peter Winn, looking up, saw that the pigeon was outdistancing the machine. Then he saw something else. The aeroplane suddenly and instantly became smaller. It had reefed. Its high-speed plane-design was now revealed. Instead of the generous spread of surface with which it had taken the air, it was now a lean and hawklike monoplane balanced on long and exceedingly narrow wings.

*

When young Winn reefed down so suddenly, he received a surprise. It was his first trial of the new device, and while he was prepared for increased speed he was not prepared for such an astonishing increase. It was better than he dreamed, and, before he knew it, he was hard upon the pigeon. That little creature, frightened by this, the most monstrous hawk it had ever seen, immediately darted upward, after the manner of pigeons that strive always to rise above a hawk.

In great curves the monoplane followed upward, higher and higher into the blue. It was difficult, from underneath to see the pigeon. and young Winn dared not lose it from his sight. He even shook out his reefs in order to rise more quickly. Up, up they went, until the pigeon, true to its instinct, dropped and struck at what it to be the back of its pursuing enemy. Once was enough, for, evidently finding no life in the smooth cloth surface of the machine, it ceased soaring and straightened out on its eastward course.

A carrier pigeon on a passage can achieve a high rate of speed, and Winn reefed again. And again, to his satisfaction, be found that he was beating the pigeon. But this time he quickly shook out a portion of his reefed sustaining surface and slowed down in time. From then on he knew he had the chase safely in hand, and from then on a chant rose to his lips which he continued to sing at intervals, and unconsciously, for the rest of the passage. It was: "Going some; going some; what did I tell you!—going some."

Even so, it was not all plain sailing. The air is an unstable medium at best, and quite without warning, at an acute angle, he entered an aerial tide which he recognized as the gulf stream of wind that poured through the drafty-mouthed Golden Gate. His right wing caught it first—a sudden, sharp puff that lifted and tilted the monoplane and threatened to capsize it. But he rode with a sensitive "loose curb," and quickly, but not too quickly, he shifted the angles of his wing-tips, depressed the front horizontal rudder, and swung over the rear vertical rudder to meet the tilting thrust of the wind. As the machine came back to an even keel, and he knew that he was now wholly in the invisible stream, he readjusted the wing-tips, rapidly away from him during the several moments of his discomfiture.

The pigeon drove straight on for the Alameda County shore, and it was near this shore that Winn had another experience. He fell into an air-hole. He had fallen into air-holes before, in previous flights, but this was a far larger one than he had ever encountered. With his eyes strained on the ribbon attached to the pigeon, by that fluttering bit of color he marked his fall. Down he went, at the pit of his stomach that old sink sensation which he had known as a boy he first negotiated quick-starting elevators. But Winn, among other secrets of aviation, had learned that to go up it was sometimes necessary first to go down. The air had refused to hold him. Instead of struggling futilely and perilously against this lack of sustension, he yielded to it. With steady head and hand, he depressed the forward horizontal rudder—just recklessly enough and not a fraction more—and the monoplane dived head foremost and sharply down the void. It was falling with the keenness of a knife-blade. Every instant the speed accelerated frightfully. Thus he accumulated the momentum that would save him. But few instants were required, when, abruptly shifting the double horizontal rudders forward and astern, he shot upward on the tense and straining plane and out of the pit.

At an altitude of five hundred feet, the pigeon drove on over the town of Berkeley and lifted its flight to the Contra Costa hills. Young Winn noted the campus and buildings of the University of California—his university—as he rose after the pigeon.

Once more, on these Contra Costa hills, he early came to grief. The pigeon was now flying low, and where a grove of eucalyptus presented a solid front to the wind, the bird was suddenly sent fluttering wildly upward for a distance of a hundred feet. Winn knew what it meant. It had been caught in an air-surf that beat upward hundreds of feet where the fresh west wind smote the upstanding wall of the grove. He reefed hastily to the uttermost, and at the same time depressed the angle of his flight to meet that upward surge. Nevertheless, the monoplane was tossed fully three hundred feet before the danger was left astern.

Two or more ranges of hills the pigeon crossed, and then Winn saw it dropping down to a landing where a small cabin stood in a hillside clearing. He blessed that clearing. Not only was it good for alighting, but, on account of the steepness of the slope, it was just the thing for rising again into the air.

A man, reading a newspaper, had just started up at the sight of the returning pigeon, when be heard the burr of Winn's engine and saw the huge monoplane, with all surfaces set, drop down upon him, stop suddenly on an air-cushion manufactured on the spur of the moment by a shift of the horizontal rudders, glide a few yards, strike ground, and come to rest not a score of feet away from him. But when he saw a young man, calmly sitting in the machine and leveling a pistol at him, the man turned to run. Before he could make the comer of the cabin, a bullet through the leg brought him down in a sprawling fall.

"What do you want!" he demanded sullenly, as the other stood over him.

"I want to take you for a ride in my new machine," Winn answered. "Believe me, she is a loo-loo."

The man did not argue long, for this strange visitor had most convincing ways. Under Winn's instructions, covered all the time by the pistol, the man improvised a tourniquet and applied it to his wounded leg. Winn helped him to a seat in the machine, then went to the pigeon-loft and took possession of the bird with the ribbon still fast to its leg.

A very tractable prisoner, the man proved. Once up in the air, he sat close, in an ecstasy of fear. An adept at winged blackmail, he had no aptitude for wings himself, and when he gazed down at the flying land and water far beneath him, he did not feel moved to attack his captor, now defenseless, both hands occupied with flight.

Instead, the only way the man felt moved was to sit closer.

*

Peter Winn, Senior, scanning the heavens with powerful glasses, saw the monoplane leap into view and grow large over the rugged backbone of Angel Island. Several minutes later he cried out to the waiting detectives that the machine carried a passenger. Dropping swiftly and piling up an abrupt air-cushion, the monoplane landed.

"That reefing device is a winner!" young Winn cried, as he climbed out. "Did you see me at the start? I almost ran over the pigeon. Going some, dad! Going some! What did I tell you? Going some!"

"But who is that with you?" his father demanded.

The young man looked back at his prisoner and remembered.

"Why, that's the pigeon-fancier," he said. "I guess the officers can take care of him."

Peter Winn gripped his son's hand in grim silence, and fondled the pigeon which his son had passed to him. Again he fondled the pretty creature. Then he spoke.

"Exhibit A, for the People," he said.

From *The Night-Born* (1913)
(First published in *The Lever*, Sept, 1910)

WHEN THE WORLD WAS YOUNG

I

He was a very quiet, self-possessed sort of man, sitting a moment on top of the wall to sound the damp darkness for warnings of the dangers it might conceal. But the plummet of his hearing brought nothing to him save the moaning of wind through invisible trees and the rustling of leaves on swaying branches. A heavy fog drifted and drove before the wind, and though he could not see this fog, the wet of it blew upon his face, and the wall on which he sat was wet.

Without noise he had climbed to the top of the wall from the outside, and without noise he dropped to the ground on the inside. From his pocket he drew an electric night-stick, but he did not use it. Dark as the way was, he was not anxious for light. Carrying the night-stick in his hand, his finger on the button, he advanced through the darkness. The ground was velvety and springy to his feet, being carpeted with dead pine-needles and leaves and mold which evidently bad been undisturbed for years. Leaves and branches brushed against his body, but so dark was it that he could not avoid them. Soon he walked with his hand stretched out gropingly before him, and more than once the hand fetched up against the solid trunks of massive trees. All about him he knew were these trees; he sensed the loom of them everywhere; and he experienced a strange feeling of microscopic smallness in the midst of great bulks leaning toward him to crush him. Beyond, he knew, was the house, and he expected to find some trail or winding path that would lead easily to it.

Once, he found himself trapped. On every side he groped against trees and branches, or blundered into thickets of underbrush, until there seemed no way out. Then he turned on his light, circumspectly, directing its rays to the ground at his feet. Slowly and carefully he moved it about him, the white brightness showing in sharp detail all the obstacles to his progress. He saw an opening between huge-trunked trees, and advanced through it, putting out the light and treading on dry footing as yet protected from the drip of the fog by the dense foliage overhead. His sense of direction was good, and he knew he was going toward the house.

And then the thing happened—the thing unthinkable and unexpected. His descending foot came down upon something that was soft and alive, and that arose with a snort under the weight of his body. He sprang clear, and crouched for another spring, anywhere, tense and expectant, keyed for the onslaught of the unknown. He waited a moment, wondering what manner of animal it was that had arisen from under his foot and that now made no sound nor movement and that must be crouching and waiting just as tensely and expectantly as he. The strain became unbearable. Holding the night-stick before him, he pressed the button, saw, and screamed aloud in terror. He was prepared for anything, from a frightened calf or fawn to a belligerent lion, but he was not prepared for what he saw. In that instant his tiny searchlight, sharp and white, had shown him what a thousand years would not enable him to forget—a man, huge and blond, yellow-haired and yellow-bearded, naked except for soft-tanned moccasins and what seemed a goat-skin about his middle. Arms and legs were bare, as were his shoulders and most of his chest. The skin was smooth and hairless, but browned by sun and wind, while under it heavy muscles were knotted like fat snakes.

Still, this alone, unexpected as it well was, was not what had made the man scream out. What had caused his terror was the unspeakable ferocity of the face, the wild-animal glare of the blue eyes scarcely dazzled by the light, the pine-needles matted and clinging in the beard and hair, and the whole formidable body crouched and in the act of springing at him. Practically in the instant he saw all this, and while his scream still rang, the thing leaped, he flung his night-stick full at it, and threw himself to the ground. He felt its feet and shins strike against his ribs, and he bounded up and away while the thing itself hurled onward in a heavy crashing fall into the underbrush.

As the noise of the fall ceased, the man stopped and on hands and knees waited. He could hear the thing moving about, searching for him, and he was afraid to advertise his location by attempting further flight. He knew that inevitably he would crackle the underbrush and be pursued. Once he drew out his revolver, then changed his mind. He had recovered his composure and hoped to get away without noise. Several times he heard the thing beating up the thickets for him, and there were moments when it, too, remained still and listened. This gave an idea to the man. One of his hands was resting on a chunk of dead wood. Carefully, first feeling about him in the darkness to know that the full swing of his arm was clear, he raised the chunk of wood and threw it. It was not a large piece, and it went far, landing noisily in a bush. He heard the thing bound into the bush, and at the same time himself crawled steadily away. And on hands and knees, slowly and cautiously, he crawled on, till his knees were wet on the soggy mold, When he listened he heard naught but the moaning wind and the drip-drip of the fog from the branches. Never abating his caution, he stood erect and went on to the stone wall, over which he climbed and dropped down to the road outside.

Feeling his way in a clump of bushes, he drew out a bicycle and prepared to mount. He was in the act of driving the gear around with his foot for the purpose of getting the opposite pedal in position, when he heard the thud of a heavy body that landed lightly and evidently on its feet. He did not wait for more, but ran, with hands on the handles of his bicycle, until he was able to vault astride the saddle, catch the pedals, and start a spurt. Behind he could hear the quick thud-thud of feet on the dust of the road, but he drew away from it and lost it. Unfortunately, he had started away from the direction of town and was heading higher up into the hills. He knew that on this particular road there were no cross roads. The only way back was past that terror, and he could not steel himself to face it. At the end of half an hour, finding himself on an ever increasing grade, he dismounted. For still greater safety, leaving the wheel by the roadside, he climbed through a fence into what he decided was a hillside pasture, spread a newspaper on the ground, and sat down.

"Gosh!" he said aloud, mopping the sweat and fog from his face.

And "Gosh!" he said once again, while rolling a cigarette and as he pondered the problem of getting back.

But he made no attempt to go back. He was resolved not to face that road in the dark, and with head bowed on knees, he dozed, waiting for daylight.

How long afterward he did not know, he was awakened by the yapping bark of a young coyote. As he looked about and located it on the brow of the hill behind him, he noted the change that had come over the face of the night. The fog was gone; the stars and moon were out; even the wind had died down. It had transformed into a balmy California summer night. He tried to doze again, but the yap of the coyote disturbed him. Half asleep, he heard a wild and eery chant. Looking about him, he noticed that the coyote had ceased its noise and was running away along the crest of the hill, and behind it, in full pursuit, no longer chanting, ran the naked creature he had encountered in the garden. It was a young coyote, and it was being overtaken when the chase passed from view. The man trembled as with a chill as he started to his feet, clambered over the fence, and mounted his wheel. But it was his chance and he knew it. The terror was no longer between him and Mill Valley.

He sped at a breakneck rate down the hill, but in the turn at the bottom, in the deep shadows, he encountered a chuck-hole and pitched headlong over the handle bar.

"It's sure not my night," he muttered, as he examined the broken fork of the machine

Shouldering the useless wheel, he trudged on. In time he came to the stone wall, and, half disbelieving his experience, he sought in the road for tracks, and found them—moccasin tracks, large ones, deep-bitten into the dust at the toes. It was while bending over them, examining, that again he heard the eery chant. He had seen the thing pursue the coyote, and he knew he had no chance on a straight run. He did not attempt it, contenting himself with hiding in the shadows on the off side of the road.

And again he saw the thing that was like a naked man, running

243

swiftly and lightly and singing as it ran. Opposite him it paused, and his heart stood still. But instead of coming toward his hiding-place, it leaped into the air, caught the branch of a roadside tree, and swung swiftly upward, from limb to limb, like an ape. It swung across the wall, and a dozen feet above the top, into the branches of another tree, and dropped out of sight to the ground. The man waited a few wondering minutes, then started on.

II

Dave Slotter leaned belligerently against the desk that barred the way to the private office of James Ward, senior partner of the firm of Ward, Knowles & Co. Dave was angry. Every one in the outer office had looked him over suspiciously, and the man who faced him was excessively suspicious.

"You just tell Mr. Ward it's important," he urged.

"I tell you he is dictating and cannot be disturbed," was the answer. "Come to-morrow."

"To-morrow will be too late. You just trot along and tell Mr. Ward it's a matter of life and death."

The secretary hesitated and Dave seized the advantage.

"You just tell him I was across the bay in Mill Valley last night, and that I want to put him wise to something."

"What name?" was the query.

"Never mind the name. He don't know me."

When Dave was shown into the private office, he was still in the belligerent frame of mind, but when he saw a large fair man whirl in a revolving chair from dictating to a stenographer to face him, Dave's demeanor abruptly changed. He did not know why it changed, and he was secretly angry with himself.

"You are Mr. Ward?" Dave asked with a fatuousness that still further irritated him. He had never intended it at all.

"Yes," came the answer. "And who are you?"

"Harry Bancroft," Dave lied. "You don't know me, and my name don't matter."

"You sent in word that you were in Mill Valley last night?"

"You live there, don't you?" Dave countered, looking suspiciously at the stenographer.

"Yes. What do you mean to see me about? I am very busy."

"I'd like to see you alone, sir."

Mr. Ward gave him a quick, penetrating look, hesitated, then made up his mind.

"That will do for a few minutes, Miss Potter."

The girl arose, gathered her notes together, and passed out. Dave looked at Mr. James Ward wonderingly, until that gentleman broke his train of inchoate thought.

"Well?"

"I was over in Mill Valley last night," Dave began confusedly.

"I've heard that before. What do you want?"

And Dave proceeded in the face of a growing conviction that was unbelievable. "I was at your house, or in the grounds, I mean."

"What were you doing there?"

"I came to break in," Dave answered in all frankness. "I heard you lived all alone with a Chinaman for cook, and it looked good to me. Only I didn't break in. Something happened that prevented. That's why I'm here. I come to warn you. I found a wild man loose in your grounds—a regular devil. He could pull a guy like me to pieces. He gave me the run of my life. He don't wear any clothes to speak of, he climbs trees like a monkey, and he runs like a deer. I saw him chasing a coyote, and the last I saw of it, by God, he was gaining on it."

Dave paused and looked for the effect that would follow his words. But no effect came. James Ward was quietly curious, and that was all.

"Very remarkable, very remarkable," he murmured. "A wild man, you say. Why have you come to tell me?"

"To warn you of your danger. I'm something of a hard proposition myself, but I don't believe in killing people . . . that is, unnecessarily. I realized that you was in danger. I thought I'd warn you. Honest, that's the game. Of course, if you wanted to give me anything for my trouble, I'd take it. That was in my mind, too. But I don't care whether you give me anything or not. I've warned you any way, and done my duty."

Mr. Ward meditated and drummed on the surface of his desk. Dave noticed they were large, powerful hands, withal well-cared for despite their dark sunburn. Also, he noted what had already caught his eye before—a tiny strip of flesh-colored courtplaster on the forehead over one eve. And still the thought that forced itself into his mind was unbelievable.

Mr. Ward took a wallet from his inside coat pocket, drew out a greenback, and passed it to Dave, who noted as he pocketed it that it was for twenty dollars.

"Thank you," said Mr. Ward, indicating that the interview was at an end. "I shall have the matter investigated. A wild man running loose *is* dangerous."

But so quiet a man was Mr. Ward, that Dave's courage returned. Besides, a new theory had suggested itself. The wild man was evidently Mr. Ward's brother, a lunatic privately confined. Dave had heard of such things. Perhaps Mr. Ward wanted it kept quiet. That was why he had given him the twenty dollars.

"Say," Dave began, "now I come to think of it that wild man looked a lot like you—"

That was as far as Dave got, for at that moment he witnessed a transformation and found himself gazing into the same unspeakably ferocious blue eyes of the night before, at the same clutching talon-like hands, and at the same formidable bulk in the act of springing upon him. But this time Dave had no night-stick to throw, and he was caught by the biceps of both arms in a grip so terrific that it made him groan with pain. He saw the large white teeth exposed, for all the world as a dog's about to bite. Mr. Ward's beard brushed his face as the teeth went in for the grip on his throat. But the bite was not given. Instead, Dave felt the other's body stiffen as with an iron restraint, and then he was flung aside, without effort but with such force that only the wall stopped his momentum and dropped him gasping to the floor.

"What do you mean by coming here and trying to blackmail me?" Mr. Ward was snarling at him. "Here, give me back that money."

Dave passed the bill back without a word.

"I thought you came here with good intentions. I know you now. Let me see and hear no more of you, or I'll put you in prison where you belong. Do you understand?"

"Yes, sir," Dave gasped.

"Then go."

And Dave went, without further word, both his biceps aching intolerably from the bruise of that tremendous grip. As his hand rested on the door knob, he was stopped.

"You were lucky," Mr. Ward was saying, and Dave noted that his face and eyes were cruel and gloating and proud. "You were lucky. Had I wanted, I could have torn your muscles out of your arms and thrown them in the waste basket there."

"Yes, sir," said Dave; and absolute conviction vibrated in his voice.

He opened the door and passed out. The secretary looked at him interrogatively.

"Gosh!" was all Dave vouchsafed, and with this utterance passed out of the offices and the story.

III

James J. Ward was forty years of age, a successful business man, and very unhappy. For forty years he had vainly tried to solve a problem that was really himself and that with increasing years became more and more a woeful affliction. In himself he was two men, and, chronologically speaking, these men were several thousand years or so apart. He had studied the question of dual personality probably more profoundly than any half dozen of the leading specialists in that intricate and mysterious psychological field. In himself he was a different case from any that had been recorded. Even the most fanciful flights of the fiction-writers had not quite hit upon him. He was not a Dr. Jekyll and Mr. Hyde, nor was he like the unfortunate young man in Kipling's "Greatest Story in the World." His two personalities were so mixed that they were practically aware of themselves and of each other all the time.

His one self was that of a man whose rearing and education

were modern and who had lived through the latter part of the nineteenth century and well into the first decade of the twentieth.

His other self he had located as a savage and a barbarian living under the primitive conditions of several thousand years before. But which self was he, and which was the other, he could never tell. For he was both selves, and both selves all the time. Very rarely indeed did it happen that one self did not know what the other was doing. Another thing was that he had no visions nor memories of the past in which that early self had lived. That early self lived in the present; but while it lived in the present, it was under the compulsion to live the way of life that must have been in that distant past.

In his childhood he had been a problem to his father and mother, and to the family doctors, though never had they come within a thousand miles of hitting upon the clue to his erratic conduct. Thus, they could not understand his excessive somnolence in the forenoon, nor his excessive activity at night. When they found him wandering along the hallways at night, or climbing over giddy roofs, or running in the hills, they decided he was a somnambulist. In reality he was wide-eyed awake and merely under the nightroaming compulsion of his early self. Questioned by an obtuse medico, he once told the truth and suffered the ignominy of having the revelation contemptuously labeled and dismissed as "dreams."

The point was, that as twilight and evening came on he became wakeful. The four walls of a room were an irk and a restraint. He heard a thousand voices whispering to him through the darkness. The night called to him, for he was, for that period of the twenty-four hours, essentially a night-prowler. But nobody understood, and never again did he attempt to explain. They classified him as a sleep-walker and took precautions accordingly—precautions that very often were futile. As his childhood advanced, he grew more cunning, so that the major portion of all his nights were spent in the open at realizing his other self. As a result, he slept in the forenoons. Morning studies and schools were impossible, and it was discovered that only in the afternoons, under private teachers, could he be taught anything. Thus was his modern self educated and developed.

But a problem, as a child, he ever remained. He was known as a little demon, of insensate cruelty and viciousness. The family medicos privately adjudged him a mental monstrosity and degenerate. Such few boy companions as he had, hailed him as a wonder, though they were all afraid of him. He could outclimb, outswim, outrun, outdevil any of them; while none dared fight with him. He was too terribly strong, madly furious.

When nine years of age he ran away to the hills, where he flourished, night-prowling, for seven weeks before he was discovered and brought home. The marvel was how he had managed to subsist and keep in condition during that time. They did not know, and he never told them, of the rabbits he had killed, of the quail, young and old, he had captured and devoured, of the farmers' chicken-roosts he had raided, nor of the cave-lair he had made and carpeted with dry leaves and grasses and in which he had slept in warmth and comfort through the forenoons of many days.

At college he was notorious for his sleepiness and stupidity during the morning lectures and for his brilliance in the afternoon. By collateral reading and by borrowing the notebook of his fellow students he managed to scrape through the detestable morning courses, while his afternoon courses were triumphs. In football he proved a giant and a terror, and, in almost every form of track athletics, save for strange Berserker rages that were sometimes displayed, he could be depended upon to win. But his fellows were afraid to box with him, and he signalized his last wrestling bout by sinking his teeth into the shoulder of his opponent.

After college, his father, in despair, sent him among the cow-punchers of a Wyoming ranch. Three months later the doughty cowmen confessed he was too much for them and telegraphed his father to come and take the wild man away. Also, when the father arrived to take him away, the cowmen allowed that they would vastly prefer chumming with howling cannibals, gibbering lunatics, cavorting gorillas, grizzly bears, and man-eating tigers than with this particular Young college product with hair parted in the middle.

There was one exception to the lack of memory of the life of his early self, and that was language. By some quirk of atavism, a certain portion of that early self's language had come down to him as a racial memory. In moments of happiness, exaltation, or battle, he was prone to burst out in wild barbaric songs or chants. It was by this means that he located in time and space that strayed half of him who should have been dead and dust for thousands of years. He sang, once, and deliberately, several of the ancient chants in the presence of Professor Wertz, who gave courses in old Saxon and who was a philogist of repute and passion. At the first one, the professor pricked up his ears and demanded to know what mongrel tongue or hog-German it was. When the second chant was rendered, the professor was highly excited. James Ward then concluded the performance by giving a song that always irresistibly

251

rushed to his lips when he was engaged in fierce struggling or fighting. Then it was that Professor Wertz proclaimed it no hog-German, but early German, or early Teuton, of a date that must far precede anything that had ever been discovered and handed down by the scholars. So early was it that it was beyond him; yet it was filled with haunting reminiscences of word-forms he knew and which his trained intuition told him were true and real. He demanded the source of the songs, and asked to borrow the precious book that contained them. Also, he demanded to know why young Ward had always posed as being profoundly ignorant of the German language. And Ward could neither explain his ignorance nor lend the book. Whereupon, after pleadings and entreaties that extended through weeks, Professor Wert took a dislike to the young man, believed him a liar, and classified him as a man of monstrous selfishness for not giving him a glimpse of this wonderful screed that was older than the oldest any philologist had ever known or dreamed.

But little good did it do this much-mixed young man to know that half of him was late American and the other half early Teuton. Nevertheless, the late American in him was no weakling, and he (if he were a he and had a shred of existence outside of these two) compelled an adjustment or compromise between his one self that was a nightprowling savage that kept his other self sleepy of mornings, and that other self that was cultured and refined and that wanted to be normal and live and love and prosecute business like other people. The afternoons and early evenings he gave to the one, the nights to the other; the forenoons and parts of the nights were devoted to sleep for the twain. But in the mornings he slept in bed like a civilized man. In the night time he slept like a wild animal, as he had slept Dave Slotter stepped on him in the woods.

Persuading his father to advance the capital, he went into business and keen and successful business he made of it, devoting his afternoons whole-souled to it, while his partner devoted the mornings. The early evenings he spent socially, but, as the hour grew to nine or ten, an irresistible restlessness overcame him and he disappeared from the haunts of men until the next afternoon. Friends and acquaintances thought that he spent much of his time in sport. And they were right, though they never would have dreamed of the nature of the sport, even if they had seen him running coyotes in night-chases over the hills of Mill Valley. Neither were the schooner captains believed when they reported seeing, on cold winter mornings, a man swimming in the tide-rips of Raccoon Straits or in the swift currents between Goat island and Angel Island miles from shore.

In the bungalow at Mill Valley he lived alone, save for Lee Sing, the Chinese cook and factotum, who knew much about the strangeness of his master, who was paid well for saying nothing, and who never did say anything. After the satisfaction of his nights, a morning's sleep, and a breakfast of Lee Sing's, James Ward crossed the bay to San Francisco on a midday ferryboat and went to the club and on to his office, as normal and conventional a man of business as could be found in the city. But as the evening lengthened, the night called to him. There came a quickening of all his perceptions and a restlessness. His hearing was suddenly acute; the myriad night-noises told him a luring and familiar story; and, if alone, he would begin to pace up and down the narrow room like any caged animal from the wild.

Once, he ventured to fall in love. He never permitted himself that diversion again. He was afraid. And for many a day the young lady, scared at least out of a portion of her young ladyhood, bore on her arms and shoulders and wrists divers black-and-blue bruises— tokens of caresses which he had bestowed in all fond gentleness but too late at night. There was the mistake. Had he ventured love- making in the afternoon, all would have been well, for it would have been as the quiet gentleman that he would have made love— but at night it was the uncouth, wife-stealing savage of the dark German forests. Out of his wisdom, he decided that afternoon love- making could be prosecuted successfully; but out of the same wisdom he was convinced that marriage as would prove a ghastly failure. He found it appalling to imagine being married and encountering his wife after dark.

So he had eschewed all love-making, regulated his dual life, cleaned up a million in business, fought shy of match-making mamas and bright-eyed and eager young ladies of various ages, met Lilian Gersdale and made it a rigid observance never to see her later than eight o'clock in the evening, run of nights after his coyotes, and slept in forest lairs—and through it all had kept his secret safe save Lee Sing . . . and now, Dave Slotter. It was the latter's discovery of both his selves that frightened him. In spite of the counter fright he had given the burglar, the latter might talk. And even if he did not, sooner or later he would be found out by some one else.

Thus it was that James Ward made a fresh and heroic effort to control the Teutonic barbarian that was half of him. So well did he make it a point to see Lilian in the afternoons, that the time came when she accepted him for better or worse, and when he prayed privily and fervently that it was not for worse. During this period no prize-fighter ever trained more harshly and faithfully for a contest than he trained to subdue the wild savage in him. Among other things, he strove to exhaust himself during the day, so that sleep would render him deaf to the call of the night. He took a vacation from the office and went on long hunting trips, following the deer through the most inaccessible and rugged country he could find—and always in the daytime. Night found him indoors and tired. At home he installed a score of exercise machines, and where other men might go through a particular movement ten times, he went hundreds. Also, as a compromise, he built a sleeping porch on the second story. Here he at least breathed the blessed night air. Double screens prevented him from escaping into the woods, and each night Lee Sing locked him in and each morning let him out.

The time came, in the month of August, when he engaged additional servants to assist Lee Sing and dared a house party in his Mill Valley bungalow. Lilian, her mother and brother, and half a dozen mutual friends, were the guests. For two days and nights all went well. And on the third night, playing bridge till eleven o'clock, he had reason to be proud of himself. His restlessness fully hid, but as luck would have it, Lilian Gersdale was his opponent on his right. She was a frail delicate flower of a woman, and in his night-mood her very frailty incensed him. Not that he loved her less, but that he felt almost irresistibly impelled to reach out and paw and maul her. Especially was this true when she was engaged in playing a winning hand against him.

He had one of the deer-hounds brought in and, when it seemed he must fly to pieces with the tension, a caressing hand laid on the animal brought him relief. These contacts with the hairy coat gave him instant easement and enabled him to play out the evening. Nor did anyone guess the terrible struggle their host was making, the

255

while he laughed so carelessly and played so keenly and deliberately.

When they separated for the night, he saw to it that he parted from Lilian in the presence of the others. Once on his sleeping porch and safely locked in, he doubled and tripled and even quadrupled his exercises until, exhausted, he lay down on the couch to woo sleep and to ponder two problems that especially troubled him. One was this matter of exercise. It was a paradox. The more he exercised in this excessive fashion, the stronger he became. While it was true that he thus quite tired out his night-running Teutonic self, it seemed that he was merely setting back the fatal day when his strength would be too much for him and overpower him, and then it would be a strength more terrible than he had yet known. The other problem was that of his marriage and of the stratagems he must employ in order to avoid his wife after dark. And thus, fruitlessly pondering, he fell asleep.

Now, where the huge grizzly bear came from that night was long a mystery, while the people of the Springs Brothers' Circus, showing at Sausalito, searched long and vainly for "Big Ben, the Biggest Grizzly in Captivity." But Big Ben escaped, and, out of the mazes of half a thousand bungalows and country estates, selected the grounds of James J. Ward for visitation. The first Mr. Ward knew was when he found himself on his feet, quivering and tense, a surge of battle in his breast and on his lips the old war-chant. From without came a wild baying and bellowing of the hounds. And sharp as a knife-thrust through the pandemonium came the agony of a stricken dog—his dog, he knew.

Not stopping for slippers, pajama-clad, he burst through the door Lee Sing had so carefully locked, and sped down the stairs and

256

out into the night. As his naked feet struck the graveled driveway, he stopped abruptly, reached under the steps to a hiding-place he knew well, and pulled forth a huge knotty club—his old companion on many a mad night adventure on the hills. The frantic hullabaloo of the dogs was coming nearer, and, swinging the club, he sprang straight into the thickets to meet it.

The aroused household assembled on the wide veranda. Somebody turned on the electric lights, but they could see nothing but one another's frightened faces. Beyond the brightly illuminated driveway the trees formed a wall of impenetrable blackness. Yet somewhere in that blackness a terrible struggle was going on. There was an infernal outcry of animals, a great snarling and growling, the sound of blows being struck and a smashing and crashing of underbrush by heavy bodies.

The tide of battle swept out from among the trees and upon the driveway just beneath the onlookers. Then they saw. Mrs. Gersdale cried out and clung fainting to her son. Lilian, clutching the railing so spasmodically that a bruising hurt was left in her finger-ends for days, gazed horror-stricken at a yellow-haired, wild-eyed giant whom she recognized as the man who was to be her husband. He was swinging a great club, and fighting furiously and calmly with a shaggy monster that was bigger than any bear she had ever seen. One rip of the beast's claws had dragged away Ward's pajama-coat and streaked his flesh with blood.

While most of Lilian Gersdale's fright was for the man beloved, there was a large portion of it due to the man himself. Never had she dreamed so formidable and magnificent a savage lurked under the starched shirt and conventional garb of her betrothed. And never had she had any conception of how a man battled. Such a battle was certainly not modern; nor was she there beholding a modern man, though she did not know it. For this was not Mr. James J. Ward, the San Francisco business man, but one, unnamed and unknown, a crude, rude savage creature who, by some freak of chance, lived again after thrice a thousand years.

The hounds, ever maintaining their mad uproar, circled about the fight, or dashed in and out, distracting the bear. When the animal turned to meet such flanking assaults, the man leaped in and the club came down. Angered afresh by every such blow, the bear would rush, and the man, leaping and skipping, avoiding the dogs, went backwards or circled to one side or the other. Whereupon the dogs, taking advantage of the opening, would again spring in and draw the animal's wrath to them.

The end came suddenly. Whirling, the grizzly caught a hound with a wide sweeping cuff that sent the brute, its ribs caved in and its back broken, hurtling twenty feet. Then the human brute went mad. A foaming rage flecked the lips that parted with a wild inarticulate cry, as it sprang in, swung the club mightily in both hands, and brought it down full on the head of the uprearing grizzly. Not even the skull of a grizzly could withstand the crushing force of such a blow, and the animal went down to meet the worrying of the hounds. And through their scurrying leaped the man, squarely upon the body, where, in the white electric light, resting on his club, he chanted a triumph in an unknown tongue—a song so ancient that Professor Wertz would have given ten years of his life for it.

His guests rushed to possess him and acclaim him, but James Ward, suddenly looking out of the eyes of the early Teuton, saw the fair frail Twentieth Century girl he loved, and felt something snap in his brain. He staggered weakly toward her, dropped the club, and nearly fell. Something had gone wrong with him. Inside his brain was an intolerable agony. It seemed as if the soul of him were flying asunder. Following the excited gaze of the others, he glanced back and saw the carcass of the bear. The sight filled him with fear. He uttered a cry and would have fled, had they not restrained him and led him into the bungalow.

James J. Ward is still at the head of the firm of Ward, Knowles & Co. But he no longer lives in the country; nor does he run of nights after the coyotes under the moon. The early Teuton in him died the night of the Mill Valley fight with the bear. James J. Ward is now wholly James J. Ward, and he shares no part of his being with any vagabond anachronism from the younger world. And so wholly is James J. Ward modern, that he knows in all its bitter fullness the curse of civilized fear. He is now afraid of the dark, and night in the forest is to him a thing of abysmal terror. His city house is of the spick and span order, and he evinces a great interest in burglarproof devices. His home is a tangle of electric wires, and after bed-time a guest can scarcely breathe without setting off an alarm. Also, he had invented a combination keyless door-lock that travelers may carry in their vest pockets and apply immediately and successfully under all circumstances. But his wife does not deem him a coward. She knows better. And, like any hero, he is content to rest on his laurels. His bravery is never questioned by those friends who are aware of the Mill Valley episode.

from *The Night-Born* (1913)
(First published in *The Saturday Evening Post*, Sept 10, 1910)

THE PRODIGAL FATHER

I

Josiah Childs was ordinarily an ordinary-appearing, prosperous business man. He wore a sixty-dollar, business-man's suit, his shoes were comfortable and seemly and made from the current last, his tie, collars and cuffs were just what all prosperous business men wore, and an up-to-date, business-man's derby was his wildest adventure in head-gear. Oakland, California, is no sleepy country town, and Josiah Childs, as the leading grocer of a rushing Western metropolis of three hundred thousand, appropriately lived, acted, and dressed the part.

But on this morning, before the rush of custom began, his appearance at the store, while it did not cause a riot, was sufficiently startling to impair for half an hour the staff's working efficiency. He nodded pleasantly to the two delivery drivers loading their wagons for the first trip of the morning, and cast upward the inevitable, complacent glance at the sign that ran across the front of the building—CHILDS' CASH STORE. The lettering, not too large, was of dignified black and gold, suggestive of noble spices, aristocratic condiments, and everything of the best (which was no more than to be expected of a scale of prices ten per cent. higher than any other grocery in town). But what Josiah Childs did not see as he turned his back on the drivers and entered, was the helpless and mutual fall of surprise those two worthies perpetrated on each other's necks. They clung together for support.

"Did you catch the kicks, Bill?" one moaned.

"Did you pipe the head-piece?" Bill moaned back.

"Now if he was goin' to a masquerade ball...."

"Or attendin' a reunion of the Rough Riders...."

"Or goin' huntin' bear...."

"Or swearin' off his taxes...."

"Instead of goin' all the way to the effete East—Monkton says he's going clear to Boston...."

The two drivers held each other apart at arm's length, and fell limply together again.

For Josiah Childs' outfit was all their actions connotated. His hat was a light fawn, stiff-rimmed John B. Stetson, circled by a band of Mexican stamped leather. Over a blue flannel shirt, set off by a drooping Windsor tie, was a rough-and-ready coat of large-ribbed corduroy. Pants of the same material were thrust into high-laced shoes of the sort worn by surveyors, explorers, and linemen.

A clerk at a near counter almost petrified at sight of his employer's bizarre rig. Monkton, recently elevated to the managership, gasped, swallowed, and maintained his imperturbable attentiveness. The lady bookkeeper, glancing down from her glass eyrie on the inside balcony, took one look and buried her giggles in the day book. Josiah Childs saw most of all this, but he did not mind. He was starting on his vacation, and his head and heart were buzzing with plans and anticipations of the most adventurous vacation he had taken in ten years. Under his eyelids burned visions of East Falls, Connecticut, and of all the home scenes he had been born to and brought up in. Oakland, he was thoroughly aware, was more modern than East Falls, and the excitement caused by his garb was only to be expected. Undisturbed by the sensation he knew he was creating among his employés, he moved about, accompanied by his manager, making last suggestions, giving final instructions, and radiating fond, farewell glances at all the loved details of the business he had built out of nothing.

He had a right to be proud of Childs' Cash Store. Twelve years before he had landed in Oakland with fourteen dollars and forty-three cents. Cents did not circulate so far West, and after the fourteen dollars were gone, he continued to carry the three pennies in his pocket for a weary while. Later, when he had got a job clerking in a small grocery for eleven dollars a week, and had begun sending a small monthly postal order to one, Agatha Childs, East Falls, Connecticut, he invested the three coppers in postage stamps. Uncle Sam could not reject his own lawful coin of the realm.

Having spent all his life in cramped New England, where sharpness and shrewdness had been whetted to razor-edge on the harsh stone of meagre circumstance, he had found himself abruptly in the loose and free-and-easy West, where men thought in thousand-dollar bills and newsboys dropped dead at sight of copper cents. Josiah Childs bit like fresh acid into the new industrial and business conditions. He had vision. He saw so many ways of making money all at once, that at first his brain was in a whirl.

At the same time, being sane and conservative, he had resolutely avoided speculation. The solid and substantial called to him. Clerking at eleven dollars a week, he took note of the lost opportunities, of the openings for safe enterprise, of the countless leaks in the business. If, despite all this, the boss could make a good living, what couldn't he, Josiah Childs, do with his Connecticut training? It was like a bottle of wine to a thirsty hermit, this coming to the active, generous-spending West after thirty-five years in East Falls, the last fifteen of which had been spent in humdrum clerking in the humdrum East Falls general store. Josiah Childs' head buzzed with the easy possibilities he saw. But he did not lose his head. No detail was overlooked. He spent his spare hours in studying Oakland, its people, how they made their money, and why they spent it and where. He walked the central streets, watching the drift of the buying crowds, even counting them and compiling the statistics in various notebooks. He studied the general credit system of the trade, and the particular credit systems of the different districts. He could tell to a dot the average wage or salary earned by the householders of any locality, and he made it a point of thoroughness to know every locality from the waterfront slums to the aristocratic Lake Merritt and Piedmont sections, from West Oakland, where dwelt the railroad employés, to the semi-farmers of Fruitvale at the opposite end of the city.

Broadway, on the main street and in the very heart of the shopping district, where no grocer had ever been insane enough to dream of establishing a business, was his ultimate selection. But that required money, while he had to start from the smallest of beginnings. His first store was on lower Filbert, where lived the nail-workers. In half a year, three other little corner groceries went out of business while he was compelled to enlarge his premises. He understood the principle of large sales at small profits, of stable qualities of goods, and of a square deal. He had glimpsed, also, the secret of advertising. Each week he set forth one article that sold at a loss to him. This was not an advertised loss, but an absolute loss.

His one clerk prophesied impending bankruptcy when butter, that cost Childs thirty cents, was sold for twenty-five cents, when twenty-two-cent coffee was passed across the counter at eighteen cents. The neighbourhood housewives came for these bargains and remained to buy other articles that sold at a profit. Moreover, the whole neighbourhood came quickly to know Josiah Childs, and the busy crowd of buyers in his store was an attraction in itself.

But Josiah Childs made no mistake. He knew the ultimate foundation on which his prosperity rested. He studied the nail works until he came to know as much about them as the managing directors. Before the first whisper had stirred abroad, he sold his store, and with a modest sum of ready cash went in search of a new location. Six months later the nail works closed down, and closed down forever.

His next store was established on Adeline Street, where lived a comfortable, salaried class. Here, his shelves carried a higher-grade and a more diversified stock. By the same old method, he drew his crowd. He established a delicatessen counter. He dealt directly with the farmers, so that his butter and eggs were not only always dependable but were a shade better than those sold by the finest groceries in the city. One of his specialties was Boston baked beans, and so popular did it become that the Twin Cabin Bakery paid him better than handsomely for the privilege of taking it over. He made time to study the farmers, the very apples they grew, and certain farmers he taught how properly to make cider. As a side-line, his New England apple cider proved his greatest success, and before long, after he had invaded San Francisco, Berkeley, and Alameda, he ran it as an independent business.

But always his eyes were fixed on Broadway. Only one other

intermediate move did he make, which was to as near as he could get to the Ashland Park Tract, where every purchaser of land was legally pledged to put up no home that should cost less than four thousand dollars. After that came Broadway. A strange swirl had come in the tide of the crowd. The drift was to Washington Street, where real estate promptly soared while on Broadway it was as if the bottom had fallen out. One big store after another, as the leases expired, moved to Washington.

The crowd will come back, Josiah Childs said, but he said it to himself. He knew the crowd. Oakland was growing, and he knew why it was growing. Washington Street was too narrow to carry the increasing traffic. Along Broadway, in the physical nature of things, the electric cars, ever in greater numbers, would have to run. The realty dealers said that the crowd would never come back, while the leading merchants followed the crowd. And then it was, at a ridiculously low figure, that Josiah Childs got a long lease on a modern, Class A building on Broadway, with a buying option at a fixed price. It was the beginning of the end for Broadway, said the realty dealers, when a grocery was established in its erstwhile sacred midst. Later, when the crowd did come back, they said Josiah Childs was lucky. Also, they whispered among themselves that he had cleared at least fifty thousand on the transaction.

It was an entirely different store from his previous ones. There were no more bargains. Everything was of the superlative best, and superlative best prices were charged. He catered to the most expensive trade in town. Only those who could carelessly afford to pay ten per cent. more than anywhere else, patronised him, and so excellent was his service that they could not afford to go elsewhere. His horses and delivery wagons were more expensive and finer than any one else's in town. He paid his drivers, and clerks, and bookkeepers higher wages than any other store could dream of paying. As a result, he got more efficient men, and they rendered him and his patrons a more satisfying service. In short, to deal at Childs' Cash Store became almost the infallible index of social status.

To cap everything, came the great San Francisco earthquake and fire, which caused one hundred thousand people abruptly to come across the Bay and live in Oakland. Not least to profit from so extraordinary a boom, was Josiah Childs. And now, after twelve years' absence, he was departing on a visit to East Falls, Connecticut. In the twelve years he had not received a letter from Agatha, nor had he seen even a photograph of his and Agatha's boy.

Agatha and he had never got along together. Agatha was masterful. Agatha had a tongue. She was strong on old-fashioned morality. She was unlovely in her rectitude. Josiah never could quite make out how he had happened to marry her. She was two years his senior, and had long ranked as an old maid. She had taught school, and was known by the young generation as the sternest disciplinarian in its experience. She had become set in her ways, and when she married it was merely an exchange of a number of pupils for one. Josiah had to stand the hectoring and nagging that thitherto had been distributed among many. As to how the marriage came about, his Uncle Isaac nearly hit it off one day when he said in confidence: "Josiah, when Agatha married you it was a case of marrying a struggling young man. I reckon you was overpowered. Or maybe you broke your leg and couldn't get away."

"Uncle Isaac," Josiah answered, "I didn't break my leg. I ran my dangdest, but she just plum run me down and out of breath."

"Strong in the wind, eh?" Uncle Isaac chuckled.

"We've ben married five years now," Josiah agreed, "and I've never known her to lose it."

"And never will," Uncle Isaac added.

This conversation had taken place in the last days, and so dismal an outlook proved too much for Josiah Childs. Meek he was, under Agatha's firm tuition, but he was very healthy, and his promise of life was too long for his patience. He was only thirty-three, and he came of a long-lived stock. Thirty-three more years with Agatha and Agatha's nagging was too hideous to contemplate. So, between a sunset and a rising, Josiah Childs disappeared from East Falls. And from that day, for twelve years, he had received no letter from her. Not that it was her fault. He had carefully avoided letting her have his address. His first postal money orders were sent to her from Oakland, but in the years that followed he had arranged his remittances so that they bore the scattered postmarks of most of the states west of the Rockies.

But twelve years, and the confidence born of deserved success, had softened his memories. After all, she was the mother of his boy, and it was incontestable that she had always meant well. Besides, he was not working so hard now, and he had more time to think of things besides his business. He wanted to see the boy, whom he had never seen and who had turned three before his father ever learned he was a father. Then, too, homesickness had begun to crawl in him. In a dozen years he had not seen snow, and he was always wondering if New England fruits and berries had not a finer tang than those of California. Through hazy vistas he saw the old New England life, and he wanted to see it again in the flesh before he died.

And, finally, there was duty. Agatha was his wife. He would bring her back with him to the West. He felt that he could stand it. He was a man, now, in the world of men. He ran things, instead of being run, and Agatha would quickly find it out. Nevertheless, he wanted Agatha to come to him for his own sake. So it was that he had put on his frontier rig. He would be the prodigal father, returning as penniless as when he left, and it would be up to her whether or not she killed the fatted calf. Empty of hand, and looking it, he would come back wondering if he could get his old job in the general store. Whatever followed would be Agatha's affair.

By the time he said good-bye to his staff and emerged on the sidewalk, five more of his delivery wagons were backed up and loading.

He ran his eye proudly over them, took a last fond glance at the black-and-gold letters, and signalled the electric car at the corner.

II

He ran up to East Falls from New York. In the Pullman smoker he became acquainted with several business men. The conversation, turning on the West, was quickly led by him. As president of the Oakland Chamber of Commerce, he was an authority. His words carried weight, and he knew what he was talking about, whether it was Asiatic trade, the Panama Canal, or the Japanese coolie question. It was very exhilarating, this stimulus of respectful attention accorded him by these prosperous Eastern men, and before he knew it he was at East Falls.

He was the only person who alighted, and the station was

deserted. Nobody was there expecting anybody. The long twilight of a January evening was beginning, and the bite of the keen air made him suddenly conscious that his clothing was saturated with tobacco smoke. He shuddered involuntarily. Agatha did not tolerate tobacco. He half-moved to toss the fresh-lighted cigar away, then it was borne in upon him that this was the old East Falls atmosphere overpowering him, and he resolved to combat it, thrusting the cigar between his teeth and gripping it with the firmness of a dozen years of Western resolution.

A few steps brought him into the little main street. The chilly, stilted aspect of it shocked him. Everything seemed frosty and pinched, just as the cutting air did after the warm balminess of California. Only several persons, strangers to his recollection, were abroad, and they favoured him with incurious glances. They were wrapped in an uncongenial and frosty imperviousness. His first impression was surprise at his surprise. Through the wide perspective of twelve years of Western life, he had consistently and steadily discounted the size and importance of East Falls; but this was worse than all discounting. Things were more meagre than he had dreamed. The general store took his breath away. Countless myriads of times he had contrasted it with his own spacious emporium, but now he saw that in justice he had overdone it. He felt certain that it could not accommodate two of his delicatessen counters, and he knew that he could lose all of it in one of his storerooms.

He took the familiar turning to the right at the head of the street, and as he plodded along the slippery walk he decided that one of the first things he must do was to buy sealskin cap and gloves. The thought of sleighing cheered him for a moment, until, now on the outskirts of the village, he was sanitarily perturbed by the adjacency of dwelling houses and barns. Some were even connected. Cruel memories of bitter morning chores oppressed him. The thought of chapped hands and chilblains was almost terrifying, and his heart sank at sight of the double storm-windows, which he knew were solidly fastened and unraisable, while the small ventilating panes, the size of ladies' handkerchiefs, smote him with sensations of suffocation. Agatha'll like California, he thought, calling to his mind visions of roses in dazzling sunshine and the wealth of flowers that bloomed the twelve months round.

And then, quite illogically, the years were bridged and the whole leaden weight of East Falls descended upon him like a damp sea fog. He fought it from him, thrusting it off and aside by sentimental thoughts on the "honest snow," the "fine elms," the "sturdy New England spirit," and the "great homecoming." But at sight of Agatha's house he wilted. Before he knew it, with a recrudescent guilty pang, he had tossed the half-smoked cigar away and slackened his pace until his feet dragged in the old lifeless, East Falls manner. He tried to remember that he was the owner of Childs' Cash Store, accustomed to command, whose words were listened to with respect in the Employers' Association, and who wielded the gavel at the meetings of the Chamber of Commerce. He strove to conjure visions of the letters in black and gold, and of the string of delivery wagons backed up to the sidewalk. But Agatha's New England spirit was as sharp as the frost, and it travelled to him through solid house-walls and across the intervening hundred yards.

Then he became aware that despite his will he had thrown the cigar away. This brought him an awful vision. He saw himself going out in the frost to the woodshed to smoke. His memory of Agatha he found less softened by the lapse of years than it had been when three thousand miles intervened. It was unthinkable. No; he couldn't do it. He was too old, too used to smoking all over the house, to do the woodshed stunt now. And everything depended on how he began. He would put his foot down. He would smoke in the house that very night ... in the kitchen, he feebly amended. No, by George, he would smoke now. He would arrive smoking. Mentally imprecating the cold, he exposed his bare hands and lighted another cigar. His manhood seemed to flare up with the match. He would show her who was boss. Right from the drop of the hat he would show her.

Josiah Childs had been born in this house. And it was long before he was born that his father had built it. Across the low stone fence, Josiah could see the kitchen porch and door, the connected woodshed, and the several outbuildings. Fresh from the West, where everything was new and in constant flux, he was astonished at the lack of change. Everything was as it had always been. He could almost see himself, a boy, doing the chores. There, in the woodshed, how many cords of wood had he bucksawed and split! Well, thank the Lord, that was past.

The walk to the kitchen showed signs of recent snow-shovelling. That had been one of his tasks. He wondered who did it now, and suddenly remembered that his own son must be twelve. In another moment he would have knocked at the kitchen door, but the skreek of a bucksaw from the woodshed led him aside. He looked in and saw a boy hard at work. Evidently, this was his son. Impelled by the wave of warm emotion that swept over him, he all but rushed in upon the lad. He controlled himself with an effort.

272

"Father here?" he asked curtly, though from under the stiff brim of his John B. Stetson he studied the boy closely.

Sizable for his age, he thought. A mite spare in the ribs maybe, and that possibly due to rapid growth. But the face strong and pleasing and the eyes like Uncle Isaac's. When all was said, a darn good sample.

"No, sir," the boy answered, resting on the saw-buck.

"Where is he?"

"At sea," was the answer.

Josiah Childs felt a something very akin to relief and joy tingle through him. Agatha had married again—evidently a seafaring man. Next, came an ominous, creepy sensation. Agatha had committed bigamy. He remembered Enoch Arden, read aloud to the class by the teacher in the old schoolhouse, and began to think of himself as a hero. He would do the heroic. By George, he would. He would sneak away and get the first train for California. She would never know.

But there was Agatha's New England morality, and her New England conscience. She received a regular remittance. She knew he was alive. It was impossible that she could have done this thing. He groped wildly for a solution. Perhaps she had sold the old home, and this boy was somebody else's boy.

"What is your name?" Josiah asked.

"Johnnie," came the reply.

"Last name I mean?"

"Childs, Johnnie Childs."

"And your father's name?—first name?"

"Josiah Childs."

"And he's away at sea, you say?"

"Yes, sir."

This set Josiah wondering again.

"What kind of a man is he?"

"Oh, he's all right—a good provider, Mom says. And he is. He always sends his money home, and he works hard for it, too, Mom says. She says he always was a good worker, and he's better'n other men she ever saw. He don't smoke, or drink, or swear, or do anything he oughtn't. And he never did. He was always that way, Mom says, and she knew him all her life before ever they got married. He's a very kind man, and never hurts anybody's feelings. Mom says he's the most considerate man she ever knew."

Josiah's heart went weak. Agatha had done it after all—had taken a second husband when she knew her first was still alive. Well, he had learned charity in the West, and he could be charitable. He would go quietly away. Nobody would ever know. Though it was rather mean of her, the thought flashed through him, that she should go on cashing his remittances when she was married to so model and steady-working a seafaring husband who brought his wages home. He cudgelled his brains in an effort to remember such a man out of all the East Falls men he had known.

"What's he look like?"

"Don't know. Never saw him. He's at sea all the time. But I know how tall he is. Mom says I'm goin' to be bigger'n him, and he was five feet eleven. There's a picture of him in the album. His face is thin, and he has whiskers."

A great illumination came to Josiah. He was himself five feet eleven. He had worn whiskers, and his face had been thin in those days. And Johnnie had said his father's name was Josiah Childs. He, Josiah, was this model husband who neither smoked, swore, nor drank. He was this seafaring man whose memory had been so carefully shielded by Agatha's forgiving fiction. He warmed toward her. She must have changed mightily since he left. He glowed with penitence. Then his heart sank as he thought of trying to live up to this reputation Agatha had made for him. This boy with the trusting blue eyes would expect it of him. Well, he'd have to do it. Agatha had been almighty square with him. He hadn't thought she had it in her.

The resolve he might there and then have taken was doomed never to be, for he heard the kitchen door open to give vent to a woman's nagging, irritable voice.

"Johnnie!—you!" it cried.

How often had he heard it in the old days: "Josiah!—you!" A shiver went through him. Involuntarily, automatically, with a guilty start, he turned his hand back upward so that the cigar was hidden. He felt himself shrinking and shrivelling as she stepped out on the stoop. It was his unchanged wife, the same shrew wrinkles, with the same sour-drooping corners to the thin-lipped mouth. But there was more sourness, an added droop, the lips were thinner, and the shrew wrinkles were deeper. She swept Josiah with a hostile, withering stare.

"Do you think your father would stop work to talk to tramps?" she demanded of the boy, who visibly quailed, even as Josiah.

"I was only answering his questions," Johnnie pleaded doggedly but hopelessly. "He wanted to know—"

"And I suppose you told him," she snapped. "What business is it of his prying around? No, and he gets nothing to eat. As for you, get to work at once. I'll teach you, idling at your chores. Your father wa'n't like that. Can't I ever make you like him?"

275

Johnnie bent his back, and the bucksaw resumed its protesting skreek. Agatha surveyed Josiah sourly. It was patent she did not recognise him.

"You be off," she commanded harshly. "None of your snooping around here."

Josiah felt the numbness of paralysis creeping over him. He moistened his lips and tried to say something, but found himself bereft of speech.

"You be off, I say," she rasped in her high-keyed voice, "or I'll put the constable after you."

Josiah turned obediently. He heard the door slam as he went down the walk. As in a nightmare he opened the gate he had opened ten thousand times and stepped out on the sidewalk. He felt dazed. Surely it was a dream. Very soon he would wake up with a sigh of relief. He rubbed his forehead and paused indecisively. The monotonous complaint of the bucksaw came to his ears. If that boy had any of the old Childs spirit in him, sooner or later he'd run away. Agatha was beyond the endurance of human flesh. She had not changed, unless for the worse, if such a thing were possible. That boy would surely run for it, maybe soon. Maybe now.

Josiah Childs straightened up and threw his shoulders back. The great-spirited West, with its daring and its carelessness of consequences when mere obstacles stand in the way of its desire, flamed up in him. He looked at his watch, remembered the time table, and spoke to himself, solemnly, aloud. It was an affirmation of faith:

"I don't care a hang about the law. That boy can't be crucified. I'll give her a double allowance, four times, anything, but he goes with me. She can follow on to California if she wants, but I'll draw up an agreement, in which what's what, and she'll sign it, and live up to it, by George, if she wants to stay. And she will," he added grimly. "She's got to have somebody to nag."

He opened the gate and strode back to the woodshed door. Johnnie looked up, but kept on sawing.

"What'd you like to do most of anything in the world?" Josiah demanded in a tense, low voice.

Johnnie hesitated, and almost stopped sawing. Josiah made signs for him to keep it up.

"Go to sea," Johnnie answered. "Along with my father."

Josiah felt himself trembling.

"Would you?" he asked eagerly.

"Would I!"

The look of joy on Johnnie's face decided everything.

"Come here, then. Listen. I'm your father. I'm Josiah Childs. Did you ever want to run away?"

Johnnie nodded emphatically.

"That's what I did," Josiah went on. "I ran away." He fumbled for his watch hurriedly. "We've just time to catch the train for California. I live there now. Maybe Agatha, your mother, will come along afterward. I'll tell you all about it on the train. Come on."

He gathered the half-frightened, half-trusting boy into his arms for a moment, then, hand in hand, they fled across the yard, out of the gate, and down the street. They heard the kitchen door open, and the last they heard was:

"Johnnie!—you! Why ain't you sawing? I'll attend to your case directly!"

277

from *The Turtles of Tasman* (1916)
(First published in *Woman's World*, May, 1912)

THE BENEFIT OF THE DOUBT

I

Carter Watson, a current magazine under his arm, strolled slowly along, gazing about him curiously. Twenty years had elapsed since he had been on this particular street, and the changes were great and stupefying. This Western city of three hundred thousand souls had contained but thirty thousand, when, as a boy, he had been wont to ramble along its streets. In those days the street he was now on had been a quiet residence street in the respectable working-class quarter. On this late afternoon he found that it had been submerged by a vast and vicious tenderloin. Chinese and Japanese shops and dens abounded, all confusedly intermingled with low white resorts and boozing dens. This quiet street of his youth had become the toughest quarter of the city.

He looked at his watch. It was half-past five. It was the slack time of the day in such a region, as he well knew, yet he was curious to see. In all his score of years of wandering and studying social conditions over the world, he had carried with him the memory of his old town as a sweet and wholesome place. The metamorphosis he now beheld was startling. He certainly must continue his stroll and glimpse the infamy to which his town had descended.

Another thing: Carter Watson had a keen social and civic

consciousness. Independently wealthy, he had been loath to dissipate his energies in the pink teas and freak dinners of society, while actresses, race-horses, and kindred diversions had left him cold. He had the ethical bee in his bonnet and was a reformer of no mean pretension, though his work had been mainly in the line of contributions to the heavier reviews and quarterlies and to the publication over his name of brightly, cleverly written books on the working classes and the slum-dwellers. Among the twenty-seven to his credit occurred titles such as, "If Christ Came to New Orleans," " The Worked-out Worker," "Tenement Reform in Berlin," "The Rural Slums of England," "The people of the East Side," "Reform Versus Revolution," "The University Settlement as a Hot Bed of Radicalism' and "The Cave Man of Civilization."

But Carter Watson was neither morbid nor fanatic. He did not lose his head over the horrors he encountered, studied, and exposed. No hair brained enthusiasm branded him. His humor saved him, as did his wide experience and his conservative philosophic temperament. Nor did he have any patience with lightning change reform theories. As he saw it, society would grow better only through the painfully slow and arduously painful processes of evolution. There were no short cuts, no sudden regenerations. The betterment of mankind must be worked out in agony and misery just as all past social betterments had been worked out.

But on this late summer afternoon, Carter Watson was curious. As he moved along he paused before a gaudy drinking place. The sign above read, "The Vendome." There were two entrances. One evidently led to the bar. This he did not explore. The other was a narrow hallway. Passing through this he found himself in a huge room, filled with chair-encircled tables and quite deserted. In the dim light he made out a piano in the distance. Making a mental note that he would come back some time and study the class of persons that must sit and drink at those multitudinous tables, he proceeded to circumnavigate the room.

Now, at the rear, a short hallway led off to a small kitchen, and here, at a table, alone, sat Patsy Horan, proprietor of the Vendome, consuming a hasty supper ere the evening rush of business. Also, Patsy Horan was angry with the world. He had got out of the wrong side of bed that morning, and nothing had gone right all day. Had his barkeepers been asked, they would have described his mental condition as a grouch. But Carter Watson did not know this. As he passed the little hallway, Patsy Horan's sullen eyes lighted on the magazine he carried under his arm. Patsy did not know Carter Watson, nor did he know that what he carried under his arm was a magazine. Patsy, out of the depths of his grouch, decided that this stranger was one of those pests who marred and scarred the walls of his back rooms by tacking up or pasting up advertisements. The color on the front cover of the magazine convinced him that it was such an advertisement. Thus the trouble began. Knife and fork in hand, Patsy leaped for Carter Watson.

"Out wid yeh!" Patsy bellowed. "I know yer game!"

Carter Watson was startled. The man had come upon him like the eruption of a jack-in-the-box.

"A defacin' me walls," cried Patsy, at the same time emitting a string of vivid and vile, rather than virile, epithets of opprobrium.

"If I have given any offense I did not mean to—"

But that was as far as the visitor got. Patsy interrupted.

"Get out wid yeh; yeh talk too much wid yer mouth," quoted

Patsy, emphasizing his remarks with flourishes of the knife and fork.

Carter Watson caught a quick vision of that eating-fork inserted uncomfortably between his ribs, knew that it would be rash to talk further with his mouth, and promptly turned to go. The sight of his meekly retreating back must have further enraged Patsy Horan, for that worthy, dropping the table implements, sprang upon him.

Patsy weighed one hundred and eighty pounds. So did Watson. In this they were equal. But Patsy was a rushing, rough-and-tumble saloon-fighter, while Watson was a boxer. In this the latter had the advantage, for Patsy came in wide open, swinging his right in a perilous sweep. All Watson had to do was to straight-left him and escape. But Watson had another advantage. His boxing, and his experience in the slums and ghettos of the world, had taught him restraint.

He pivoted on his feet, and, instead of striking, ducked the other's swinging blow and went into a clinch. But Patsy, charging like a bull, had the momentum of his rush, while Watson, whirling to meet him, had no momentum. As a result, the pair of them went down, with all their three hundred and sixty pounds of weight, in a long crashing fall, Watson underneath. He lay with his head touching the rear wall of the large room. The street was a hundred and fifty feet away, and he did some quick thinking. His first thought was to avoid trouble. He had no wish to get into the papers of this, his childhood town, where many of his relatives and family friends still lived.

So it was that he locked his arms around the man on top of him, held him close, and waited for the help to come that must come in response to the crash of the fall. The help came—that is, six men ran in from the bar and formed about in a semi-circle.

'Take him off, fellows," Watson said. "I haven't struck him, and I don't want any fight."

But the semi-circle remained silent. Watson held on and waited. Patsy, after various vain efforts to inflict damage, made an overture.

"Leggo o' me an' I'll get off o' yeh," said he.

Watson let go, but when Patsy scrambled to his feet he stood over his recumbent foe, ready to strike.

"Get up," Patsy commanded.

His voice was stern and implacable, like the voice of God calling to judgment, and Watson knew there was no mercy there.

"Stand back and I'll get up," he countered.

"If yer a gentleman, get up," quoth Patsy, his pale blue eyes aflame with wrath, his fist ready for a crushing blow.

At the same moment he drew his foot back to kick the other in the face. Watson blocked the kick with his crossed arms and sprang to his feet so quickly that he was in a clinch with his antagonist before the latter could strike. Holding him, Watson spoke to the onlookers:

"Take him away from me, fellows. You see I am not striking him. I don't want to fight. I want to get out of here."

The circle did not move nor speak. Its silence was ominous and sent a chill to Watson's heart.

Patsy made an effort to throw him, which culminated in his putting Patsy on his back. Tearing loose from him, Watson sprang to his feet and made for the door. But the circle of men was interposed a wall. He noticed the white, pasty faces, the kind that never see the sun, and knew that the men who barred his way were the nightprowlers and preying beasts of the city jungle. By them he

283

was thrust back upon the pursuing, bull-rushing Patsy.

Again it was a clinch, in which, in momentary safety, Watson appealed to the gang. And again his words fell on deaf ears. Then it was that he knew fear. For he had known of many similar situations, in low dens like this, when solitary men were man-handled, their ribs and features caved in, themselves beaten and kicked to death. And he knew, further, that if he were to escape he must neither strike his assailant nor any of the men who opposed him.

Yet in him was righteous indignation. Under no circumstances could seven to one be fair. Also, he was angry, and there stirred in him the fighting beast that is in all men. But he remembered his wife and children, his unfinished book, the ten thousand rolling acres of the up-country ranch he loved so well. He even saw in flashing visions the blue of the sky, the golden sun pouring down on his flower-spangled meadows, the lazy cattle knee-deep in the brooks, and the flash of trout in the riffles. Life was good-too good for him to risk it for a moment's sway of the beast. In short, Carter Watson was cool and scared.

His opponent, locked by his masterly clinch, was striving to throw him. Again Watson put him on the floor, broke away, and was thrust back by the pasty-faced circle to duck Patsy's swinging right and effect another clinch. This happened many times. And Watson grew even cooler, while the baffled Patsy, unable to inflict punishment, raged wildly and more wildly. He took to batting with his head in the clinches. The first time, he landed his forehead flush on Watson's nose. After that, the latter, in the clinches, buried his face in Patsy's breast. But the enraged Patsy batted on, striking his own eye and nose and cheek on the top of the other's head. The more he was thus injured, the more and the harder did Patsy bat.

This one-sided contest continued for twelve or fifteen minutes. Watson never struck a blow, and strove only to escape. Sometimes, in the free moments, circling about among the tables as he tried to win the door, the pasty-faced men gripped his coat-tails and flung him back at the swinging right of the on-rushing Patsy. Time upon time, and times without end, he clinched and put Patsy on his back, each time first whirling him around and putting him down in the direction of the door and gaining toward that goal by the length of the fall.

In the end, hatless, disheveled, with streaming nose and one eye closed, Watson won to the sidewalk and into the arms of a policeman.

"Arrest that man," Watson panted.

"Hello, Patsy," said the policeman. "What's the mix-up?"

"Hello, Charley," was the answer. "This guy comes in—"

"Arrest that man, officer," Watson repeated.

"G'wan! Beat it!" said Patsy.

"Beat it!" added the policeman. "If you don't, I'll pull you in."

"Not unless you arrest that man. He has committed a violent and unprovoked assault on me."

"Is it so, Patsy?" was the officer's query.

"Nah. Lemme tell you, Charley, an' I got the witnesses to prove it, so help me God. I was settin' in me kitchen eatin' a bowl of soup, when this guy comes in an' gets gay wid me. I never seen him in me born days before. He was drunk—"

"Look at me, officer," protested the indignant sociologist. "Am I drunk?"

The officer looked at him with sullen, menacing eyes and

nodded to Patsy to continue.

"This guy gets gay wid me. 'I'm Tim McGrath,' says he, 'an' I can do the like to you,' says he. 'Put up yer hands.' I smiles, an' wid that, biff biff, he lands me twice an' spills me soup. Look at me eye. I'm fair murdered."

"What are you going to do, officer?" Watson demanded.

"Go on, beat it," was the answer, "or I'll pull you sure."

The civic righteousness of Carter Watson flamed up.

"Mr. Officer, I protest—"

But at that moment the policeman grabbed his arm with a savage jerk that nearly overthrew him.

"Come on, you're pulled."

"Arrest him, too," Watson demanded.

"Nix on that play," was the reply.

"What did you assault him for, him a peacefully eatin' his soup?"

II

Carter Watson was genuinely angry. Not only had he been wantonly assaulted, badly battered, and arrested, but the morning papers without exception came out with lurid accounts of his drunken brawl with the proprietor of the notorious Vendome. Not one accurate or truthful line was published. Patsy Horan and his satellites described the battle in detail. The one incontestable thing was that Carter Watson had been drunk. Thrice he had been thrown out of the place and into the gutter, and thrice he had come back, breathing blood and fire and announcing that he was going to clean out the place. "EMINENT SOCIOLOGIST JAGGED AND JUGGED," was the first head-line he read, on the front page, accompanied by a large portrait of himself. Other headlines were: "CARTER WATSON ASPIRED TO CHAMPIONSHIP HONORS"; "CARTER WATSON GETS HIS"; "NOTED SOCIOLOGIST ATTEMPTS TO CLEAN OUT A TENDERLOIN CAFE"; and "CARTER WATSON KNOCKED OUT BY PATSY HORAN IN THREE ROUNDS."

At the police court, next morning, under bail, appeared Carter Watson to answer the complaint of the People Versus Carter Watson, for the latter's assault and battery on one Patsy Horan. But first, the Prosecuting Attorney, who was paid to prosecute all offenders against the People, drew him aside and talked with him privately.

"Why not let it drop!" said the Prosecuting Attorney. "I tell you what you do, Mr. Watson: Shake hands with Mr. Horan and make it up, and we'll drop the case right here. A word to the Judge, and the case against you will be dismissed."

"But I don't want it dismissed," was the answer. "Your office being what it is, you should be prosecuting me instead of asking me to make up with this—this fellow."

"Oh, I'll prosecute you all right," retorted the Prosecuting Attorney.

"Also you will have to prosecute this Patsy Horan," Watson advised; "for I shall now have him arrested for assault and battery."

"You'd better shake and make up," the Prosecuting Attorney repeated, and this time there was almost a threat in his voice.

The trials of both men were set for a week later, on the same morning, in Police Judge Witberg's court.

"You have no chance," Watson was told by an old friend of his boyhood, the retired manager of the biggest paper in the city. "Everybody knows you were beaten up by this man. His reputation

287

is most unsavory. But it won't help you in the least. Both cases will be dismissed. This will be because you are you. Any ordinary man would be convicted."

"But I do not understand," objected the perplexed sociologist. "Without warning I was attacked by this man; and badly beaten. I did not strike a blow. I—"

"That has nothing to do with it," the other cut him off.

"Then what is there that has anything to do with it?"

"I'll tell you. You are now up against the local police and political machine. Who are you? You are not even a legal resident in this town. You live up in the country. You haven't a vote of your own here. Much less do you swing any votes. This dive proprietor swings a string of votes in his precincts—a mighty long string."

"Do you mean to tell me that this Judge Witberg will violate the sacredness of his office and oath by letting this brute off?" Watson demanded.

"Watch him," was the grim reply. "Oh, he'll do it nicely enough. He will give an extra-legal, extra-judicial decision, abounding in every word in the dictionary that stands for fairness and right."

"But there are the newspapers," Watson cried.

"They are not fighting the administration at present. They'll give it to you hard. You see what they have already done to you."

"Then these snips of boys on the police detail won't write the truth?"

"They will write something so near like the truth that the public will believe it. They write their stories under instruction, you know. They have their orders to twist and color, and there won't be much left of you when they get done. Better drop the whole thing right now. You are in bad."

"But the trials are set."

"Give the word and they'll drop them now. A man can't fight a machine unless he has a machine behind him."

III

But Carter Watson was stubborn. He was convinced that the machine would beat him, but all his days he had sought social experience, and this was certainly something new.

The morning of the trial the Prosecuting Attorney made another attempt to patch up the affair.

"If you feel that way, I should like to get a lawyer to prosecute the case," said Watson.

"No, you don't," said the Prosecuting Attorney. "I am paid by the People to prosecute, and prosecute I will. But let me tell you. You have no chance. We shall lump both cases into one, and you watch out."

Judge Witberg looked good to Watson. A fairly young man, short, comfortably stout, smooth-shaven and with an intelligent face, he seemed a very nice man indeed. This good impression was added to by the smiling lips and the wrinkles of laughter in the corners of his black eyes. Looking at him and studying him, Watson felt almost sure that his old friend's prognostication was wrong.

But Watson was soon to learn. Patsy Horan and two of his satellites testified to a most colossal aggregation of perjuries. Watson could not have believed it possible without having experienced it. They denied the existence of the other four men. And of the two that testified, one claimed to have been in the kitchen, a witness to Watson's unprovoked assault on Patsy, while the other, remaining in the bar, had witnessed Watson's second and third rushes into the place as he attempted to annihilate the unoffending Patsy. The vile language ascribed to Watson was so voluminously and unspeakably vile, that he felt they were injuring their own case. It was so impossible that he should utter such things. But when they described the brutal blows he had rained on poor Patsy's face, and the chair he demolished when he vainly attempted to kick Patsy, Watson waxed secretly hilarious and at the same time sad. The trial was a farce, but such lowness of life was depressing to contemplate when he considered the long upward climb humanity must make.

Watson could not recognize himself, nor could his worst enemy have recognized him, in the swashbuckling, rough-housing picture that was painted of him. But, as in all cases of complicated perjury, rifts and contradictions in the various stories appeared. The Judge somehow failed to notice them, while the Prosecuting Attorney and Patsy's attorney shied off from them gracefully. Watson had not bothered to get a lawyer for himself, and he was now glad that he had not.

Still, he retained a semblance of faith in Judge Witberg when he went himself on the stand and started to tell his story.

"I was strolling casually along the street, your Honor," Watson began, but was interrupted by the Judge.

"We are not here to consider your previous actions," bellowed Judge Witberg. "Who struck the first blow?"

"Your Honor," Watson pleaded, "I have no witnesses of the actual fray, and the truth of my story can only be brought out by telling the story fully–"

Again he was interrupted.

290

"We do not care to publish any magazines here," Judge Witberg roared, looking at him so fiercely and malevolently that Watson could scarcely bring himself to believe that this was same man he had studied a few minutes previously.

"Who struck the first blow?" Patsy's attorney asked.

The Prosecuting Attorney interposed, demanding to know which of the two cases lumped together this was, and by what right Patsy's lawyer, at that stage of the proceedings, should take the witness. Patsy's attorney fought back. Judge Witberg interfered, professing no knowledge of any two cases being lumped together. All this had to be explained. Battle royal raged, terminating in both attorneys apologizing to the Court and to each other. And so it went, and to Watson it had the seeming of a group of pickpockets ruffling and bustling an honest man as they took his purse. The machine was working, that was all.

"Why did you enter this place of unsavory reputations?" was asked him.

"It has been my custom for many years, as a student of economics and sociology, to acquaint myself—"

But this was as far as Watson got.

"We want none of your ologies here," snarled Judge Witberg. "It is a plain question. Answer it plainly. Is it true or not true that you were drunk? That is the gist of the question."

When Watson attempted to tell how Patsy had injured his face in his attempts to bat with his head, Watson was openly scouted and flouted, and Judge Witberg again took him in hand.

"Are you aware of the solemnity of the oath you took to testify to nothing but the truth on this witness stand?" the Judge demanded. "This is a fairy story you are telling. It is not reasonable

291

that a man would so injure himself, and continue to injure himself, by striking the soft and sensitive parts of his face against your head. You are a sensible man. It is unreasonable, is it not?"

"Men are unreasonable when they are angry," Watson answered meekly.

Then it was that Judge Witberg was deeply outraged and righteously wrathful.

"What right have you to say that?" he cried. "It is gratuitous. It has no bearing on the case. You are here as a witness, sir, of events that have transpired. The Court does not wish to hear any expressions of opinion from you at all."

"I but answered your question, your Honor," Watson protested humbly.

"You did nothing of the sort," was the next blast. "And let me warn you, sir, let me warn you, that you are laying yourself liable to contempt by such insolence. And I will have you know that we know how to observe the law and the rules of courtesy down here in this little courtroom. I am ashamed of you."

And, while the next punctilious legal wrangle between the attorneys interrupted his tale of what happened in the Vendome, Carter Watson, without bitterness, amused and at the same time sad, saw rise before him the machine, large and small, that dominated his country, the unpunished and shameless grafts of a thousand cities perpetrated by the spidery and vermin-like creatures of the machines. Here it was before him, a courtroom and a judge, bowed down in subservience by the machine to a dive-keeper who swung a string of votes. Petty and sordid as it was, it was one face of the many-faced machine that loomed colossally, in every city and state, in a thousand guises overshadowing the land.

A familiar phrase rang in his ears: "It is to laugh." At the height of the wrangle, he giggled, once, aloud, and earned a sullen frown from Judge Witberg. Worse, a myriad times, he decided, were these bullying lawyers and this bullying judge then the bucko mates in first quality hell-ships, who not only did their own bullying but protected themselves as well. These petty rapscallions, on the other hand, sought protection behind the majesty of the law. They struck, but no one was permitted to strike back, for behind them were the prison cells and the clubs of the stupid policemen—paid and professional fighters and beaters-up of men. Yet he was not bitter. The grossness and the sliminess of it was forgotten in the simple grotesqueness of it, and he had the saving sense of humor.

Nevertheless, hectored and heckled though he was, he managed in the end to give a simple, straightforward version of the affair, and, despite a belligerent cross-examination, his story was not shaken in any particular. Quite different it was from the perjuries that had shouted aloud from the perjuries of Patsy and his two witnesses.

Both Patsy's attorney and the Prosecuting Attorney rested their cases, letting everything go before the Court without argument. Watson protested against this, but was silenced when the Prosecuting Attorney told him that he was the Public Prosecutor and knew his business.

"Patrick Horan has testified that he was in danger of his life and that he was compelled to defend himself," Judge Witberg's verdict began. "Mr. Watson has testified to the same thing. Each has sworn that the other struck the first blow; each has sworn that the other made an unprovoked assault on him. It is an axiom of the law that the defendant should be given the benefit of the doubt. A very

293

reasonable doubt exists. Therefore, in the case of the People Versus Carter Watson the benefit of the doubt is given to said Carter Watson and he is herewith ordered discharged from custody. The same reasoning applies to the case of the People Versus Patrick Horan. He is given the benefit of the doubt and discharged from custody. My recommendation is that both defendants shake hands and make up."

In the afternoon papers the first headline that caught Watson's eye was: "CARTER WATSON ACQUITTED." In the second paper it was: "CARTER WATSON ESCAPES A FINE." But what capped everything was the one beginning: "CARTER WATSON A GOOD FELLOW." In the text he read how Judge Witberg had advised both fighters to shake hands, which they promptly did. Further, he read:

"'Let's have a nip on it,' said Patsy Horan.

"'Sure,' said Carter Watson.

"And, arm in arm, they ambled for the nearest saloon."

IV

Now, from the whole adventure, Watson carried away no bitterness. It was a social experience of a new order, and it led to the writing of another book, which he entitled, "POLICE COURT PROCEDURE: A Tentative Analysis."

One summer morning a year later, on his ranch, he left his horse and himself clambered on through a miniature canyon to inspect some rock ferns he had planted the previous winter. Emerging from the upper end of the canyon, he came out on one of his flower-spangled meadows, a delightful isolated spot, screened from the world by low hills and clumps of trees. And here he found a man, evidently on a stroll from the summer hotel down at the little town a mile away. They met face to face and the recognition was mutual. It was Judge Witberg. Also, it was a clear case of trespass, for Watson had trespass signs upon his boundaries, though he never enforced them.

Judge Witberg held out his hand, which Watson refused to see.

"Politics is a dirty trade, isn't it, Judge?" he remarked. "Oh, yes, I see your hand, but I don't care to take it. The papers said I shook hands with Patsy Horan after the trial. You know I did not, but let me tell you that I'd a thousand times rather shake hands with him and his vile following of curs, than with you."

Judge Witberg was painfully flustered, and as he hemmed and hawed and essayed to speak, Watson, looking at him, was struck by a sudden whim, and he determined on a grim and facetious antic.

"I should scarcely expect any animus from a man of your acquirements and knowledge of the world," the Judge was saying.

"Animus?" Watson replied. "Certainly not. I haven't such a thing in my nature. And to prove it, let me show you something curious, something you have never seen before." Casting about him, Watson picked up a rough stone the size of his fist. "See this. Watch me."

So saying, Carter Watson tapped himself a sharp blow on the cheek. The stone laid the flesh open to the bone and the blood spurted forth.

"The stone was too sharp," he announced to the astounded police judge, who thought he had gone mad.

"I must bruise it a trifle. There is nothing like being realistic in such matters."

Whereupon Carter Watson found a smooth stone and with it pounded his cheek nicely several times.

"Ah," he cooed. "That will turn beautifully green and black in a few hours. It will be most convincing."

"You are insane," Judge Witberg quavered.

"Don't use such vile language to me," said Watson. "You see my bruised and bleeding face? You did that, with that right hand of yours. You hit me twice—biff, biff. It is a brutal and unprovoked assault. I am in danger of my life. I must protect myself."

Judge Witberg backed away in alarm before the menacing fists of the other.

"If you strike me I'll have you arrested," Judge Witberg threatened.

"That is what I told Patsy," was the answer. "And do you know what he did when I told him that?"

"No."

"That!"

And at the same moment Watson's right fist landed flush on Judge Witberg's nose, putting that legal gentleman over on his back on the grass.

"Get up!" commanded Watson. "If you are a gentleman, get up—that's what Patsy told me, you know."

Judge Witberg declined to rise, and was dragged to his feet by the coat-collar, only to have one eye blacked and be put on his back again. After that it was a red Indian massacre. Judge Witberg was humanely and scientifically beaten up. His checks were boxed, his cars cuffed, and his face was rubbed in the turf. And all the time Watson exposited the way Patsy Horan had done it. Occasionally, and very carefully, the facetious sociologist administered a real bruising blow. Once, dragging the poor Judge to his feet, he deliberately bumped his own nose on the gentleman's head. The nose promptly bled.

"See that!" cried Watson, stepping back and deftly shedding his blood all down his own shirt front. "You did it. With your fist you did it. It is awful. I am fair murdered. I must again defend myself."

And once more Judge Witberg impacted his features on a fist and was sent to grass.

"I will have you arrested," he sobbed as he lay.

"That's what Patsy said."

"A brutal—-sniff, sniff,—and unprovoked—sniff, sniff— assault."

"That's what Patsy said."

"I will surely have you arrested."

"Speaking slangily, not if I can beat you to it."

And with that, Carter Watson departed down the canyon, mounted his horse, and rode to town.

An hour later, as Judge Witberg limped up the grounds to his hotel, he was arrested by a village constable on a charge of assault and battery preferred by Carter Watson.

V

"Your Honor," Watson said next day to the village Justice, a well to do farmer and graduate, thirty years before, from a cow college, "since this Sol Witberg has seen fit to charge me with battery, following upon my charge of battery against him, I would suggest that both cases be lumped together. The testimony and the facts are the same in both cases."

To this the Justice agreed, and the double case proceeded. Watson, as prosecuting witness, first took the stand and told his story.

"I was picking flowers," he testified. "Picking flowers on my own land, never dreaming of danger. Suddenly this man rushed upon me from behind the trees. 'I am the Dodo,' he says, 'and I can do you to a frazzle. Put up your hands.' I smiled, but with that, biff, biff, he struck me, knocking me down and spilling my flowers. The language he used was frightful. It was an unprovoked and brutal assault. Look at my cheek. Look at my nose—I could not understand it. He must have been drunk. Before I recovered from my surprise he had administered this beating. I was in danger of my life and was compelled to defend himself. That is all, Your Honor, though I must say, in conclusion, that I cannot get over my perplexity. Why did he say he was the Dodo? Why did he so wantonly attack me?"

And thus was Sol Witberg given a liberal education in the art of perjury. Often, from his high seat, he had listened indulgently to police court perjuries in cooked-up cases; but for the first time perjury was directed against him, and he no longer sat above the court, with the bailiffs, the Policemen's clubs, and the prison cells behind him.

"Your Honor," he cried, "never have I heard such a pack of lies told by so bare-faced a liar—!'

Watson here sprang to his feet.

"Your Honor, I protest. It is for your Honor to decide truth or falsehood. The witness is on the stand to testify to actual events that have transpired. His personal opinion upon things in general, and upon me, has no bearing on the case whatever."

The Justice scratched his head and waxed phlegmatically indignant.

"The point is well taken," he decided. "I am surprised at you, Mr. Witberg, claiming to be a judge and skilled in the practice of the law, and yet being guilty of such unlawyerlike conduct. Your manner, sir, and your methods, remind me of a shyster. This is a simple case of assault and battery. We are here to determine who struck the first blow, and we are not interested in your estimates of Mr. Watson's personal character. Proceed with your story."

Sol Witberg would have bitten his bruised and swollen lip in chagrin, had it not hurt so much. But he contained himself and told a simple, straightforward, truthful story.

"Your Honor," Watson said, "I would suggest that you ask him what he was doing on my premises."

"A very good question. What were you doing, sir, on Mr. Watson's premises?"

"I did not know they were his premises."

"It was a trespass, your Honor," Watson cried. "The warnings are posted conspicuously."

"I saw no warnings," said Sol Witberg.

"I have seen them myself," snapped the Justice. "They are very conspicuous. And I would warn you, sir, that if you palter with the truth in such little matters you may darken your more important statements with suspicion. Why did you strike Mr. Watson?"

"Your Honor, as I have testified, I did not strike a blow."

The Justice looked at Carter Watson's bruised and swollen visage, and turned to glare at Sol Witberg.

"Look at that man's cheek!" he thundered. "If you did not strike a blow how comes it that he is so disfigured and injured?"

"As I testified—"

"Be careful," the Justice warned.

"I will be careful, sir. I will say nothing but the truth. He struck himself with a rock. He struck himself with two different rocks."

"Does it stand to reason that a man, any man not a lunatic, would so injure himself, and continue to injure himself, by striking the soft and sensitive parts of his face with a stone?" Carter Watson demanded

"It sounds like a fairy story," was the Justice's comment.

"Mr. Witberg, had you been drinking?"

"No, sir."

"Do you never drink?"

"On occasion."

The Justice meditated on this answer with an air of astute profundity.

Watson took advantage of the opportunity to wink at Sol Witberg, but that much-abused gentleman saw nothing humorous in the situation.

"A very peculiar case, a very peculiar case," the Justice announced, as he began his verdict. "The evidence of the two parties is flatly contradictory. There are no witnesses outside the two principals. Each claims the other committed the assault, and I have no legal way of determining the truth. But I have my private opinion, Mr. Witberg, and I would recommend that henceforth you keep off of Mr. Watson's premises and keep away from this section of the country—"

"This is an outrage!" Sol Witberg blurted out.

"Sit down, sir!" was the Justice's thundered command. "If you interrupt the Court in this manner again, I shall fine you for contempt. And I warn you I shall fine you heavily—you, a judge yourself, who should be conversant with the courtesy and dignity of courts. I shall now give my verdict:

"It is a rule of law that the defendant shall be given the benefit of the doubt. As I have said, and I repeat, there is no legal way for me to determine who struck the first blow. Therefore, and much to my regret,"—here he paused and glared at Sol Witberg—"in each of these cases I am compelled to give the defendant the benefit of the doubt. Gentlemen, you are both dismissed."

"Let us have a nip on it," Watson said to Witberg, as they left the courtroom; but that outraged person refused to lock arms and amble to the nearest saloon.

From *The Night-Born* (1913)
(First published in *The Saturday Evening Post*, Nov 12, 1910)

IV. SAN FRANCISCO

PAST AND FUTURE

from *JOHN BARLEYCORN*

I liked saloons. Especially I liked the San Francisco saloons. They had the most delicious dainties for the taking—strange breads and crackers, cheeses, sausages, sardines—wonderful foods that I never saw on our meagre home-table. And once, I remember, a barkeeper mixed me a sweet temperance drink of syrup and soda- water. My father did not pay for it. It was the barkeeper's treat, and he became my ideal of a good, kind man. I dreamed day- dreams of him for years. Although I was seven years old at the time, I can see him now with undiminished clearness, though I never laid eyes on him but that one time. The saloon was south of Market Street in San Francisco. It stood on the west side of the street. As you entered, the bar was on the left. On the right, against the wall, was the free lunch counter. It was a long, narrow room, and at the rear, beyond the beer kegs on tap, were small, round tables and chairs. The barkeeper was blue-eyed, and had fair, silky hair peeping out from under a black silk skull- cap. I remember he wore a brown Cardigan jacket, and I know precisely the spot, in the midst of the array of bottles, from which he took the bottle of red-coloured syrup. He and my father talked long, and I sipped my sweet drink and worshipped him. And for years afterward I worshipped the memory of him.

Despite my two disastrous experiences, here was John Barleycorn, prevalent and accessible everywhere in the community, luring and drawing me. Here were connotations of the saloon making deep indentations in a child's mind. Here was a child, forming its first judgments of the world, finding the saloon a delightful and desirable place. Stores, nor public buildings, nor all the dwellings of men ever opened their doors to me and let me warm by their fires or permitted me to eat the food of the gods from narrow shelves against the wall. Their doors were ever closed to me; the saloon's doors were ever open. And always and everywhere I found saloons, on highway and byway, up narrow alleys and on busy thoroughfares, bright-lighted and cheerful, warm in winter, and in summer dark and cool. Yes, the saloon was a mighty fine place, and it was more than that.

1913

from *THE SEA WOLF*

I scarcely know where to begin, though I sometimes facetiously place the cause of it all to Charley Furuseth's credit. He kept a summer cottage in Mill Valley, under the shadow of Mount Tamalpais, and never occupied it except when he loafed through the winter months and read Nietzsche and Schopenhauer to rest his brain. When summer came on, he elected to sweat out a hot and dusty existence in the city and to toil incessantly. Had it not been my custom to run up to see him every Saturday afternoon and to stop over till Monday morning, this particular January Monday morning would not have found me afloat on San Francisco Bay.

Not but that I was afloat in a safe craft, for the *Martinez* was a new ferry-steamer, making her fourth or fifth trip on the run between Sausalito and San Francisco. The danger lay in the heavy fog which blanketed the bay, and of which, as a landsman, I had little apprehension. In fact, I remember the placid exaltation with which took up my position on the forward upper deck, directly beneath the pilot-house, and allowed the mystery of the fog to lay hold of my imagination. A fresh breeze was blowing, and for a time I was alone in the moist obscurity; yet not alone, for I was dimly conscious of the presence of the pilot, and of what I took to be the captain, in the glass house above my head.

I remember thinking how comfortable it was, this division of labor which made it unnecessary for me to study fogs, winds, tides, and navigation, in order to visit my friend who lived across an arm of the sea. It was good that men should be specialists, I mused. The peculiar knowledge of the pilot and captain sufficed for many thousands of people who knew no more of the sea and navigation than I knew. On the other hand, instead of having to devote my energy to the learning of a multitude of things, I concentrated it upon a few particular things, such as, for instance, the analysis of Poe's place in American literature, an essay of mine, by the way, in the current Atlantic. Coming aboard, as I passed through the cabin, I had noticed with greedy eyes a stout gentleman reading the Atlantic, which was open at my very essay. And there it was again, the division of labor, the special knowledge of the pilot and captain which permitted the stout gentleman to read my special knowledge on Poe while they carried him safely from Sausalito to San Francisco.

A red-faced man, slamming the cabin door behind him and stumping out on the deck, interrupted my reflections, though I made a mental note of the topic for use in a projected essay which I had thought of calling "The Necessity for Freedom: A Plea for the Artist." The red-faced man shot a glance up at the pilot-house, gazed around at the fog, stumped across the deck and back (he evidently had artificial legs), and stood still by my side, legs wide apart, and with an expression of keen enjoyment on his face. I was not wrong when decided that his days had been spent on the sea.

"It's nasty weather like this here that turns heads gray before their time," he said, with a nod toward the pilot-house.

"I had not thought there was any particular strain," answered. "It seems as simple as A, B, C. They know the direction by compass, the distance, and the speed. I should not call it anything more than mathematical certainty."

"Strain!" he snorted. "Simple as A, B, C! Mathematical certainty!"

He seemed to brace himself up and lean backward against the air as he stared at me. "How about this here tide that's rushin' out through the Golden Gate?" he demanded, or bellowed, rather. "How fast is she ebbin'? What's the drift, eh? Listen to that, will you? A bell-buoy, and we're a-top of it! See 'em alterin' the course!"

From out of the fog came the mournful tolling of a bell, and could see the pilot turning the wheel with great rapidity. The bell, which had seemed straight ahead, was now sounding from the side. Our own whistle was blowing hoarsely, and from time to time the sound of other whistles came to us from out of the fog.

"That's a ferry-boat of some sort," the newcomer said, indicating a whistle off to the right. "And there! D'ye hear that? Blown by mouth. Some scow schooner, most likely. Better watch out, Mr. Schooner-man. Ah, I thought so. Now hell's a-poppin' for somebody!"

The unseen ferry-boat was blowing blast after blast, and the mouth-blown horn was tooting in terror-stricken fashion.

"And now they're payin' their respects to each other and tryin' to get clear," the red-faced man went on, as the hurried whistling ceased.

His face was shining, his eyes flashing with excitement, as he translated into articulate language the speech of the horns and sirens. "That's a steam siren a-goin' it over there to the left. And you hear that fellow with a frog in his throat — a steam schooner as near as can judge, crawlin' in from the Heads against the tide."

A shrill little whistle, piping as if gone mad, came from directly ahead and from very near at hand. Gongs sounded on the *Martinez*.

309

Our paddle-wheels stopped, their pulsing beat died away, and then they started again. The shrill little whistle, like the chirping of a cricket amid the cries of great beasts, shot through the fog from more to the side and swiftly grew faint and fainter. I looked to my companion for enlightenment.

"One of them dare-devil launches," he said. "I almost wish we'd sunk him, the little rip! They're the cause of more trouble. And what good are they? Any jackass gets aboard one and runs it from hell to breakfast, blowin' his whistle to beat the band and tellin' the rest of the world to look out for him, because he's comin' and can't look out for himself! Because he's comin'! And you've got to look out, too! Right of way! Common decency! They don't know the meanin' of it!"

I felt quite amused at his unwarranted choler, and while he stumped indignantly up and down I fell to dwelling upon the romance of the fog. And romantic it certainly was — the fog, like the gray shadow of infinite mystery, brooding over the whirling speck of earth; and men, mere motes of light and sparkle, cursed with an insane relish for work, riding their steeds of wood and steel through the heart of the mystery, groping their way blindly through the Unseen, and clamoring and clanging in confident speech the while their hearts are heavy with incertitude and fear.

The voice of my companion brought me back to myself with a laugh. I too had been groping and floundering, the while I thought rode clear-eyed through the mystery.

"Hello; somebody comin' our way," he was saying. "And d'ye hear that? He's comin' fast. Walking right along. Guess he don't hear us yet. Wind's in wrong direction."

The fresh breeze was blowing right down upon us, and I could hear the whistle plainly, off to one side and a little ahead.

"Ferry-boat?" I asked.

He nodded, then added, "Or he wouldn't be keepin' up such a clip." He gave a short chuckle. "They're gettin' anxious up there."

I glanced up. The captain had thrust his head and shoulders out of the pilot-house, and was staring intently into the fog as though by sheer force of will he could penetrate it. His face was anxious, as was the face of my companion, who had stumped over to the rail and was gazing with a like intentness in the direction of the invisible danger.

Then everything happened, and with inconceivable rapidity. The fog seemed to break away as though split by a wedge, and the bow of a steamboat emerged, trailing fog-wreaths on either side like seaweed on the snout of Leviathan. I could see the pilot-house and a white-bearded man leaning partly out of it, on his elbows. He was clad in a blue uniform, and I remember noting how trim and quiet he was. His quietness, under the circumstances, was terrible. He accepted Destiny, marched hand in hand with it, and coolly measured the stroke. As he leaned there, he ran a calm and speculative eye over us, as though to determine the precise point of the collision, and took no notice whatever when our pilot, white with rage, shouted, "Now you've done it!"

On looking back, I realize that the remark was too obvious to make rejoinder necessary.

"Grab hold of something and hang on," the red-faced man said to me. All his bluster had gone, and he seemed to have caught the contagion of preternatural calm. "And listen to the women scream," he said grimly, almost bitterly, I thought, as though he had been through the experience before.

311

The vessels came together before I could follow his advice. We must have been struck squarely amidships, for I saw nothing, the strange steamboat having passed beyond my line of vision. The *Martinez* heeled over, sharply, and there was a crashing and rending of timber. I was thrown flat on the wet deck, and before I could scramble to my feet I heard the scream of the women. This it was, I am certain, — the most indescribable of blood-curdling sounds, — that threw me into a panic. I remembered the life-preservers stored in the cabin, but was met at the door and swept backward by a wild rush of men and women. What happened in the next few minutes I do not recollect, though I have a clear remembrance of pulling down life-preservers from the overhead racks, while the red-faced man fastened them about the bodies of an hysterical group of women. This memory is as distinct and sharp as that of any picture I have seen. It is a picture, and I can see it now, — the jagged edges of the hole in the side of the cabin, through which the gray fog swirled and eddied; the empty upholstered seats, littered with all the evidences of sudden flight, such as packages, hand satchels, umbrellas, and wraps; the stout gentleman who had been reading my essay, encased in cork and canvas, the magazine still in his hand, and asking me with monotonous insistence if I thought there was any danger; the red-faced man, stumping gallantly around on his artificial legs and buckling life-preservers on all comers; and finally, the screaming bedlam of women.

This it was, the screaming of the women, that most tried my nerves. It must have tried, too, the nerves of the red-faced man, for have another picture which will never fade from my mind. The stout gentleman is stuffing the magazine into his overcoat pocket and looking on curiously. A tangled mass of women, with drawn, white faces and open mouths, is shrieking like a chorus of lost souls; and the red-faced man, his face now purplish with wrath, and with arms extended overhead as in the act of hurling thunderbolts, is shouting, "Shut up! Oh, shut up!"

I remember the scene impelled me to sudden laughter, and in the next instant I realized I was becoming hysterical myself; for these were women of my own kind, like my mother and sisters, with the fear of death upon them and unwilling to die. And I remember that the sounds they made reminded me of the squealing of pigs under the knife of the butcher, and I was struck with horror at the vividness of the analogy. These women, capable of the most sublime emotions, of the tenderest sympathies, were open-mouthed and screaming. They wanted to live, they were helpless, like rats in a trap, and they screamed.

The horror of it drove me out on deck. I was feeling sick and squeamish, and sat down on a bench. In a hazy way I saw and heard men rushing and shouting as they strove to lower the boats. It was just as I had read descriptions of such scenes in books. The tackles jammed. Nothing worked. One boat lowered away with the plugs out, filled with women and children and then with water, and capsized. Another boat had been lowered by one end, and still hung in the tackle by the other end, where it had been abandoned. Nothing was to be seen of the strange steamboat which had caused the disaster, though I heard men saying that she would undoubtedly send boats to our assistance.

I descended to the lower deck. The *Martinez* was sinking fast, for the water was very near. Numbers of the passengers were leaping overboard. Others, in the water, were clamoring to be taken aboard again. No one heeded them. A cry arose that we were sinking. was seized by the consequent panic, and went over the side in a surge of bodies. How I went over I do not know, though I did know, and instantly, why those in the water were so desirous of getting back on the steamer. The water was cold — so cold that it was painful. The pang, as I plunged into it, was as quick and sharp as that of fire. It bit to the marrow. It was like the grip of death. I gasped with the anguish and shock of it, filling my lungs before the life-preserver popped me to the surface. The taste of the salt was strong in my mouth, and I was strangling with the acrid stuff in my throat and lungs.

But it was the cold that was most distressing. I felt that could survive but a few minutes. People were struggling and floundering in the water about me. I could hear them crying out to one another. And I heard, also, the sound of oars. Evidently the strange steamboat had lowered its boats. As the time went by I marvelled that I was still alive. I had no sensation whatever in my lower limbs, while a chilling numbness was wrapping about my heart and creeping into it. Small waves, with spiteful foaming crests, continually broke over me and into my mouth, sending me off into more strangling paroxysms.

The noises grew indistinct, though I heard a final and despairing chorus of screams in the distance and knew that the *Martinez* had gone down. Later, — how much later I have no knowledge, — I came to myself with a start of fear. I was alone. I could hear no calls or cries — only the sound of the waves, made weirdly hollow and reverberant by the fog. A panic in a crowd, which partakes of a sort of community of interest, is not so terrible as a panic when one is by oneself; and such a panic I now suffered. Whither was I drifting? The red-faced man had said that the tide was ebbing through the

Golden Gate. Was I, then, being carried out to sea? And the life-preserver in which I floated? Was it not liable to go to pieces at any moment? I had heard of such things being made of paper and hollow rushes which quickly became saturated and lost all buoyancy. And I could not swim a stroke. And I was alone, floating, apparently, in the midst of a gray primordial vastness. I confess that a madness seized me, that I shrieked aloud as the women had shrieked, and beat the water with my numb hands.

How long this lasted I have no conception, for a blankness intervened, of which I remember no more than one remembers of troubled and painful sleep. When I aroused, it was as after centuries of time; and I saw, almost above me and emerging from the fog, the bow of a vessel, and three triangular sails, each shrewdly lapping the other and filled with wind. Where the bow cut the water there was a great foaming and gurgling, and I seemed directly in its path. I tried to cry out, but was too exhausted. The bow plunged down, just missing me and sending a swash of water clear over my head. Then the long, black side of the vessel began slipping past, so near that I could have touched it with my hands. I tried to reach it, in a mad resolve to claw into the wood with my nails, but my arms were heavy and lifeless. Again I strove to call out, but made no sound.

The stern of the vessel shot by, dropping, as it did so, into a hollow between the waves; and I caught a glimpse of a man standing at the wheel, and of another man who seemed to be doing little else than smoke a cigar. I saw the smoke issuing from his lips as he slowly turned his head and glanced out over the water in my direction. It was a careless, unpremeditated glance, one of those haphazard things men do when they have no immediate call to do anything in particular, but act because they are alive and must do

315

something.

But life and death were in that glance. I could see the vessel being swallowed up in the fog; I saw the back of the man at the wheel, and the head of the other man turning, slowly turning, as his gaze struck the water and casually lifted along it toward me. His face wore an absent expression, as of deep thought, and I became afraid that if his eyes did light upon me he would nevertheless not see me. But his eyes did light upon me, and looked squarely into mine; and he did see me, for he sprang to the wheel, thrusting the other man aside, and whirled it round and round, hand over hand, at the same time shouting orders of some sort. The vessel seemed to go off at a tangent to its former course and leapt almost instantly from view into the fog.

I felt myself slipping into unconsciousness, and tried with all the power of my will to fight above the suffocating blankness and darkness that was rising around me. A little later I heard the stroke of oars, growing nearer and nearer, and the calls of a man. When he was very near I heard him crying, in vexed fashion, "Why in hell don't you sing out?" This meant me, I thought, and then the blankness and darkness rose over me.

1904

SOUTH OF THE SLOT

Old San Francisco, which is the San Francisco of only the other day, the day before the Earthquake, was divided midway by the Slot. The Slot was an iron crack that ran along the center of Market street, and from the Slot arose the burr of the ceaseless, endless cable that was hitched at will to the cars it dragged up and down. In truth, there were two slots, but in the quick grammar of the West time was saved by calling them, and much more that they stood for, "The Slot." North of the Slot were the theaters, hotels, and shopping district, the banks and the staid, respectable business houses. South of the Slot were the factories, slums, laundries, machine-shops, boiler works, and the abodes of the working class.

The Slot was the metaphor that expressed the class cleavage of Society, and no man crossed this metaphor, back and forth, more successfully than Freddie Drummond. He made a practice of living in both worlds, and in both worlds he lived signally well. Freddie Drummond was a professor in the Sociology Department of the University of California, and it was as a professor of sociology that he first crossed over the Slot, lived for six months in the great labor-ghetto, and wrote "The Unskilled Laborer" — a book that was hailed everywhere as an able contribution to the literature of progress, and as a splendid reply to the literature of discontent. Politically and economically it was nothing if not orthodox. Presidents of great railway systems bought whole editions of it to give to their employees. The Manufacturers' Association alone distributed fifty thousand copies of it. In a way, it was almost as immoral as the far-famed and notorious "Message to Garcia," while in its pernicious preachment of thrift and content it ran "Mrs. Wiggs of the Cabbage Patch" a close second.

At first, Freddie Drummond found it monstrously difficult to get along among the working people. He was not used to their ways, and they certainly were not used to his. They were suspicious. He had no antecedents. He could talk of no previous jobs. His hands were soft. His extraordinary politeness was ominous. His first idea of the role he would play was that of a free and independent American who chose to work with his hands and no explanations given. But it wouldn't do, as he quickly discovered. At the beginning they accepted him, very provisionally, as a freak. A little later, as he began to know his way about better, he insensibly drifted into the role that would work — namely, he was a man who had seen better days, very much better days, but who was down in his luck, though, to be sure, only temporarily.

He learned many things, and generalized much and often erroneously, all of which can be found in the pages of "The Unskilled Laborer." He saved himself, however, after the sane and conservative manner of his kind, by labeling his generalizations as "tentative." One of his first experiences was in the great Wilmax Cannery, where he was put on piece-work making small packing cases. A box factory supplied the parts, and all Freddie Drummond had to do was to fit the parts into a form and drive in the wire nails with a light hammer.

It was not skilled labor, but it was piece-work. The ordinary laborers in the cannery got a dollar and a half per day. Freddie

Drummond found the other men on the same job with him jogging along and earning a dollar and seventy-five cents a day. By the third day he was able to earn the same. But he was ambitious. He did not care to jog along and, being unusually able and fit, on the fourth day earned two dollars. The next day, having keyed himself up to an exhausting high-tension, he earned two dollars and a half. His fellow workers favored him with scowls and black looks, and made remarks, slangily witty and which he did not understand, about sucking up to the boss and pace-making and holding her down when the rains set in. He was astonished at their malingering on piece-work, generalized about the inherent laziness of the unskilled laborer, and proceeded next day to hammer out three dollars' worth of boxes.

And that night, coming out of the cannery, he was interviewed by his fellow workmen, who were very angry and incoherently slangy. He failed to comprehend the motive behind their action. The action itself was strenuous. When he refused to ease down his pace and bleated about freedom of contract, independent Americanism, and the dignity of toil, they proceeded to spoil his pace-making ability. It was a fierce battle, for Drummond was a large man and an athlete, but the crowd finally jumped on his ribs, walked on his face, and stamped on his fingers, so that it was only after lying in bed for a week that he was able to get up and look for another job. All of which is duly narrated in that first book of his, in the chapter entitled "The Tyranny of Labor."

A little later, in another department of the Wilmax Cannery, lumping as a fruit-distributor among the women, he essayed to carry two boxes of fruit at a time, and was promptly reproached by the other fruit-lumpers. It was palpable malingering; but he was there, he decided, not to change conditions, but to observe. So he lumped one box thereafter, and so well did he study the art of shirking that he wrote a special chapter on it, with the last several paragraphs devoted to tentative generalizations.

In those six months he worked at many jobs and developed into a very good imitation of a genuine worker. He was a natural linguist, and he kept notebooks, making a scientific study of the workers' slang or argot, until he could talk quite intelligibly. This language also enabled him more intimately to follow their mental processes, and thereby to gather much data for a projected chapter in some future book which he planned to entitle "Synthesis of Working-Class Psychology."

Before he arose to the surface from that first plunge into the underworld he discovered that he was a good actor and demonstrated the plasticity of his nature. He was himself astonished at his own fluidity. Once having mastered the language and conquered numerous fastidious qualms, he found that he could flow into any nook of working-class life and fit it so snugly as to feel comfortably at home. As he said, in the preface to his second book, "The Toiler," he endeavored really to know the working people, and the only possible way to achieve this was to work beside them, eat their food, sleep in their beds, be amused with their amusements, think their thoughts, and feel their feelings.

He was not a deep thinker. He had no faith in new theories. All his norms and criteria were conventional. His Thesis, on the French Revolution, was noteworthy in college annals, not merely for its painstaking and voluminous accuracy, but for the fact that it was the dryest, deadest, most formal, and most orthodox screed ever written on the subject. He was a very reserved man, and his natural inhibition was large in quantity and steel-like in quality. He had but few friends. He was too undemonstrative, too frigid. He had no vices, nor had anyone ever discovered any temptations. Tobacco he detested, beer he abhorred, and he was never known to drink anything stronger than an occasional light wine at dinner.

When a freshman he had been baptized "Ice-Box" by his warmer-blooded fellows. As a member of the faculty he was known as "Cold-Storage." He had but one grief, and that was "Freddie." He had earned it when he played full-back on the `Varsity eleven', and his formal soul had never succeeded in living it down. "Freddie" he would ever be, except officially, and through nightmare vistas he looked into a future when his world would speak of him as "Old Freddie."

For he was very young to be a Doctor of Sociology, only twenty-seven, and he looked younger. In appearance and atmosphere he was a strapping big college man, smooth-faced and easy-mannered, clean and simple and wholesome, with a known record of being a splendid athlete and an implied vast possession of cold culture of the inhibited sort. He never talked shop out of class and committee rooms, except later on, when his books showered him with distasteful public notice and he yielded to the extent of reading occasional papers before certain literary and economic societies. He did everything right — too right; and in dress and comportment was inevitably correct. Not that he was a dandy. Far from it. He was a college man, in dress and carriage as like as a pea to the type that of late years is being so generously turned out of our institutions of higher learning. His handshake was satisfyingly strong and stiff. His blue eyes were coldly blue and convincingly sincere. His voice, firm and masculine, clean and crisp of enunciation, was pleasant to the ear. The one drawback to Freddie Drummond was his inhibition. He never unbent. In his football days, the higher the tension of the game, the cooler he grew. He was noted as a boxer, but he was regarded as an automaton, with the inhuman precision of a machine judging distance and timing blows, guarding, blocking, and stalling. He was rarely punished himself, while he rarely punished an opponent. He was too clever and too controlled to permit himself to put a pound more weight into a punch than he intended. With him it was a matter of exercise. It kept him fit.

As time went by, Freddie Drummond found himself more frequently crossing the Slot and losing himself in South of Market. His summer and winter holidays were spent there, and, whether it was a week or a week-end, he found the time spent there to be valuable and enjoyable. And there was so much material to be gathered. His third book, "Mass and Master," became a text-book in the American universities; and almost before he knew it, he was at work on a fourth one, "The Fallacy of the Inefficient."

Somewhere in his make-up there was a strange twist or quirk. Perhaps it was a recoil from his environment and training, or from the tempered seed of his ancestors, who had been bookmen generation preceding generation; but at any rate, he found enjoyment in being down in the working-class world. In his own world he was "Cold-Storage," but down below he was "Big" Bill Totts, who could drink and smoke, and slang and fight, and be an all-around favorite. Everybody liked Bill, and more than one working girl made love to him. At first he had been merely a good actor, but as time went on, simulation became second nature. He no longer played a part, and he loved sausages, sausages and bacon, than which, in his own proper sphere, there was nothing more loathsome in the way of food.

From doing the thing for the need's sake, he came to doing the thing for the thing's sake. He found himself regretting as the time drew near for him to go back to his lecture-room and his inhibition. And he often found himself waiting with anticipation for the dreamy time to pass when he could cross the Slot and cut loose and play the devil. He was not wicked, but as "Big" Bill Totts he did a myriad things that Freddie Drummond would never have been permitted to do. Moreover, Freddie Drummond never would have wanted to do them. That was the strangest part of his discovery. Freddie Drummond and Bill Totts were two totally different creatures. The desires and tastes and impulses of each ran counter to the other's. Bill Totts could shirk at a job with clear conscience, while Freddie Drummond condemned shirking as vicious, criminal, and un-American, and devoted whole chapters to condemnation of the vice. Freddie Drummond did not care for dancing, but Bill Totts never missed the nights at the various dancing clubs, such as The Magnolia, The Western Star, and The Elite; while he won a massive silver cup, standing thirty inches high, for being the best-sustained character at the Butchers and Meat Workers' annual grand masked ball. And Bill Totts liked the girls and the girls liked him, while Freddie Drummond enjoyed playing the ascetic in this particular, was open in his opposition to equal suffrage, and cynically bitter in his secret condemnation of coeducation.

Freddie Drummond changed his manners with his dress, and without effort. When he entered the obscure little room used for his transformation scenes, he carried himself just a bit too stiffly. He was too erect, his shoulders were an inch too far back, while his face was grave, almost harsh, and practically expressionless. But when

323

he emerged in Bill Totts's clothes he was another creature. Bill Totts did not slouch, but somehow his whole form limbered up and became graceful. The very sound of the voice was changed, and the laugh was loud and hearty, while loose speech and an occasional oath were as a matter of course on his lips. Also, Bill Totts was a trifle inclined to later hours, and at times, in saloons, to be good-naturedly bellicose with other workmen. Then, too, at Sunday picnics or when coming home from the show, either arm betrayed a practiced familiarity in stealing around girls' waists, while he displayed a wit keen and delightful in the flirtatious badinage that was expected of a good fellow in his class.

So thoroughly was Bill Totts himself, so thoroughly a workman, a genuine denizen of South of the Slot, that he was as class-conscious as the average of his kind, and his hatred for a scab even exceeded that of the average loyal union man. During the Water Front Strike, Freddie Drummond was somehow able to stand apart from the unique combination, and, coldly critical, watch Bill Totts hilariously slug scab long-shoremen. For Bill Totts was a dues-paying member of the Longshoremen Union and had a right to be indignant with the usurpers of his job. "Big" Bill Totts was so very big, and so very able, that it was "Big" Bill to the front when trouble was brewing. From acting outraged feelings, Freddie Drummond, in the role of his other self, came to experience genuine outrage, and it was only when he returned to the classic atmosphere of the university that he was able, sanely and conservatively, to generalize upon his underworld experiences and put them down on paper as a trained sociologist should. That Bill Totts lacked the perspective to raise him above class-consciousness, Freddie Drummond clearly saw. But Bill Totts could not see it. When he saw a scab taking his job away, he saw red at the same time, and little else did he see. It was Freddie Drummond, irreproachably clothed and comported, seated at his study desk or facing his class in "Sociology 17," who saw Bill Totts, and all around Bill Totts, and all around the whole scab and union-labor problem and its relation to the economic welfare of the United States in the struggle for the world market. Bill Totts really wasn't able to see beyond the next meal and the prize-fight the following night at the Gaiety Athletic Club.

It was while gathering material for "Women and Work" that Freddie received his first warning of the danger he was in. He was too successful at living in both worlds. This strange dualism he had developed was after all very unstable, and, as he sat in his study and meditated, he saw that it could not endure. It was really a transition stage, and if he persisted he saw that he would inevitably have to drop one world or the other. He could not continue in both. And as he looked at the row of volumes that graced the upper shelf of his revolving book-case, his volumes, beginning with his Thesis and ending with "Women and Work," he decided that that was the world he would hold to and stick by. Bill Totts had served his purpose, but he had become a too dangerous accomplice. Bill Totts would have to cease.

Freddie Drummond's fright was due to Mary Condon, President of the International Glove Workers' Union No. 974. He had seen her, first, from the spectators' gallery, at the annual convention of the Northwest Federation of Labor, and he had seen her through Bill Totts' eyes, and that individual had been most favorably impressed by her. She was not Freddie Drummond's sort at all. What if she were a royal-bodied woman, graceful and sinewy as a panther, with amazing black eyes that could fill with fire or laughter-love, as the mood might dictate? He detested women with a too exuberant vitality and a lack of . . . well, of inhibition. Freddie Drummond accepted the doctrine of evolution because it was quite universally accepted by college men, and he flatly believed that man had climbed up the ladder of life out of the weltering muck and mess of lower and monstrous organic things. But he was a trifle ashamed of this genealogy, and preferred not to think of it. Wherefore, probably, he practiced his iron inhibition and preached it to others, and preferred women of his own type, who could shake free of this bestial and regrettable ancestral line and by discipline and control emphasize the wideness of the gulf that separated them from what their dim forbears had been.

Bill Totts had none of these considerations. He had liked Mary Condon from the moment his eyes first rested on her in the convention hall, and he had made it a point, then and there, to find out who she was. The next time he met her, and quite by accident, was when he was driving an express wagon for Pat Morrissey. It was in a lodging house in Mission Street, where he had been called to take a trunk into storage. The landlady's daughter had called him and led him to the little bedroom, the occupant of which, a glove-maker, had just been removed to hospital. But Bill did not know this. He stooped, up-ended the trunk, which was a large one, got it on his shoulder, and struggled to his feet with his back toward the open door. At that moment he heard a woman's voice.

"Belong to the union?" was the question asked.

"Aw, what's it to you?" he retorted. "Run along now, an' git outa my way. I wanta turn round."

The next he knew, big as he was, he was whirled half around and sent reeling backward, the trunk overbalancing him, till he fetched up with a crash against the wall. He started to swear, but at the same instant found himself looking into Mary Condon's flashing, angry eyes.

"Of course I b'long to the union," he said. "I was only kiddin' you."

"Where's your card?" she demanded in business-like tones.

"In my pocket. But I can't git it out now. This trunk's too damn heavy. Come on down to the wagon an' I'll show it to you."

"Put that trunk down," was the command.

"What for? I got a card, I'm tellin' you."

"Put it down, that's all. No scab's going to handle that trunk. You ought to be ashamed of yourself, you big coward, scabbing on honest men. Why don't you join the union and be a man?"

Mary Condon's color had left her face, and it was apparent that she was in a rage.

"To think of a big man like you turning traitor to his class. I suppose you're aching to join the militia for a chance to shoot down union drivers the next strike. You may belong to the militia already, for that matter. You're the sort — "

"Hold on, now, that's too much!" Bill dropped the trunk to the floor with a bang, straightened up, and thrust his hand into his inside coat pocket. "I told you I was only kiddin'. There, look at that."

It was a union card properly enough.

"All right, take it along," Mary Condon said. "And the next time don't kid."

Her face relaxed as she noticed the ease with which he got the big trunk to his shoulder, and her eyes glowed as they glanced over the graceful massiveness of the man. But Bill did not see that. He was too busy with the trunk.

The next time he saw Mary Condon was during the Laundry Strike. The Laundry Workers, but recently organized, were green at the business, and had petitioned Mary Condon to engineer the strike. Freddie Drummond had had an inkling of what was coming, and had sent Bill Totts to join the union and investigate. Bill's job was in the wash-room, and the men had been called out first, that morning, in order to stiffen the courage of the girls; and Bill chanced to be near the door to the mangle-room when Mary Condon started to enter. The superintendent, who was both large and stout, barred her way. He wasn't going to have his girls called out, and he'd teach her a lesson to mind her own business. And as Mary tried to squeeze past him he thrust her back with a fat hand on her shoulder. She glanced around and saw Bill.

"Here you, Mr. Totts," she called. "Lend a hand. I want to get in."

Bill experienced a startle of warm surprise. She had remembered his name from his union card. The next moment the superintendent had been plucked from the doorway raving about rights under the law, and the girls were deserting their machines. During the rest of that short and successful strike, Bill constituted himself Mary Condon's henchman and messenger, and when it was over returned to the University to be Freddie Drummond and to wonder what Bill Totts could see in such a woman.

Freddie Drummond was entirely safe, but Bill had fallen in love. There was no getting away from the fact of it, and it was this fact that had given Freddie Drummond his warning. Well, he had done his work, and his adventures could cease. There was no need for him to cross the Slot again. All but the last three chapters of his latest, "Labor Tactics and Strategy," was finished, and he had sufficient material on hand adequately to supply those chapters.

Another conclusion he arrived at, was that in order to sheet-anchor himself as Freddie Drummond, closer ties and relations in his own social nook were necessary. It was time that he was married, anyway, and he was fully aware that if Freddie Drummond didn't get married, Bill Totts assuredly would, and the complications were too awful to contemplate. And so, enters Catherine Van Vorst. She was a college woman herself, and her father, the one wealthy member of the faculty, was the head of the Philosophy Department as well. It would be a wise marriage from every standpoint, Freddie Drummond concluded when the engagement was consummated and announced. In appearance cold and reserved, aristocratic and wholesomely conservative, Catherine Van Vorst, though warm in her way, possessed an inhibition equal to Drummond's.

All seemed well with him, but Freddie Drummond could not quite shake off the call of the underworld, the lure of the free and open, of the unhampered, irresponsible life South of the Slot. As the time of his marriage approached, he felt that he had indeed sowed wild oats, and he felt, moreover, what a good thing it would be if he could have but one wild fling more, play the good fellow and the wastrel one last time, ere he settled down to gray lecture-rooms and sober matrimony. And, further to tempt him, the very last chapter of "Labor Tactics and Strategy" remained unwritten for lack of a trifle more of essential data which he had neglected to gather.

So Freddie Drummond went down for the last time as Bill Totts, got his data, and, unfortunately, encountered Mary Condon. Once more installed in his study, it was not a pleasant thing to look back upon. It made his warning doubly imperative. Bill Totts had behaved abominably. Not only had he met Mary Condon at the Central Labor Council, but he had stopped in at a chop-house with her, on the way home, and treated her to oysters. And before they parted at her door, his arms had been about her, and he had kissed her on the lips and kissed her repeatedly. And her last words in his ear, words uttered softly with a catchy sob in the throat that was nothing more nor less than a love cry, were "Bill . . . dear, dear Bill."

Freddie Drummond shuddered at the recollection. He saw the pit yawning for him. He was not by nature a polygamist, and he was appalled at the possibilities of the situation. It would have to be put an end to, and it would end in one only of two ways: either he must become wholly Bill Totts and be married to Mary Condon, or he must remain wholly Freddie Drummond and be married to Catherine Van Vorst. Otherwise, his conduct would be beneath contempt and horrible.

In the several months that followed, San Francisco was torn with labor strife. The unions and the employers' associations had locked horns with a determination that looked as if they intended to settle the matter, one way or the other, for all time. But Freddie Drummond corrected proofs, lectured classes, and did not budge. He devoted himself to Catherine Van Vorst, and day by day found more to respect and admire in her — nay, even to love in her. The Street Car Strike tempted him, but not so severely as he would have expected; and the great Meat Strike came on and left him cold. The ghost of Bill Totts had been successfully laid, and Freddie Drummond with rejuvenescent zeal tackled a brochure, long-planned, on the topic of "diminishing returns."

The wedding was two weeks off, when, one afternoon, in San Francisco, Catherine Van Vorst picked him up and whisked him away to see a Boys' Club, recently instituted by the settlement workers with whom she was interested. It was her brother's machine, but they were alone with the exception of the chauffeur. At the junction with Kearny Street, Market and Geary Streets intersect like the sides of a sharp-angled letter "V." They, in the auto, were coming down Market with the intention of negotiating the sharp apex and going up Geary. But they did not know what was coming down Geary, timed by fate to meet them at the apex. While aware from the papers that the Meat Strike was on and that it was an exceedingly bitter one, all thought of it at that moment was farthest from Freddie Drummond's mind. Was he not seated beside Catherine? And, besides, he was carefully expositing to her his views on settlement work — views that Bill Totts' adventures had played a part in formulating.

Coming down Geary Street were six meat wagons. Beside each scab driver sat a policeman. Front and rear, and along each side of this procession, marched a protecting escort of one hundred police. Behind the police rear guard, at a respectful distance, was an orderly but vociferous mob, several blocks in length, that congested the street from sidewalk to sidewalk. The Beef Trust was making an effort to supply the hotels, and, incidentally, to begin the breaking of the strike. The St. Francis had already been supplied, at a cost of many broken windows and broken heads, and the expedition was marching to the relief of the Palace Hotel.

All unwitting, Drummond sat beside Catherine, talking settlement work, as the auto, honking methodically and dodging traffic, swung in a wide curve to get around the apex. A big coal wagon, loaded with lump coal and drawn by four huge horses, just debouching from Kearny Street as though to turn down Market,

331

blocked their way. The driver of the wagon seemed undecided, and the chauffeur, running slow but disregarding some shouted warning from the crossing policemen, swerved the auto to the left, violating the traffic rules, in order to pass in front of the wagon.

At that moment Freddie Drummond discontinued his conversation. Nor did he resume it again, for the situation was developing with the rapidity of a transformation scene. He heard the roar of the mob at the rear, and caught a glimpse of the helmeted police and the lurching meat wagons. At the same moment, laying on his whip and standing up to his task, the coal driver rushed horses and wagon squarely in front of the advancing procession, pulled the horses up sharply, and put on the big brake. Then he made his lines fast to the brake-handle and sat down with the air of one who had stopped to stay. The auto had been brought to a stop, too, by his big panting leaders which had jammed against it.

Before the chauffeur could back clear, an old Irishman, driving a rickety express wagon and lashing his one horse to a gallop, had locked wheels with the auto. Drummond recognized both horse and wagon, for he had driven them often himself. The Irishman was Pat Morrissey. On the other side a brewery wagon was locking with the coal wagon, and an east-bound Kearny-Street car, wildly clanging its gong, the motorman shouting defiance at the crossing policeman, was dashing forward to complete the blockade. And wagon after wagon was locking and blocking and adding to the confusion. The meat wagons halted. The police were trapped. The roar at the rear increased as the mob came on to the attack, while the vanguard of the police charged the obstructing wagons.

"We're in for it," Drummond remarked coolly to Catherine.

"Yes," she nodded, with equal coolness. "What savages they are."

His admiration for her doubled on itself. She was indeed his sort. He would have been satisfied with her even if she had screamed and clung to him, but this — this was magnificent. She sat in that storm center as calmly as if it had been no more than a block of carriages at the opera.

The police were struggling to clear a passage. The driver of the coal wagon, a big man in shirt sleeves, lighted a pipe and sat smoking. He glanced down complacently at a captain of police who was raving and cursing at him, and his only acknowledgment was a shrug of the shoulders. From the rear arose the rat-tat-tat of clubs on heads and a pandemonium of cursing, yelling, and shouting. A violent accession of noise proclaimed that the mob had broken through and was dragging a scab from a wagon. The police captain reinforced from his vanguard, and the mob at the rear was repelled. Meanwhile, window after window in the high office building on the right had been opened, and the class-conscious clerks were raining a shower of office furniture down on the heads of police and scabs. Waste-baskets, ink-bottles, paper-weights, typewriters — anything and everything that came to hand was filling the air.

A policeman, under orders from his captain, clambered to the lofty seat of the coal wagon to arrest the driver. And the driver, rising leisurely and peacefully to meet him, suddenly crumpled him in his arms and threw him down on top of the captain. The driver was a young giant, and when he climbed on top his load and poised a lump of coal in both hands, a policeman, who was just scaling the wagon from the side, let go and dropped back to earth. The captain ordered half a dozen of his men to take the wagon. The teamster, scrambling over the load from side to side, beat them down with

333

huge lumps of coal.

The crowd on the sidewalks and the teamsters on the locked wagons roared encouragement and their own delight. The motorman, smashing helmets with his controller bar, was beaten into insensibility and dragged from his platform. The captain of police, beside himself at the repulse of his men, led the next assault on the coal wagon. A score of police were swarming up the tall-sided fortress. But the teamster multiplied himself. At times there were six or eight policemen rolling on the pavement and under the wagon. Engaged in repulsing an attack on the rear end of his fortress, the teamster turned about to see the captain just in the act of stepping on to the seat from the front end. He was still in the air and in most unstable equilibrium, when the teamster hurled a thirty-pound lump of coal. It caught the captain fairly on the chest, and he went over backward, striking on a wheeler's back, tumbling on to the ground, and jamming against the rear wheel of the auto.

Catherine thought he was dead, but he picked himself up and charged back. She reached out her gloved hand and patted the flank of the snorting, quivering horse. But Drummond did not notice the action. He had eyes for nothing save the battle of the coal wagon, while somewhere in his complicated psychology, one Bill Totts was heaving and straining in an effort to come to life. Drummond believed in law and order and the maintenance of the established, but this riotous savage within him would have none of it. Then, if ever, did Freddie Drummond call upon his iron inhibition to save him. But it is written that the house divided against itself must fall. And Freddie Drummond found that he had divided all the will and force of him with Bill Totts, and between them the entity that constituted the pair of them was being wrenched in twain.

334

Freddie Drummond sat in the auto, quite composed, alongside Catherine Van Vorst; but looking out of Freddie Drummond's eyes was Bill Totts, and somewhere behind those eyes, battling for the control of their mutual body, were Freddie Drummond, the sane and conservative sociologist, and Bill Totts, the class-conscious and bellicose union workingman. It was Bill Totts, looking out of those eyes, who saw the inevitable end of the battle on the coal wagon. He saw a policeman gain the top of the load, a second, and a third. They lurched clumsily on the loose footing, but their long riot-clubs were out and swinging. One blow caught the teamster on the head. A second he dodged, receiving it on the shoulder. For him the game was plainly up. He dashed in suddenly, clutched two policemen in his arms, and hurled himself a prisoner to the pavement, his hold never relaxing on his two captors.

Catherine Van Vorst was sick and faint at sight of the blood and brutal fighting. But her qualms were vanquished by the sensational and most unexpected happening that followed. The man beside her emitted an unearthly and uncultured yell and rose to his feet. She saw him spring over the front seat, leap to the broad rump of the wheeler, and from there gain the wagon. His onslaught was like a whirlwind. Before the bewildered officer on top the load could guess the errand of this conventionally clad but excited-seeming gentleman, he was the recipient of a punch that arched him back through the air to the pavement. A kick in the face led an ascending policeman to follow his example. A rush of three more gained the top and locked with Bill Totts in a gigantic clinch, during which his scalp was opened up by a club, and coat, vest, and half his starched shirt were torn from him. But the three policemen were flung wide and far, and Bill Totts, raining down lumps of coal, held the fort.

The captain led gallantly to the attack, but was bowled over by a chunk of coal that burst on his head in black baptism. The need of the police was to break the blockade in front before the mob could break in at the rear, and Bill Totts' need was to hold the wagon till the mob did break through. So the battle of the coal went on.

The crowd had recognized its champion. "Big" Bill, as usual, had come to the front, and Catherine Van Vorst was bewildered by the cries of "Bill! O you Bill!" that arose on every hand. Pat Morrissey, on his wagon seat, was jumping and screaming in an ecstasy, "Eat 'em, Bill! Eat 'em! Eat 'em alive!" From the sidewalk she heard a woman's voice cry out, "Look out, Bill — front end!" Bill took the warning and with well-directed coal cleaned the front end of the wagon of assailants. Catherine Van Vorst turned her head and saw on the curb of the sidewalk a woman with vivid coloring and flashing black eyes who was staring with all her soul at the man who had been Freddie Drummond a few minutes before.

The windows of the office building became vociferous with applause. A fresh shower of office chairs and filing cabinets descended. The mob had broken through on one side the line of wagons, and was advancing, each segregated policeman the center of a fighting group. The scabs were torn from their seats, the traces of the horses cut, and the frightened animals put in flight. Many policemen crawled under the coal wagon for safety, while the loose horses, with here and there a policeman on their backs or struggling at their heads to hold them, surged across the sidewalk opposite the jam and broke into Market Street.

Catherine Van Vorst heard the woman's voice calling in warning. She was back on the curb again, and crying out:

"Beat it, Bill! Now's your time! Beat it!"

The police for the moment had been swept away. Bill Totts leaped to the pavement and made his way to the woman on the sidewalk. Catherine Van Vorst saw her throw her arms around him and kiss him on the lips; and Catherine Van Vorst watched him curiously as he went on down the sidewalk, one arm around the woman, both talking and laughing, and he with a volubility and abandon she could never have dreamed possible.

The police were back again and clearing the jam while waiting for reinforcements and new drivers and horses. The mob had done its work and was scattering, and Catherine Van Vorst, still watching, could see the man she had known as Freddie Drummond. He towered a head above the crowd. His arm was still about the woman. And she in the motorcar, watching, saw the pair cross Market Street, cross the Slot, and disappear down Third Street into the labor ghetto.

*

In the years that followed no more lectures were given in the University of California by one Freddie Drummond, and no more books on economics and the labor question appeared over the name of Frederick A. Drummond. On the other hand there arose a new labor leader, William Totts by name. He it was who married Mary Condon, President of the International Glove Workers' Union No. 974; and he it was who called the notorious Cooks and Waiters' Strike, which, before its successful termination, brought out with it scores of other unions, among which, of the more remotely allied, were the Chicken Pickers and the Undertakers.

337

from *The Strength of the Strong* (1914)

(First published in *The Saturday Evening Post*, Vol. 181, May, 1909)

THE DREAM OF DEBS

I awoke fully an hour before my customary time. This in itself was remarkable, and I lay very wide awake, pondering over it. Something was the matter, something was wrong - I knew not what. I was oppressed by a premonition of something terrible that had happened or was about to happen. But what was it? I strove to orient myself. I remembered that at the time of the Great Earthquake of 1906 many claimed they awakened some moments before the first shock and that during these moments they experienced strange feelings of dread. Was San Francisco again to be visited by earthquake?

I lay for a full minute, numbly expectant, but there occurred no reeling of walls nor shock and grind of falling masonry. All was quiet. That was it! The silence! No wonder I had been perturbed. The hum of the great live city was strangely absent. The surface cars passed along my street, at that time of day, on an average of one every three minutes; but in the ten succeeding minutes not a car passed. Perhaps it was a street-railway strike, was my thought; or perhaps there had been an accident and the power was shut off. But no, the silence was too profound. I heard no jar and rattle of waggon wheels, nor stamp of iron-shod hoofs straining up the steep cobble-stones.

Pressing the push-button beside my bed, I strove to hear the sound of the bell, though I well knew it was impossible for the

339

sound to rise three stories to me even if the bell did ring. It rang all right, for a few minutes later Brown entered with the tray and morning paper. Though his features were impassive as ever, I noted a startled, apprehensive light in his eyes. I noted, also, that there was no cream on the tray.

"The Creamery did not deliver this morning," he explained; "nor did the bakery."

I glanced again at the tray. There were no fresh French rolls - only slices of stale graham bread from yesterday, the most detestable of bread so far as I was concerned.

"Nothing was delivered this morning, sir," Brown started to explain apologetically; but I interrupted him.

"The paper?"

"Yes, sir, it was delivered, but it was the only thing, and it is the last time, too. There won't be any paper to-morrow. The paper says so. Can I send out and get you some condensed milk?"

I shook my head, accepted the coffee black, and spread open the paper. The headlines explained everything - explained too much, in fact, for the lengths of pessimism to which the journal went were ridiculous. A general strike, it said, had been called all over the United States; and most foreboding anxieties were expressed concerning the provisioning of the great cities.

I read on hastily, skimming much and remembering much of labour troubles in the past. For a generation the general strike had been the dream of organized labour, which dream had arisen originally in the mind of Debs, one of the great labour leaders of thirty years before. I recollected that in my young college-settlement days I had even written an article on the subject for one of the magazines and that I had entitled it "The Dream of Debs." And I must confess that I had treated the idea very cavalierly and academically as a dream and nothing more. Time and the world had rolled on, Gompers was gone, the American Federation of Labour was gone, and gone was Debs with all his wild revolutionary ideas; but the dream had persisted, and here it was at last realized in fact. But I laughed, as I read, at the journal's gloomy outlook. I knew better. I had seen organized labour worsted in too many conflicts. It would be a matter only of days when the thing would be settled. This was a national strike, and it wouldn't take the Government long to break it.

I threw the paper down and proceeded to dress. It would certainly be interesting to be out in the streets of San Francisco when not a wheel was turning and the whole city was taking an enforced vacation.

"I beg your pardon, sir," Brown said, as he handed me my cigar-case, "but Mr. Harmmed has asked to see you before you go out."

"Send him in right away," I answered.

Harmmed was the butler. When he entered I could see he was labouring under controlled excitement. He came at once to the point.

"What shall I do, sir? There will be needed provisions, and the delivery drivers are on strike. And the electricity is shut off - I guess they're on strike, too."

"Are the shops open?" I asked.

"Only the small ones, sir. The retail clerks are out, and the big ones can't open; but the owners and their families are running the little ones themselves."

"Then take the machine," I said, "and go the rounds and make your purchases. Buy plenty of everything you need or may need.

Get a box of candles - no, get half-a-dozen boxes. And, when you're done, tell Harrison to bring the machine around to the club for me - not later than eleven."

Harmmed shook his head gravely. "Mr. Harrison has struck along with the Chauffeurs' Union, and I don't know how to run the machine myself."

"Oh, ho, he has, has he?" said. "Well, when next Mister Harrison happens around you tell him that he can look elsewhere for a position."

"Yes, sir."

"You don't happen to belong to a Butlers' Union, do you, Harmmed?"

"No, sir," was the answer. "And even if I did I'd not desert my employer in a crisis like this. No, sir, I would - "

"All right, thank you," I said. "Now you get ready to accompany me. I'll run the machine myself, and we'll lay in a stock of provisions to stand a siege."

It was a beautiful first of May, even as May days go. The sky was cloudless, there was no wind, and the air was warm - almost balmy. Many autos were out, but the owners were driving them themselves. The streets were crowded but quiet. The working class, dressed in its Sunday best, was out taking the air and observing the effects of the strike. It was all so unusual, and withal so peaceful, that I found myself enjoying it. My nerves were tingling with mild excitement. It was a sort of placid adventure. I passed Miss Chickering. She was at the helm of her little runabout. She swung around and came after me, catching me at the corner.

"Oh, Mr. Corf!'" she hailed. "Do you know where I can buy candles? I've been to a dozen shops, and they're all sold out. It's dreadfully awful, isn't it?"

But her sparkling eyes gave the lie to her words. Like the rest of us, she was enjoying it hugely. Quite an adventure it was, getting those candles. It was not until we went across the city and down into the working-class quarter south of Market Street that we found small corner groceries that had not yet sold out. Miss Chickering thought one box was sufficient, but I persuaded her into taking four. My car was large, and I laid in a dozen boxes. There was no telling what delays might arise in the settlement of the strike. Also, I filled the car with sacks of flour, baking-powder, tinned goods, and all the ordinary necessaries of life suggested by Harmmed, who fussed around and clucked over the purchases like an anxious old hen.

The remarkable thing, that first day of the strike, was that no one really apprehended anything serious. The announcement of organized labour in the morning papers that it was prepared to stay out a month or three months was laughed at. And yet that very first day we might have guessed as much from the fact that the working class took practically no part in the great rush to buy provisions. Of course not. For weeks and months, craftily and secretly, the whole working class had been laying in private stocks of provisions. That was why we were permitted to go down and buy out the little groceries in the working-class neighbourhoods.

It was not until I arrived at the club that afternoon that I began to feel the first alarm. Everything was in confusion. There were no olives for the cocktails, and the service was by hitches and jerks. Most of the men were angry, and all were worried. A babel of voices greeted me as I entered. General Folsom, nursing his capacious paunch in a window-seat in the smoking-room was defending himself against half-a-dozen excited gentlemen who were demanding that he should do something.

"What can I do more than I have done?" he was saying. "There are no orders from Washington. If you gentlemen will get a wire through I'll do anything I am commanded to do. But I don't see what can be done. The first thing I did this morning, as soon as I learned of the strike, was to order in the troops from the Presidio - three thousand of them. They're guarding the banks, the Mint, the post office, and all the public buildings. There is no disorder whatever. The strikers are keeping the peace perfectly. You can't expect me to shoot them down as they walk along the streets with wives and children all in their best bib and tucker."

"I'd like to know what's happening on Wall Street," I heard Jimmy Wombold say as I passed along. I could imagine his anxiety, for I knew that he was deep in the big Consolidated-Western deal.

"Say, Corf," Atkinson bustled up to me, "is your machine running?"

"Yes," I answered, "but what's the matter with your own?"

"Broken down, and the garages are all closed. And my wife's somewhere around Truckee, I think, stalled on the overland. Can't get a wire to her for love or money. She should have arrived this evening. She may be starving. Lend me your machine."

"Can't get it across the bay," Halstead spoke up. "The ferries aren't running. But I tell you what you can do. There's Rollinson - oh, Rollinson, come here a moment. Atkinson wants to get a machine across the bay. His wife is stuck on the overland at Truckee. Can't you bring the *Lurlette* across from Tiburon and carry the machine over for him?"

The *Lurlette* was a two-hundred-ton, ocean-going schooner-yacht.

Rollinson shook his head. "You couldn't get a longshoreman to land the machine on board, even if I could get the *Lurlette* over, which I can't, for the crew are members of the Coast Seamen's Union, and they're on strike along with the rest."

"But my wife may be starving," I could hear Atkinson wailing as I moved on.

At the other end of the smoking-room I ran into a group of men bunched excitedly and angrily around Bertie Messener. And Bertie was stirring them up and prodding them in his cool, cynical way. Bertie didn't care about the strike. He didn't care much about anything. He was blase - at least in all the clean things of life; the nasty things had no attraction for him. He was worth twenty millions, all of it in safe investments, and he had never done a tap of productive work in his life - inherited it all from his father and two uncles. He had been everywhere, seen everything, and done everything but get married, and this last in the face of the grim and determined attack of a few hundred ambitious mammas. For years he had been the greatest catch, and as yet he had avoided being caught. He was disgracefully eligible. On top of his wealth he was young, handsome, and, as I said before, clean. He was a great athlete, a young blond god that did everything perfectly and admirably with the solitary exception of matrimony. And he didn't care about anything, had no ambitions, no passions, no desire to do the very things he did so much better than other men.

"This is sedition!" one man in the group was crying. Another called it revolt and revolution, and another called it anarchy.

"I can't see it," Bertie said. "I have been out in the streets all morning. Perfect order reigns. I never saw a more law-abiding populace. There's no use calling it names. It's not any of those things. It's just what it claims to be, a general strike, and it's your turn to play, gentlemen."

"And we'll play all right!" cried Garfield, one of the traction millionaires. "We'll show this dirt where its place is - the beasts! Wait till the Government takes a hand."

"But where is the Government?" Bertie interposed. "It might as well be at the bottom of the sea so far as you're concerned. You don't know what's happening at Washington. You don't know whether you've got a Government or not."

"Don't you worry about that," Garfield blurted out.

"I assure you I'm not worrying," Bertie smiled languidly. "But it seems to me it's what you fellows are doing. Look in the glass, Garfield."

Garfield did not look, but had he looked he would have seen a very excited gentleman with rumpled, iron-grey hair, a flushed face, mouth sullen and vindictive, and eyes wildly gleaming.

"It's not right, I tell you," little Hanover said; and from his tone I was sure that he had already said it a number of times.

"Now that's going too far, Hanover," Bertie replied. "You fellows make me tired. You're all open-shop men. You've eroded my eardrums with your endless gabble for the open shop and the right of a man to work. You've harangued along those lines for years. Labour is doing nothing wrong in going out on this general strike. It is violating no law of God nor man. Don't you talk, Hanover. You've been ringing the changes too long on the God-given right to work . . . or not to work; you can't escape the corollary. It's a dirty little sordid scrap, that's all the whole thing is. You've got labour down and gouged it, and now labour's got you down and is gouging you, that's all, and you're squealing."

Every man in the group broke out in indignant denials that labour had ever been gouged.

"No, sir!" Garfield was shouting. "We've done the best for labour. Instead of gouging it, we've given it a chance to live. We've made work for it. Where would labour be if it hadn't been for us?"

"A whole lot better off," Bertie sneered. "You've got labour down and gouged it every time you got a chance, and you went out of your way to make chances."

"No! No!" were the cries.

"There was the teamsters' strike, right here in San Francisco," Bertie went on imperturbably. "The Employers' Association precipitated that strike. You know that. And you know I know it, too, for I've sat in these very rooms and heard the inside talk and news of the fight. First you precipitated the strike, then you bought the Mayor and the Chief of Police and broke the strike. A pretty spectacle, you philanthropists getting the teamsters down and gouging them.

"Hold on, I'm not through with you. It's only last year that the labour ticket of Colorado elected a governor. He was never seated. You know why. You know how your brother philanthropists and capitalists of Colorado worked it. It was a case of getting labour down and gouging it. You kept the president of the South-western Amalgamated Association of Miners in jail for three years on trumped-up murder charges, and with him out of the way you broke up the association. That was gouging labour, you'll admit. The third time the graduated income tax was declared unconstitutional was a gouge. So was the eight-hour Bill you killed in the last Congress.

347

"And of all unmitigated immoral gouges, your destruction of the closed-shop principle was the limit. You know how it was done. You bought out Farburg, the last president of the old American Federation of Labour. He was your creature - or the creature of all the trusts and employers' associations, which is the same thing. You precipitated the big closed-shop strike. Farburg betrayed that strike. You won, and the old American Federation of Labour crumbled to pieces. You follows destroyed it, and by so doing undid yourselves; for right on top of it began the organization of the I.L.W. - the biggest and solidest organization of labour the United States has ever seen, and you are responsible for its existence and for the present general strike. You smashed all the old federations and drove labour into the I.L.W., and the I.L.W. called the general strike - still fighting for the closed shop. And then you have the effrontery to stand here face to face and tell me that you never got labour down and gouged it. Bah!"

This time there were no denials. Garfield broke out in self-defence -

"We've done nothing we were not compelled to do, if we were to win."

"I'm not saying anything about that," Bertie answered. "What I am complaining about is your squealing now that you're getting a taste of your own medicine. How many strikes have you won by starving labour into submission? Well, labour's worked out a scheme whereby to starve you into submission. It wants the closed shop, and, if it can get it by starving you, why, starve you shall."

"I notice that you have profited in the past by those very labour gouges you mention," insinuated Brentwood, one of the wiliest and most astute of our corporation lawyers. "The receiver is as bad as the thief," he sneered. "You had no hand in the gouging, but you took your whack out of the gouge."

"That is quite beside the question, Brentwood," Bertie drawled. "You're as bad as Hanover, intruding the moral element. I haven't said that anything is right or wrong. It's all a rotten game, I know; and my sole kick is that you fellows are squealing now that you're down and labour's taking a gouge out of you. Of course I've taken the profits from the gouging and, thanks to you, gentlemen, without having personally to do the dirty work. You did that for me - oh, believe me, not because I am more virtuous than you, but because my good father and his various brothers left me a lot of money with which to pay for the dirty work."

"If you mean to insinuate - " Brentwood began hotly.

"Hold on, don't get all-ruffled up," Bertie interposed insolently. "There's no use in playing hypocrites in this thieves' den. The high and lofty is all right for the newspapers, boys' clubs, and Sunday schools - that's part of the game; but for heaven's sake don't let's play it on one another. You know, and you know that I know just what jobbery was done in the building trades' strike last fall, who put up the money, who did the work, and who profited by it." (Brentwood flushed darkly.) "But we are all tarred with the same brush, and the best thing for us to do is to leave morality out of it. Again I repeat, play the game, play it to the last finish, but for goodness' sake don't squeal when you get hurt."

When I left the group Bertie was off on a new tack tormenting them with the more serious aspects of the situation, pointing out the shortage of supplies that was already making itself felt, and asking them what they were going to do about it. A little later I met him in the cloak-room, leaving, and gave him a lift home in my machine.

"It's a great stroke, this general strike," he said, as we bowled along through the crowded but orderly streets. "It's a smashing body-blow. Labour caught us napping and struck at our weakest place, the stomach. I'm going to get out of San Francisco, Corf. Take my advice and get out, too. Head for the country, anywhere. You'll have more chance. Buy up a stock of supplies and get into a tent or a cabin somewhere. Soon there'll be nothing but starvation in this city for such as we."

How correct Bertie Messener was I never dreamed. I decided that he was an alarmist. As for myself, I was content to remain and watch the fun. After I dropped him, instead of going directly home, I went on in a hunt for more food. To my surprise, I learned that the small groceries where I had bought in the morning were sold out. I extended my search to the Potrero, and by good luck managed to pick up another box of candles, two sacks of wheat flour, ten pounds of graham flour (which would do for the servants), a case of tinned corn, and two cases of tinned tomatoes. It did look as though there was going to be at least a temporary food shortage, and I hugged myself over the goodly stock of provisions I had laid in.

The next morning I had my coffee in bed as usual, and, more than the cream, I missed the daily paper. It was this absence of knowledge of what was going on in the world that I found the chief hardship. Down at the club there was little news. Rider had crossed from Oakland in his launch, and Halstead had been down to San Jose and back in his machine. They reported the same conditions in those places as in San Francisco. Everything was tied up by the strike. All grocery stocks had been bought out by the upper classes. And perfect order reigned. But what was happening over the rest of the country - in Chicago? New York? Washington? Most probably the same things that were happening with us, we concluded; but the fact that we did not know with absolute surety was irritating.

General Folsom had a bit of news. An attempt had been made to place army telegraphers in the telegraph offices, but the wires had been cut in every direction. This was, so far, the one unlawful act committed by labour, and that it was a concerted act he was fully convinced. He had communicated by wireless with the army post at Benicia, the telegraph lines were even then being patrolled by soldiers all the way to Sacramento. Once, for one short instant, they had got the Sacramento call, then the wires, somewhere, were cut again. General Folsom reasoned that similar attempts to open communication were being made by the authorities all the way across the continent, but he was non-committal as to whether or not he thought the attempt would succeed. What worried him was the wire-cutting; he could not but believe that it was an important part of the deep-laid labour conspiracy. Also, he regretted that the Government had not long since established its projected chain of wireless stations.

The days came and went, and for a while it was a humdrum time. Nothing happened. The edge of excitement had become blunted. The streets were not so crowded. The working class did not come uptown any more to see how we were taking the strike. And there were not so many automobiles running around. The repair-shops and garages were closed, and whenever a machine broke down it went out of commission. The clutch on mine broke, and neither love nor money could get it repaired. Like the rest, I was now walking. San Francisco lay dead, and we did not know what was happening over the rest of the country. But from the very fact that we did not know we could conclude only that the rest of the

351

country lay as dead as San Francisco. From time to time the city was placarded with the proclamations of organized labour - these had been printed months before, and evidenced how thoroughly the I.L.W. had prepared for the strike. Every detail had been worked out long in advance. No violence had occurred as yet, with the exception of the shooting of a few wire-cutters by the soldiers, but the people of the slums were starving and growing ominously restless.

The business men, the millionaires, and the professional class held meetings and passed resolutions, but there was no way of making the proclamations public. They could not even get them printed. One result of these meetings, however, was that General Folsom was persuaded into taking military possession of the wholesale houses and of all the flour, grain, and food warehouses. It was high time, for suffering was becoming acute in the homes of the rich, and bread-lines were necessary. I knew that my servants were beginning to draw long faces, and it was amazing - the hole they made in my stock of provisions. In fact, as I afterward surmised, each servant was stealing from me and secreting a private stock of provisions for himself.

But with the formation of the bread-lines came new troubles. There was only so much of a food reserve in San Francisco, and at the best it could not last long. Organized labour, we knew, had its private supplies; nevertheless, the whole working class joined the bread-lines. As a result, the provisions General Folsom had taken possession of diminished with perilous rapidity. How were the soldiers to distinguish between a shabby middle-class man, a member of the I.L.W., or a slum dweller? The first and the last had to be fed, but the soldiers did not know all the I.L.W. men in the city, much less the wives and sons and daughters of the I.L.W. men. The employers helping, a few of the known union men were flung out of the bread-lines; but that amounted to nothing. To make matters worse, the Government tugs that had been hauling food from the army depots on Mare Island to Angel Island found no more food to haul. The soldiers now received their rations from the confiscated provisions, and they received them first.

The beginning of the end was in sight. Violence was beginning to show its face. Law and order were passing away, and passing away, I must confess, among the slum people and the upper classes. Organized labour still maintained perfect order. It could well afford to - it had plenty to eat. I remember the afternoon at the club when I caught Halstead and Brentwood whispering in a corner. They took me in on the venture. Brentwood's machine was still in running order, and they were going out cow-stealing. Halstead had a long butcher knife and a cleaver. We went out to the outskirts of the city. Here and there were cows grazing, but always they were guarded by their owners. We pursued our quest, following along the fringe of the city to the east, and on the hills near Hunter's Point we came upon a cow guarded by a little girl. There was also a young calf with the cow. We wasted no time on preliminaries. The little girl ran away screaming, while we slaughtered the cow. I omit the details, for they are not nice - we were unaccustomed to such work, and we bungled it.

But in the midst of it, working with the haste of fear, we heard cries, and we saw a number of men running toward us. We abandoned the spoils and took to our heels. To our surprise we were not pursued. Looking back, we saw the men hurriedly cutting up the cow. They had been on the same lay as ourselves. We argued that there was plenty for all, and ran back. The scene that followed beggars description. We fought and squabbled over the division like savages. Brentwood, I remember, was a perfect brute, snarling and snapping and threatening that murder would be done if we did not get our proper share.

And we were getting our share when there occurred a new irruption on the scene. This time it was the dreaded peace officers of the I.L.W. The little girl had brought them. They were armed with whips and clubs, and there were a score of them. The little girl danced up and down in anger, the tears streaming down her cheeks, crying: "Give it to 'em! Give it to 'em! That guy with the specs - he did it! Mash his face for him! Mash his face!" That guy with the specs was I, and I got my face mashed, too, though I had the presence of mind to take off my glasses at the first. My! but we did receive a trouncing as we scattered in all directions. Brentwood, Halstead, and I fled away for the machine. Brentwood's nose was bleeding, while Halstead's cheek was cut across with the scarlet slash of a black-snake whip.

And, lo, when the pursuit ceased and we had gained the machine, there, hiding behind it, was the frightened calf. Brentwood warned us to be cautious, and crept up on it like a wolf or tiger. Knife and cleaver had been left behind, but Brentwood still had his hands, and over and over on the ground he rolled with the poor little calf as he throttled it. We threw the carcass into the machine, covered it over with a robe, and started for home. But our misfortunes had only begun. We blew out a tyre. There was no way of fixing it, and twilight was coming on. We abandoned the machine, Brentwood pulling and staggering along in advance, the calf, covered by the robe, slung across his shoulders. We took turn about carrying that calf, and it nearly killed us. Also, we lost our way. And then, after hours of wandering and toil, we encountered a gang of hoodlums. They were not I.L.W. men, and I guess they were as hungry as we. At any rate, they got the calf and we got the thrashing. Brentwood raged like a madman the rest of the way home, and he looked like one, with his torn clothes, swollen nose, and blackened eyes.

There wasn't any more cow-stealing after that. General Folsom sent his troopers out and confiscated all the cows, and his troopers, aided by the militia, ate most of the meat. General Folsom was not to be blamed; it was his duty to maintain law and order, and he maintained it by means of the soldiers, wherefore he was compelled to feed them first of all.

It was about this time that the great panic occurred. The wealthy classes precipitated the flight, and then the slum people caught the contagion and stampeded wildly out of the city. General Folsom was pleased. It was estimated that at least 200,000 had deserted San Francisco, and by that much was his food problem solved. Well do I remember that day. In the morning I had eaten a crust of bread. Half of the afternoon I had stood in the bread-line; and after dark I returned home, tired and miserable, carrying a quart of rice and a slice of bacon. Brown met me at the door. His face was worn and terrified. All the servants had fled, he informed me. He alone remained. I was touched by his faithfulness and, when I learned that he had eaten nothing all day, I divided my food with him. We cooked half the rice and half the bacon, sharing it equally and reserving the other half for morning. I went to bed with my hunger, and tossed restlessly all night. In the morning I found Brown had deserted me, and, greater misfortune still, he had stolen what remained of the rice and bacon.

It was a gloomy handful of men that came together at the club that morning. There was no service at all. The last servant was gone. I noticed, too, that the silver was gone, and I learned where it had gone. The servants had not taken it, for the reason, I presume, that the club members got to it first. Their method of disposing of it was simple. Down south of Market Street, in the dwellings of the I.L.W., the housewives had given square meals in exchange for it. I went back to my house. Yes, my silver was gone - all but a massive pitcher. This I wrapped up and carried down south of Market Street.

I felt better after the meal, and returned to the club to learn if there was anything new in the situation. Hanover, Collins, and Dakon were just leaving. There was no one inside, they told me, and they invited me to come along with them. They were leaving the city, they said, on Dakon's horses, and there was a spare one for me. Dakon had four magnificent carriage horses that he wanted to save, and General Folsom had given him the tip that next morning all the horses that remained in the city were to be confiscated for food. There were not many horses left, for tens of thousands of them had been turned loose into the country when the hay and grain gave out during the first days. Birdall, I remember, who had great draying interests, had turned loose three hundred dray horses. At an average value of five hundred dollars, this had amounted to $150,000. He had hoped, at first, to recover most of the horses after the strike was over, but in the end he never recovered one of them. They were all eaten by the people that fled from San Francisco. For that matter, the killing of the army mules and horses for food had already begun.

Fortunately for Dakon, he had had a plentiful supply of hay and grain stored in his stable. We managed to raise four saddles, and we found the animals in good condition and spirited, withal unused to being ridden. I remembered the San Francisco of the great earthquake as we rode through the streets, but this San Francisco was vastly more pitiable. No cataclysm of nature had caused this, but, rather, the tyranny of the labour unions. We rode down past Union Square and through the theatre, hotel, and shopping districts. The streets were deserted. Here and there stood automobiles, abandoned where they had broken down or when the gasolene had given out. There was no sign of life, save for the occasional policemen and the soldiers guarding the banks and public buildings. Once we came upon an I.L.W. man pasting up the latest proclamation. We stopped to read. "We have maintained an orderly strike," it ran; "and we shall maintain order to the end. The end will come when our demands are satisfied, and our demands will be satisfied when we have starved our employers into submission, as we ourselves in the past have often been starved into submission."

"Messener's very words," Collins said. "And I, for one, am ready to submit, only they won't give me a chance to submit. I haven't had a full meal in an age. I wonder what horse-meat tastes like?"

We stopped to read another proclamation: "When we think our employers are ready to submit we shall open up the telegraphs and place the employers' associations of the United States in communication. But only messages relating to peace terms shall be permitted over the wires."

We rode on, crossed Market Street, and a little later were passing through the working-class district. Here the streets were not deserted. Leaning over the gates or standing in groups were the

357

I.L.W. men. Happy, well-fed children were playing games, and stout housewives sat on the front steps gossiping. One and all cast amused glances at us. Little children ran after us, crying: "Hey, mister, ain't you hungry?" And one woman, nursing a child at her breast, called to Dakon: "Say, Fatty, I'll give you a meal for your skate - ham and potatoes, currant jelly, white bread, canned butter, and two cups of coffee."

"Have you noticed, the last few days," Hanover remarked to me, "that there's not been a stray dog in the streets?"

I had noticed, but I had not thought about it before. It was high time to leave the unfortunate city. We at last managed to connect with the San Bruno Road, along which we headed south. I had a country place near Menlo, and it was our objective. But soon we began to discover that the country was worse off and far more dangerous than the city. There the soldiers and the I.L.W. kept order; but the country had been turned over to anarchy. Two hundred thousand people had fled from San Francisco, and we had countless evidences that their flight had been like that of an army of locusts.

They had swept everything clean. There had been robbery and fighting. Here and there we passed bodies by the roadside and saw the blackened ruins of farm-houses. The fences were down, and the crops had been trampled by the feet of a multitude. All the vegetable patches had been rooted up by the famished hordes. All the chickens and farm animals had been slaughtered. This was true of all the main roads that led out of San Francisco. Here and there, away from the roads, farmers had held their own with shotguns and revolvers, and were still holding their own. They warned us away and refused to parley with us. And all the destruction and violence had been done by the slum-dwellers and the upper classes. The I.L.W. men, with plentiful food supplies, remained quietly in their homes in the cities.

Early in the ride we received concrete proof of how desperate was the situation. To the right of us we heard cries and rifle-shots. Bullets whistled dangerously near. There was a crashing in the underbrush; then a magnificent black truck-horse broke across the road in front of us and was gone. We had barely time to notice that he was bleeding and lame. He was followed by three soldiers. The chase went on among the trees on the left. We could hear the soldiers calling to one another. A fourth soldier limped out upon the road from the right, sat down on a boulder, and mopped the sweat from his face.

"Militia," Dakon whispered. "Deserters."

The man grinned up at us and asked for a match. In reply to Dakon's "What's the word?" he informed us that the militiamen were deserting. "No grub," he explained. "They're feedin' it all to the regulars." We also learned from him that the military prisoners had been released from Alcatraz Island because they could no longer be fed.

I shall never forget the next sight we encountered. We came upon it abruptly around a turn of the road. Overhead arched the trees. The sunshine was filtering down through the branches. Butterflies were fluttering by, and from the fields came the song of larks. And there it stood, a powerful touring car. About it and in it lay a number of corpses. It told its own tale. Its occupants, fleeing from the city, had been attacked and dragged down by a gang of slum dwellers - hoodlums. The thing had occurred within twenty-four hours. Freshly opened meat and fruit tins explained the reason

359

for the attack. Dakon examined the bodies.

"I thought so," he reported. "I've ridden in that car. It was Perriton - the whole family. We've got to watch out for ourselves from now on."

"But we have no food with which to invite attack," I objected.

Dakon pointed to the horse I rode, and I understood.

Early in the day Dakon's horse had cast a shoe. The delicate hoof had split, and by noon the animal was limping. Dakon refused to ride it farther, and refused to desert it. So, on his solicitation, we went on. He would lead the horse and join us at my place. That was the last we saw of him; nor did we ever learn his end.

By one o'clock we arrived at the town of Menlo, or, rather, at the site of Menlo, for it was in ruins. Corpses lay everywhere. The business part of the town, as well as part of the residences, had been gutted by fire. Here and there a residence still held out; but there was no getting near them. When we approached too closely we were fired upon. We met a woman who was poking about in the smoking ruins of her cottage. The first attack, she told us, had been on the stores, and as she talked we could picture that raging, roaring, hungry mob flinging itself on the handful of townspeople. Millionaires and paupers had fought side by side for the food, and then fought with one another after they got it. The town of Palo Alto and Stanford University had been sacked in similar fashion, we learned. Ahead of us lay a desolate, wasted land; and we thought we were wise in turning off to my place. It lay three miles to the west, snuggling among the first rolling swells of the foothills.

But as we rode along we saw that the devastation was not confined to the main roads. The van of the flight had kept to the roads, sacking the small towns as it went; while those that followed had scattered out and swept the whole countryside like a great broom. My place was built of concrete, masonry, and tiles, and so had escaped being burned, but it was gutted clean. We found the gardener's body in the windmill, littered around with empty shotgun shells. He had put up a good fight. But no trace could we find of the two Italian labourers, nor of the house-keeper and her husband. Not a live thing remained. The calves, the colts, all the fancy poultry and thoroughbred stock, everything, was gone. The kitchen and the fireplaces, where the mob had cooked, were a mess, while many camp-fires outside bore witness to the large number that had fed and spent the night. What they had not eaten they had carried away. There was not a bite for us.

We spent the rest of the night vainly waiting for Dakon, and in the morning, with our revolvers, fought off half-a-dozen marauders. Then we killed one of Dakon's horses, hiding for the future what meat we did not immediately eat. In the afternoon Collins went out for a walk, but failed to return. This was the last straw to Hanover. He was for flight there and then, and I had great difficulty in persuading him to wait for daylight. As for myself, I was convinced that the end of the general strike was near, and I was resolved to return to San Francisco. So, in the morning, we parted company, Hanover heading south, fifty pounds of horse-meat strapped to his saddle, while I, similarly loaded, headed north. Little Hanover pulled through all right, and to the end of his life he will persist, I know, in boring everybody with the narrative of his subsequent adventures.

I got as far as Belmont, on the main road back, when I was robbed of my horse-meat by three militiamen. There was no change in the situation, they said, except that it was going from bad to worse. The I.L.W. had plenty of provisions hidden away and could last out for months. I managed to get as far as Baden, when my horse was taken away from me by a dozen men. Two of them were San Francisco policemen, and the remainder were regular soldiers. This was ominous. The situation was certainly extreme when the regulars were beginning to desert. When I continued my way on foot, they already had the fire started, and the last of Dakon's horses lay slaughtered on the ground.

As luck would have it, I sprained my ankle, and succeeded in getting no farther than South San Francisco. I lay there that night in an out-house, shivering with the cold and at the same time burning with fever. Two days I lay there, too sick to move, and on the third, reeling and giddy, supporting myself on an extemporized crutch, I tottered on toward San Francisco. I was weak as well, for it was the third day since food had passed my lips. It was a day of nightmare and torment. As in a dream I passed hundreds of regular soldiers drifting along in the opposite direction, and many policemen, with their families, organized in large groups for mutual protection.

As I entered the city I remembered the workman's house at which I had traded the silver pitcher, and in that direction my hunger drove me. Twilight was falling when I came to the place. I passed around by the alleyway and crawled up the black steps, on which I collapsed. I managed to reach out with the crutch and knock on the door. Then I must have fainted, for I came to in the kitchen, my face wet with water, and whisky being poured down my throat. I choked and spluttered and tried to talk. I began saying something about not having any more silver pitchers, but that I would make it up to them afterward if they would only give me something to eat. But the housewife interrupted me.

"Why, you poor man," she said, "haven't you heard? The strike was called off this afternoon. Of course we'll give you something to eat."

She bustled around, opening a tin of breakfast bacon and preparing to fry it.

"Let me have some now, please," I begged; and I ate the raw bacon on a slice of bread, while her husband explained that the demands of the I.L.W. had been granted. The wires had been opened up in the early afternoon, and everywhere the employers' associations had given in. There hadn't been any employers left in San Francisco, but General Folsom had spoken for them. The trains and steamers would start running in the morning, and so would everything else just as soon as system could be established.

And that was the end of the general strike. I never want to see another one. It was worse than a war. A general strike is a cruel and immoral thing, and the brain of man should be capable of running industry in a more rational way. Harrison is still my chauffeur. It was part of the conditions of the I.L.W. that all of its members should be reinstated in their old positions. Brown never came back, but the rest of the servants are with me. I hadn't the heart to discharge them — poor creatures, they were pretty hard-pressed when they deserted with the food and silver. And now I can't discharge them. They have all been unionized by the I.L.W. The tyranny of organized labour is getting beyond human endurance. Something must be done.

from *The Strength of the Strong* (1914)
(First published in *The International Socialist Review,* January 9, 1909)

EPILOGUE:
18 April 1906

THE STORY OF AN EYEWITNESS

Upon receipt of the first news of the earthquake, Collier's *telegraphed to Mr. Jack London — who lives only forty miles from San Francisco — requesting him to go to the scene of the disaster and write the story of what he saw. Mr. London started at once, and he sent the following dramatic description of the tragic events he witnessed in the burning city.*

The earthquake shook down in San Francisco hundreds of thousands of dollars worth of walls and chimneys. But the conflagration that followed burned up hundreds of millions of dollars' worth of property There is no estimating within hundreds of millions the actual damage wrought. Not in history has a modern imperial city been so completely destroyed. San Francisco is gone. Nothing remains of it but memories and a fringe of dwelling-houses on its outskirts. Its industrial section is wiped out. Its business section is wiped out. Its social and residential section is wiped out. The factories and warehouses, the great stores and newspaper buildings, the hotels and the palaces of the nabobs, are all gone. Remains only the fringe of dwelling houses on the outskirts of what was once San Francisco.

Within an hour after the earthquake shock the smoke of San Francisco's burning was a lurid tower visible a hundred miles away. And for three days and nights this lurid tower swayed in the sky, reddening the sun, darkening the day, and filling the land with smoke.

On Wednesday morning at a quarter past five came the earthquake. A minute later the flames were leaping upward In a dozen different quarters south of Market Street, in the working-class ghetto, and in the factories, fires started. There was no opposing the flames. There was no organization, no communication. All the cunning adjustments of a twentieth century city had been smashed by the earthquake. The streets were humped into ridges and depressions, and piled with the debris of fallen walls. The steel rails were twisted into perpendicular and horizontal angles. The telephone and telegraph systems were disrupted. And the great water-mains had burst. All the shrewd contrivances and safeguards of man had been thrown out of gear by thirty seconds' twitching of the earth-crust.

By Wednesday afternoon, inside of twelve hours, half the heart of the city was gone. At that time I watched the vast conflagration from out on the bay. It was dead calm. Not a flicker of wind stirred. Yet from every side wind was pouring in upon the city. East, west, north, and south, strong winds were blowing upon the doomed city. The heated air rising made an enormous suck. Thus did the fire of itself build its own colossal chimney through the atmosphere. Day and night this dead calm continued, and yet, near to the flames, the wind was often half a gale, so mighty was the suck.

Wednesday night saw the destruction of the very heart of the city. Dynamite was lavishly used, and many of San Francisco proudest structures were crumbled by man himself into ruins, but there was no withstanding the onrush of the flames. Time and again successful stands were made by the fire-fighters, and every time the flames flanked around on either side or came up from the rear, and turned to defeat the hard-won victory.

An enumeration of the buildings destroyed would be a directory of San Francisco. An enumeration of the buildings undestroyed would be a line and several addresses. An enumeration of the deeds of heroism would stock a library and bankrupt the Carnegie medal fund. An enumeration of the dead-will never be made. All vestiges of them were destroyed by the flames. The number of the victims of the earthquake will never be known. South of Market Street, where the loss of life was particularly heavy, was the first to catch fire.

Remarkable as it may seem, Wednesday night while the whole city crashed and roared into ruin, was a quiet night. There were no crowds. There was no shouting and yelling. There was no hysteria, no disorder. I passed Wednesday night in the path of the advancing flames, and in all those terrible hours I saw not one woman who wept, not one man who was excited, not one person who was in the slightest degree panic stricken.

Before the flames, throughout the night, fled tens of thousands of homeless ones. Some were wrapped in blankets. Others carried bundles of bedding and dear household treasures. Sometimes a whole family was harnessed to a carriage or delivery wagon that was weighted down with their possessions. Baby buggies, toy wagons, and go-carts were used as trucks, while every other person was dragging a trunk. Yet everybody was gracious. The most perfect courtesy obtained. Never in all San Francisco's history, were her people so kind and courteous as on this night of terror.

All night these tens of thousands fled before the flames. Many of them, the poor people from the labor ghetto, had fled all day as well. They had left their homes burdened with possessions. Now and again they lightened up, flinging out upon the street clothing

369

and treasures they had dragged for miles.

They held on longest to their trunks, and over these trunks many a strong man broke his heart that night. The hills of San Francisco are steep, and up these hills, mile after mile, were the trunks dragged. Everywhere were trunks with across them lying their exhausted owners, men and women. Before the march of the flames were flung picket lines of soldiers. And a block at a time, as the flames advanced, these pickets retreated. One of their tasks was to keep the trunk-pullers moving. The exhausted creatures, stirred on by the menace of bayonets, would arise and struggle up the steep pavements, pausing from weakness every five or ten feet.

Often, after surmounting a heart-breaking hill. they would find another wall of flame advancing upon them at right angles and be compelled to change anew the line of their retreat. In the end, completely played out, after toiling for a dozen hours like giants, thousands of them were compelled to abandon their trunks. Here the shopkeepers and soft members of the middle class were at a disadvantage. But the working-men dug holes in vacant lots and backyards and buried their trunks.

At nine o'clock Wednesday evening I walked down through the very heart of the city. I walked through miles and miles of magnificent buildings and towering skyscrapers. Here was no fire. All was in perfect order. The police patrolled the streets. Every building had its watchman at the door. And yet it was doomed, all of it. There was no water. The dynamite was giving out. And at right angles two different conflagrations were sweeping down upon it.

At one o'clock in the morning I walked down through the same section Everything still stood intact. There was no fire. And yet there was a change. A rain of ashes was falling. The watchmen at the doors were gone. The police had been withdrawn. There were no firemen, no fire-engines, no men fighting with dynamite. The district had been absolutely abandoned. I stood at the corner of Kearney and Market, in the very innermost heart of San Francisco. Kearny Street was deserted. Half a dozen blocks away it was burning on both sides. The street was a wall of flame. And against this wall of flame, silhouetted sharply, were two United States cavalrymen sitting their horses, calming watching. That was all. Not another person was in sight. In the intact heart of the city two troopers sat their horses and watched.

Surrender was complete. There was no water. The sewers had long since been pumped dry. There was no dynamite. Another fire had broken out further uptown, and now from three sides conflagrations were sweeping down. The fourth side had been burned earlier in the day. In that direction stood the tottering walls of the Examiner building, the burned-out Call building, the smoldering ruins of the Grand Hotel, and the gutted, devastated, dynamited Palace Hotel.

The following will illustrate the sweep of the flames and the inability of men to calculate their spread. At eight o'clock Wednesday evening I passed through Union Square. It was packed with refugees. Thousands of them had gone to bed on the grass. Government tents had been set up, supper was being cooked, and the refugees were lining up for free meals.

At half past one in the morning three sides of Union Square were in flames. The fourth side, where stood the great St. Francis Hotel was still holding out. An hour later, ignited from top and sides the St. Francis was flaming heavenward. Union Square, heaped high with mountains of trunks, was deserted. Troops, refugees, and all had retreated.

It was at Union Square that I saw a man offering a thousand dollars for a team of horses. He was in charge of a truck piled high with trunks from some hotel. It had been hauled here into what was considered safety, and the horses had been taken out. The flames were on three sides of the Square and there were no horses.

Also, at this time, standing beside the truck, I urged a man to seek safety in flight. He was all but hemmed in by several conflagrations. He was an old man and he Was on crutches. Said he: "Today is my birthday. Last night I was worth thirty thousand dollars. I bought five bottles of wine, some delicate fish and other things for my birthday dinner. I have had no dinner, and all I own are these crutches."

I convinced him of his danger and started him limping on his way. An hour later, from a distance, I saw the truck-load of trunks burning merrily in the middle of the street.

On Thursday morning at a quarter past five, just twenty-four hours after the earthquake, I sat on the steps of a small residence on Nob Hill. With me sat Japanese, Italians, Chinese, and negroes—a bit of the cosmopolitan flotsam of the wreck of the city. All about were the palaces of the nabob pioneers of Forty-nine. To the east and south at right angles, were advancing two mighty walls of flame

I went inside with the owner of the house on the steps of which I sat. He was cool and cheerful and hospitable. "Yesterday morning," he said, "I was worth six hundred thousand dollars. This morning this house is all I have left. It will go in fifteen minutes. He pointed to a large cabinet. "That is my wife's collection of china. This rug upon which we stand is a present. It cost fifteen hundred dollars. Try that piano. Listen to its tone. There are few like it. There are no horses. The flames will be here in fifteen minutes."

Outside the old Mark Hopkins residence a palace was just catching fire. The troops were falling back and driving the refugees before them. From every side came the roaring of flames, the crashing of walls, and the detonations of dynamite.

I passed out of the house. Day was trying to dawn through the smoke-pall. A sickly light was creeping over the face of things. Once only the sun broke through the smoke-pall, blood-red, and showing quarter its usual size. The smoke-pall itself, viewed from beneath, was a rose color that pulsed and fluttered with lavender shades Then it turned to mauve and yellow and dun. There was no sun. And so dawned the second day on stricken San Francisco.

An hour later I was creeping past the shattered dome of the City Hall. Than it there was no better exhibit of the destructive force of the earthquake. Most of the stone had been shaken from the great dome, leaving standing the naked framework of steel. Market Street was piled high with the wreckage, and across the wreckage lay the overthrown pillars of the City Hall shattered into short crosswise sections.

This section of the city with the exception of the Mint and the Post-Office, was already a waste of smoking ruins. Here and there through the smoke, creeping warily under the shadows of tottering walls, emerged occasional men and women. It was like the meeting of the handful of survivors after the day of the end of the world.

On Mission Street lay a dozen steers, in a neat row stretching across the street just as they had been struck down by the flying ruins of the earthquake. The fire had passed through afterward and roasted them. The human dead had been carried away before the fire came. At another place on Mission Street I saw a milk wagon. A steel telegraph pole had smashed down sheer through the driver's seat and crushed the front wheels. The milk cans lay scattered around.

All day Thursday and all Thursday night, all day Friday and Friday night, the flames still raged on.

Friday night saw the flames finally conquered. through not until Russian Hill and Telegraph Hill had been swept and three-quarters of a mile of wharves and docks had been licked up.

The great stand of the fire-fighters was made Thursday night on Van Ness Avenue. Had they failed here, the comparatively few remaining houses of the city would have been swept. Here were the magnificent residences of the second generation of San Francisco nabobs, and these, in a solid zone, were dynamited down across the path of the fire. Here and there the flames leaped the zone, but these fires were beaten out, principally by the use of wet blankets and rugs.

San Francisco, at the present time, is like the crater of a volcano, around which are camped tens of thousands of refugees At the Presidio alone are at least twenty thousand. All the surrounding cities and towns are jammed with the homeless ones, where they are being cared for by the relief committees. The refugees were carried free by the railroads to any point they wished to go, and it is estimated that over one hundred thousand people have left the peninsula on which San Francisco stood. The Government has the situation in hand, and, thanks to the immediate relief given by the whole United States, there is not the slightest possibility of a famine. The bankers and business men hare already set about making preparations to rebuild San Francisco.

(First published in *Collier's*, May 5, 1906)